# Eternal City

# Eternal City

## Nancy Kilpatrick
### and Michael Kilpatrick

**Five Star • Waterville, Maine**

Published in 2003 in conjunction with Tekno Books and Ed Gorman.

Set in 11 pt. Plantin by Elena Picard.

Printed in the United States on permanent paper.

**Library of Congress Cataloging-in-Publication Data**

Kilpatrick, Nancy.
    Eternal city / by Nancy Kilpatrick.
        p. cm.—(Five Star speculative fiction)
    ISBN 0-7862-4960-9 (hc : alk. paper)
    ISBN 1-4104-0153-7 (sc : alk. paper)
       1. Environmental degradation—Fiction. 2. Canada—
Fiction. I. Title. II. Series.
PS3561.I4126 E86 2003
813'.54—dc21                   2002040754

To SHADOW-DWELLERS

# Prologue

Murky. Suspended in an eternal womb. Encased in the comforting aroma of one's own kind.

Tension! Rippling through him. Through all of them.

*She Disturbs Our World!*

Reluctantly THE FATHER guides him and the others out of safety into danger. They squeeze their eyes closed against the harsh glare left in the wake of the sun. The woman has forced them out here too early, when the sky can still wound. She will expose them. She is a threat. In an instant, he understands all this and more.

*She Will Suffer!*

THE FATHER'S body leads by instinct. By right. Head tilting proudly toward Heaven, body unfurling. Knees bend. Feet spring from moist cold soil.

As they accelerate, his thoughts dwindle. Exhilaration. High soaring, gliding, wind cascades along his back one second, then: turning, slicing into a wall of crisp air the next. He feels sleek. Perfectly tuned.

Through THE FATHER'S eyes he can see far. Wind chops water. Shadows erode the landscape. He feels the blessed cool darkness crawl across him and the others. He glances around. They have become iridescent jewels sparkling in the dimming sky. Night begins!

*The Hunt Begins!*

THE FATHER chastises him. The sharp odor of admonition engulfs him, separating him from the others. He bows low in shame and obedience. There is still so much to learn.

The woman's canoe attacks the whitecaps as she frantically paddles against the current. He can see remarkably well. Her old body trembles. She is desperate and pauses to scan all directions. Absently she shoves white hair from her eyes and fondles the stone hanging from her neck as if it is a talisman capable of protecting her.

She digs the paddle left, then right, then left, heading not for her own dock but for another.

The sky is rapidly turning the color of charred earth. Along the crest of the mainland a pungent army of rigid jack pines circles the lake, blocking her escape. Escape. If she gets that far, he thinks.

*She Will Not!*

THE FATHER is correct, as always. She has no hope against them. They are superior.

The water, the land, the green bubble. Buildings dot the shoreline. A road. Two silver trailers. This is their domain.

THE FATHER'S whisper carries on the dark air and, nearby, THE MOTHER responds. Pain and joy swirl through him; THEIR voices fill and heal.

The woman looks up. Her face is streaked with the terror of ignorance. The smell of fear and loathing waft from her, polluting the night. They are so many they create a second sky, full of eyes like stars. Of celestial, eternal splendor. Why can she not see?

Intuitively he understands: it is her humanness, her awareness of mortality that limits her.

She screams then stands and kicks off her shoes. She dives over the edge of the canoe even as THE FATHER and THE MOTHER together dive toward the liquid ebony. As if drawn by an invisible cord, he and the others follow.

He feels THEIR rage quiver through his body. It is terrible. Volatile. Omnipotent . . .

Wonderful!

They careen low along the chilly water's surface. THEIR cries permeate the night, delighting him, leading the chorus. Muscles stretch, elongate. He is lighter than the air he cuts through, more fluid than the water beneath him.

The woman surfaces. THE FATHER'S energy electrifies. HE swoops low, brushing up the back of her head, playing with her, seducing her. A look of horror spreads across the woman's features. She pushes herself underwater.

Freedom from the earth and all its constraints. They sail up through the air, charged particles on the wind, THE MOTHER now in the lead, THE FATHER behind and to her right. The others vibrate, maintaining a perfect symmetry and distance between them. Such intelligence overwhelms him with its simplicity and righteous beauty.

White hair bobs in black water. THE FATHER plummets. He reaches out. But the woman sinks again and for HIS efforts HE receives a handful of angel fluff. THE FATHER is impatient, his energy kinetic, throbbing, near explosion. He spreads his glory wider, soaring higher. It is as though THE FATHER'S thoughts and the woman's thoughts meld. All of their thoughts fuse and they think and act as one in this glorious cosmic dance.

HE hovers, tension barely contained.

Suddenly HE dives. They follow as a unit.

Fear contracts his body. He holds back. The angle is too

sharp. Surely they will crash. His bones will shatter. His brain fragment.

He struggles to convey this emotion to THE FATHER, to plead for reassurance.

THE FATHER is living fury. Single minded. Bent on destruction. The others synchronize psychically.

He is swept away by the collective force.

Two human hands grasp the wooden dock. In a collapsing moment he and the others stroke death. THE FATHER clamps onto her wrists then reverses course. The old woman wails. Her sound is familiar and it chills him. But THE FATHER'S victory spreads like vapor, seeping into his cells, even as it spreads through them all. They shriek triumph as one voice, obliterating the old woman's cries.

The pleasure coursing through him feels eternal. He is floating. Above this dreary earthly plane. At one with all life. Safe. Fulfilled.

They climb toward the pale moon illuminating the sky as if it is their personal beacon. If only he could have this. Always. Please! he begs.

THE MOTHER promises: *Soon!*

*When It Serves the Greater Good!* It is THE FATHER'S voice, almighty and terrible in HIS strict, loving decisions.

Pain crushes his heart. Scorching tears spurt from his eyes and he cries in shame and frustration. Fear of separation. Terror of impending cold. Loneliness gnaws at his chillingly mortal flesh.

He swears to THE FATHER: I will give *anything,* anything to be one with you. Forever.

A stern yet gentle sound vibrates through him as THE MOTHER replies: *We Know!*

THEY are pleased.

*Soon!* THE MOTHER assures him again, tenderly, her promise abiding.

THE FATHER, so firm, says nothing. His silence is eternal.

# One

The crimson Renegade with dusty Florida plates sped west along Canada's transcontinental highway 401. Four days on the road had lulled Claire into a pleasant trance she wished could last forever. Mesmerized by the dark asphalt river flowing under the Jeep, she felt connected to an eternal current.

She glanced at her twelve-year-old son as he fiddled with the radio dial. David, gangly but good looking, at that moment resembled a contortionist—one bare foot braced against the dash, the other curled under him, right hand gripping the padded roll bar behind. Claire felt the corners of her mouth turn up.

Bill would've been proud. Then she saw a mental snapshot of herself studying her offspring and smiled. Stereotype mother! Yep, that's me.

She always enjoyed this altered state induced by long distance drives. The Jeep was a womb, she and David enveloped in a warm bubble of timelessness. Poisons from the world outside couldn't touch them.

Earth and sweet manure scents filled the Jeep as farm country drifted by quickly, interspersed with small stands of maple trees. Claire hoped David would get to see the leaves turning color on their way home. She'd never realized how much like New York State this part of Canada was. Middle class homes, not much new construction, inexpensive. Three metallic butterflies in diminishing sizes seemed to be a favorite exterior decoration. The barns were old, matte grey barnboard with rusted tin roofs, hay visible through open doorways and windows.

At Highway 12 they turned north. Eventually they arrived in what Claire remembered her Aunt Lillian calling "diviner country," the land where Canadians and some Americans owned summer homes they called cottages.

As the houses became more scarce, Claire remembered driving up here from Albany as a girl with Aunt Lillian. Back then, the trip seemed to take forever, in a good way. From the moment Lillian picked her up, it was as though the two of them entered a magical world. "We're on Fantasy Island," Claire remembered telling her aunt. Lillian laughed, that wonderful full laugh from deep in her gut, not contained and restrained like most adults. Claire thought she was very old then, because of her white hair. Now she realized it had been premature and Lillian hadn't been more than forty-five.

Along the way they had stopped at cheap clapboard motels with names like *Lay-Z-Daze* or *By-The-Way-Inn*. They'd picnic by the side of the road, eating food that didn't taste familiar and therefore was suspect. Their cooler was well-stocked with Cokes for Claire and Ginger Beer, a non-alcoholic beverage from the Caribbean that Lillian loved. Claire could still taste the wild blueberries that didn't need sugar. And cherry tomatoes—she made sure to pop them whole into her mouth and keep her lips closed when she bit into them to keep the juice from squirting out.

Lillian took her time driving. She repeated jokes and told outrageous stories about the old ways, the days of her youth, and they sang songs they made up. Those memories were the most precious of Claire's childhood. She knew that what made them so special was Lillian, who had instilled in her a respect for and awe of nature that bordered on the mystical.

She glanced at her son. Nut-brown eyes. Tousled brown hair, just like Bill's. He'd been more like her when he was a baby. Now he was changing, becoming so much like his father. Her urge to hold back change intensified with the expanding fact that Bill was gone. Still, she wanted to give David the same experience of nature that Lillian had given her, something he could carry with him all his life. She wanted him to know there was a reality beyond concrete and chrome, fast food and techno gadgets. Those things were impermanent. The earth had its own rhythms and codes and had been here before all that and would remain long after the cement crumbled. She felt it strongly, in her bones, and needed to pass that knowledge on.

"MacDonalds," David said. "Maybe they got mooseburgers up here in the Arctic."

Claire shook her head. He never let her get too far away from concrete reality. She reached over to ruffle his hair but he ducked out of the way.

"No mooseburgers, no Eskimos, no Sergeant Preston of the Yukon," she told him. "Surprised?"

"Who's Sergeant Preston?"

"An early TV series. You know, from back in the Stone age."

He gave her a *look*.

"Never mind." She sighed.

"Don't worry. It's just the G gap. They'll probably show it when they do the golden oldies, from the black and white days, and you can get all nostalgic and everything."

"Golden oldies?" Claire yelled. "*I* saw it as reruns. I'm not *ancient,* my man."

David just rolled his eyes.

"Hey, Mom, we gonna sell Aunt Lillian's land?" It wasn't uncommon that David almost read her thoughts, but it always startled her.

"Probably." The letter offering to purchase the land had come soon after news of the inheritance. She had no idea of land prices up here, but Roger Bennett, her lawyer, thought that $150,000 Canadian dollars—about $75,000 US— sounded more than fair. He urged her to accept before the offer was withdrawn. God knew, she and David could use the money. Bill's insurance had paid off the mortgage. But his company went bankrupt shortly after his death and that was the end of any pension plan. With only her pottery sales and part-time teaching salary to live on and David six years away from college . . . Still, she couldn't just part with Lillian's land like that. It felt callous. The tie was too powerful. She needed to see it one last time.

Whenever Claire thought of that land, the same image, from a photograph taken at Witch Rock, came to mind: Claire, fourteen, gawky, shy. Lillian, tall, large-boned, with a high forehead, wide cheekbones, skin bronzed by the sun. "The Sorceress of the North," Lillian had called herself, "and you, my sweet niece, are the sorceress's apprentice." It had taken Claire years to accept the sixth-sense her aunt was talking about.

That picture had been taken the last summer Claire visited her aunt. After that her parents moved to Florida. That fall Claire started high school. Then, later, college. Then she traveled and worked, met Bill, had David, and, she was shocked to realize, nearly two decades had slipped by since she had seen Lillian.

The property Claire recently inherited lay far enough north that the winters were formidable and it just now occurred to her that her Aunt must have had a rough time all by herself. Lillian's last Christmas card had described the plunging temperature as "hell finally freezing over." But the tone of Lillian's note felt odd to Claire, unusually somber, and that had troubled her. Lillian's death wasn't a surprise; Claire had known a week before the phone call. She felt certain she knew the very moment Lillian died.

A blast of radio interrupted her thoughts. David turned up the volume. He was about to switch stations when she caught his hand. "Wait a minute. I want to hear this."

"It's just a commercial."

A silky-voiced woman spoke: *Nirvana, the Eternal City. More than a resort. More than a place to retire. Come to where time stands still. Where each moment stretches into infinity.*

"That's the company that wants Aunt Lillian's land." They're big, Claire thought. Very big. There were Eternal Cities in other parts of the world, usually in remote areas— the far Caribbean, and Southeast Asia. They seemed to be a cross between Club Med and a residential complex like Sun City in South Africa, but with a twist. They were supposed to be environmentally friendly.

The ad continued with an equally smooth male voice: *Tennis, Aerobics, Water Skiing, Windsurfing, your own exclusive health and beauty spa. Even a private lagoon to moor your boat, right at your back door. Life as it's meant to be lived. Experience luxury, security and contentment in a city so immaculately self-contained you'll never want to leave. You'll feel you can live here forever. And who knows?*

"Wow, tennis. Let's do it!" David said.

Claire was silent, wondering at the strange ad. The voices promised comfort and nurturing but contained an undercurrent of seduction. Corporate hype! They mocked real nurturing, what she had received from Lillian, and it irritated her.

*Nirvana. The Eternal City. Just four hours from Toronto's Pearson Airport, in the heart of the Muskokas. In the heart of the natural world. Follow your heart to Nirvana.*

"The Muskokas. That's where we're going," David said.

A road sign for Bracebridge said thirty kilometers, which translated into less than twenty miles. She checked the gas gauge. No need to stop. She wanted to reach Lillian's. Now more than ever.

*Nirvana. The Ultimate Experience.*

"Can I change it now?" David asked.

"Please."

He flipped the dial in time to catch the end of a fast food jingle and sang along, ". . . we do it all for you."

"I'd rather do it myself," Claire muttered, suddenly out of sorts. As if synchronized to the shift in her mood, the clouds darkened, lowering in the sky. The Jeep headed into a storm.

# Two

"Damn!" his mother said as the first drops splattered the windshield. "We better put the roof up."

"It's only a drizzle," David said. " 'Member when Dad bet us we wouldn't get wet and . . ." Dumb, he thought, real dumb.

They drove in silence. The scene from the past replayed in his mind like a video: *He was just a kid then, bouncing around in the back of the Jeep, his parents up front. He heard his dad's deep, reckless pirate's laugh. "Bet a buck the rain can't touch us, me laddies." The Renegade soared through the shower like a missile, its speed and windshield creating a magic airlock of protection.*

"We'd better put it up." His mother's voice snapped him back. The Jeep slid onto the shoulder. Dark clouds ate the sky. Drops as big as eyeballs fell.

Once they were back on the road, the Renegade shuddered as a wall of wind belted it head on. The weather, his mother's mood, everything had turned dark. He didn't like the feeling he had and shoved a Madonna tape into the deck.

"Honey, could you not play that now? You know the deck isn't working right, and that scratchy sound bothers me. I need to concentrate."

He wished his dad was here. His dad would have fixed the tape deck by now, or bought a new one, or better yet, he'd have put a CD-player in the Jeep! And his mom wouldn't be worried about every little thing.

The storm grew fierce as they drove into Bracebridge. His mother slowed the Jeep to a crawl and they turned north onto Highway 4, another worn, two-lane country road cut between enormous boulders of brown and rusted red, the whole thing nearly swallowed by dense forest. The rain poured too heavy to see out the window.

Suddenly, as if a faucet had been turned off, the rain stopped. He rolled down his window.

"Dry land ho!" his mother said. A weather-battered sign announced: *Welcome to Chesborough*. They passed a low building on their right with *Ontario Provincial Police* stenciled on its side.

"Civilization," he said unenthusiastically, scanning the dead-looking fields. Out here the word "sticks" really meant something.

His mom geared down and turned into a gas station. A guy—older than him, maybe eighteen—body as rigid as a skateboard, came out from one of the open bay doors of the garage. Work boots and a tan uniform with grease stains. The name *Earl* embroidered in red on an oval fabric badge stitched above his heart. "What can I do you for?" he asked in a flat voice, like he'd invented the line. The guy stared at his mom in a sleazy way David didn't like.

David only half heard his mother say to fill it up and check the oil. He was busy checking out what there was of this so-called town.

Across the road: The Queen Victoria, a rotting three-story hotel, ringed by a sagging porch and topped by a shiny yellow satellite dish; a boarded-up theater called The

Strand, except the "r" was missing; and the same tired-looking Chinese restaurant they'd spotted in every town they'd gone through.

On this side of the road the gas station was crushed between The Country Kitchen—closed forever—and Emerson's Dry Goods, Grocery, Pharmacy and Boating Supply Shop. Right, David thought. If you can't get it at Emerson's you can't get it in Chesborough. This town's putrid.

After Earl-the-Geek had been paid, they parked at the side of the garage. "What's wrong?" his mother asked.

"Whatdaya mean?"

"I mean, what's bothering you, and I know something is."

He hated it when she did this. He shifted in his seat, but there was no way out. "Nothing. Except I hate this place. A no-star town." He used his personal town-rating system to erase Chesborough.

"What's so awful about it?" Her voice was wary.

"You told me I'd like it here but it's a dump, Mom."

"This is just the town. We're not going to spend much time here."

"This isn't a town, it's a bump on the road. A bug on a map." He glared at his mother. She glared right back.

"Let me get this straight. You don't like Chesborough."

"You got it."

"It's a bump on the road."

"Yeah."

"A bug on a map."

He didn't say anything.

"A skid mark on the lousy highway of life."

"I didn't use *those* words, but you've aced this one."

"Let's be clear about this. You're accusing me of bringing you to the smelly armpit of North America."

He couldn't stay angry. "Well, you *did* make me come here."

"And you're mad at me."

"Yeah." He refused to back down.

The fierceness in his mother's eyes softened as she studied him. He realized suddenly how disappointed he felt. She had noticed even before he had.

"I am sorry, David, and I don't blame you. Chesborough looks pretty bleak to me, too. It's not at all the way I remember. The town used to seem . . . I don't know . . . bright back then. Bigger. It's changed." She looked around. "It's grey and rundown. Depressing."

He tapped the edge of the rolled down window. "Ah, well, we just got here."

"Let's go into Emerson's. May as well get all our illusions shattered at once."

They walked to the store, shoes crunching gravel underfoot.

A small sign in the left corner of a dirty window read *Fishing Licenses* and another, on the right, said *Videos*. Tacked above the door a huge real estate sign had a *SOLD* sticker across it. "I wonder if the Emersons still own the store," his mother said.

The air had gotten like a sauna, but clear. David, sweating, followed his mother inside. He glanced at a battered thermometer on the doorframe, the mercury stopped at 87 degrees. Inside felt hotter, if that was possible. The screen door slapped shut behind him.

Lemme outta here! The stink hit first, like a dead cat he'd found rotting in their back yard last summer. The dimly-lit store was dirty and musty, a cluttered food museum. Wood shelves had buckled from years of carrying more weight than they'd been built to hold. Canned food.

21

Cleaning stuff. At the back an upright cooler with milk and soda—almost empty. Next to it was a refrigerator case with one package of butter, three cartons of eggs, a few lousy-looking tomatoes and a wilted head of iceberg lettuce.

The weirdest thing they had was the five plaster Elvis busts precariously balanced on the top of one dusty shelf. There was a rack of cheap tourist caps, one with a coiled plastic turd on the peak. The place was minus zero stars!

David looked at the display of video boxes just inside the door, all thirty of them. Most were Walt Disney and other kids' stuff, the rest boring movies, ones he'd never go see or rent. He didn't expect to find any video games, even old ones, and he was right. There was a pinball machine wedged between the cooler and the potato chip rack. He felt like playing. Then he spotted two videos on the top shelf that weren't so boring: *Tramphire* and *Bad Girls Do Dance*. He studied the pictures on the boxes while pretending to be looking at a map he took from the rack nearby.

His mom did some quick shopping and moved to the cash register, waiting for the clerk to come. Eventually the faded green curtain behind the counter quivered. A man, possibly the oldest in the world, shuffled out. Brown liver spots splotched his forehead and the back of his hands. Most of his dirty yellow hair had fallen out long ago. He was stooped over, and bony as a skeleton. They must've named the lake after him, David thought, holding back a wild laugh.

The old guy's watery, grey eyes, sunk deep in their sockets, glittered with suspicion. Silently he rang up the purchases and loaded them into a white plastic bag.

"You're Mr. Emerson, aren't you?"

The old guy nodded, short and unfriendly.

"Claire Mowatt. Formerly Palmer. You probably don't remember me. I used to visit my Aunt Lillian here a long time ago. Must be twenty years now. I was just a kid, but you and Mrs. Emerson were very kind to me."

Emerson grunted. Suddenly he began coughing, so long and hard David was afraid he might bite it then and there. His mother looked like she had the same thought. She leaned over the counter and steadied him.

Emerson scowled at her and shoved her hand away. He pulled a filthy handkerchief from his pant pocket and coughed into it, finally horking up something brown or maybe dark red. Something gross!

"Hey, Mom, you ready?" David asked.

"In a minute." Her forehead was creased. Not the old friendly Mr. Emerson you used to know, is he Mom? Sure wasn't the one she talked about.

When the old guy finally got a grip, he looked worse than before. His skin, paper-thin with a bluish tint, had turned the color of grey slime. Man, I'm outta here, David thought. Come on, Mom. This guy's puke city.

But, oh no, his mother had to go and ask, "How's your wife?"

"Dead." Emerson's stare was hostile.

"Oh, I'm so sorry. I didn't know."

He didn't explain. David had the idea the old fart enjoyed his mother's embarrassment.

"Who'd you say's your aunt?"

"Lillian Palmer. Her place is just down Skeleton Lake Road."

Emerson's body stiffened. He pushed himself back from the counter. David realized where the sour odor came from.

23

"If there's nothing else, Mrs., I got work out back." Emerson looked sly and guarded and his mom seemed upset.

"Come on. Let's go," David said, but she ignored him. He shifted to his other foot, trying to think of something tough and clever to say. The screen door opened.

A man wearing an Aussie bush hat came through and, behind him, a kid about David's age. He had orange-red hair cut short in a semi-punk style and two earrings and three ear cuffs in his left ear. Freckles the size of peas were sprinkled across his face, softening the tough cut. He glanced at David and nodded. David nodded back.

"Afternoon, Mr. Emerson," the man said.

Naturally there was no answer.

The new guy nodded at David's mother. The kid looked at David again and made a face that reflected David's thoughts about Emerson, and David twisted his mouth in agreement.

"Are you finished?" the guy in the hat asked.

"I think so," his mom said.

The guy looked at David's mom then at Mr. Emerson. "Ah, the natives . . . are unfriendly." He raised a sympathetic eyebrow.

David watched his mother blush. Geez! Adults can act so dumb. Still, there was something about this guy that was okay. His hair and eyes reminded David of wet Miami sand. He seemed like a physical kind of guy but smart too, not brainy like his dad, but the kind of guy who could survive in the jungle on berries and rainwater if he had to. Maybe it was the hat.

"My aunt died recently. I'm here to settle her estate."

"That wouldn't be Lillian Palmer?"

"Did you know her?"

"You're her niece Claire?" He frowned.

"Yes."

"She told me a lot about you. I'm Gord Roberts. I own the land next to hers. Yours now."

"Nice to meet you."

His mom put out her hand and Gord Roberts' hand surrounded it. She blushed again. She's getting hot for him, David thought. The idea of his mom feeling that way about anybody but his dad made him a little sick to his stomach. He turned away.

The kid had moved to the pinball machine and David followed. Suddenly he turned and asked, "You from around here?"

"I thought *you* were."

"You kidding?" the kid said sarcastically, pressing the buttons on the machine. There was no money in it so nothing happened. "I'm from Toronto. My stepdad lives here and I come up summers. Jerry."

"David. From Miami."

"Miami? Get real!"

"Really."

"That's a long way."

"Tell me about it. We drove up."

Jerry looked impressed.

"Don't they have any video machines?" David asked, and Jerry gave a short laugh.

David moved to the front of the pinball and slipped a U.S. quarter into the slot. It worked. "Wanna play?"

"Sure."

He put in a second quarter and the board lit up for two players. "You first," he said.

Jerry pulled the plunger like a pro. The silver ball sped up the shoot and rolled slowly down through the maze of barriers, slots and other obstructions. He flipped levers and jiggled the machine gently with steely concentration, red flaring up the sides of his cheeks, finally racking up an astonishing 2,500 points.

"Not bad," David said, taking over, feeling the pressure of competition on a machine he wasn't exactly familiar with. "You guys live next door, huh?"

"Un huh."

"What's it like around here? Anything to do?"

"You're doin' it."

"That's what I was afraid of." They looked at each other and grinned. Meanwhile, the silver ball dropped to the bottom of the machine and disappeared. David looked up. Only 1,200 points. "I guess you play all the time," he said, stepping aside.

Suddenly an angry male voice said, "You don't know these people. I do! And you sure as hell don't know what's going on!" And before David had even turned around to see what was happening, Jerry's stepfather was by the machine saying, "Come on, son."

"But we just got here—"

"Let's go!" Roberts started towards the door.

David's mom looked startled. He glanced at Jerry, who shrugged his shoulders and rolled his eyes as if to say, 'Adults—what can you do?' At the door Jerry called, "See ya."

Before the screen door shut, he ducked back in. "Come on over sometime. It's the stone house."

"Okay," David said, but Jerry had already gone.

He made his way to his mom's side. Emerson was just disappearing behind the curtain, taking the bulk of the stink with him. "You okay?" he asked.

She stared at him for a moment like she wasn't seeing him, took in air and blew a big puffy-cheeked breath out.

"This *used* to be a friendly town."

"What'd that guy say?"

"I'm not sure. A difference of opinion, I think. Tell you later. Let's get out of here and look for the cottage."

Half a mile out of Chesborough a billboard advertised *Nirvana—The Eternal City.* It was almost exactly like the dozens of other billboards they'd seen since entering Canada, except this one said *Two Kilometers,* and it had an arrow pointing down a dirt road.

They turned onto that road, barely wide enough for the Jeep. Dense green trees scraped the sky and even the wild scrub bush had grown as tall as David.

"How's anybody get anywhere in the winter?" he asked.

"Snowmobiles. But, really, the locals pretty much stay put. At least Aunt Lillian did. She was extremely self-sufficient."

"How many people live here?"

"I'm not really sure. There are cottages in the summer. I'd guess no more than five hundred year-round residents."

"Five hundred? There's more kids at my school."

She laughed.

The rutted road made for a bumpy ride. The trees grew so close together he couldn't see very far in any direction. Overhead branches cut out most of the sunlight. This wasn't like Miami. He had the feeling all this green stuff could swallow the Jeep and nobody would ever know.

As his mom drove through the shadowy tunnel, he felt frustrated that he'd have to wait four more years to get his license. Driving on this road would be fun. Like speeding through a living tunnel pitted with craters on the moon.

When the lake came into view, he saw the island right away. A Plexiglas bubble covered most of it. "Hey, Mom,

27

look!" Sunlight glinted off the reflective emerald glass. It was like a movie, seeing this out here in the woods. He almost expected the top to open and cyber warriors riding unicorns to fly out. "What is it?"

She slowed, looked long enough to focus, then turned right. "Looks like a dome."

Right, Mom, he thought. I couldn't figure that out!

Another *Eternal City* sign announced that their dock was in the same direction. Every so often he spotted a "No Swimming" sign along the edge of the water. They passed a stone house with a dusty red mailbox that had G. Roberts painted across the side.

Somebody, in David's opinion, had messed up when they named Skeleton Lake. The water was living grey-blue against at least twenty shades of brilliant green. Reflected on the surface were the birds gliding across a nearly cloudless sky. Out of the corner of his eye he saw things in the lake. Things like people, floating, but there was something wrong. Now the stupid shrubs blocked his view! "Mom, stop!" he yelled.

His mother braked hard. "What? Why did you yell?" She looked around.

"Out in the water. I think there's bodies."

"Bodies? Come on, David, it's probably a group of people swimming or something . . ."

Dark forms bobbed into a clear patch. They were bodies alright, but not human.

His mother turned to him, shaking her head, looking frazzled and not about to put up with much more. "Otters. I haven't seen one since I was last here."

"But they're all dead. How come?"

She started the Jeep and sighed. "I don't know, David, and right now I don't care."

# Three

As Jack Williams strode out of the Ontario Provincial Police station, he noticed the red Renegade whoosh by, heading north into town. Woman driver. Passenger, male youth. Florida plates.

Williams climbed into his cruiser, backed away from the stucco building and fishtailed out of the packed-dirt parking lot onto Highway 4. Minutes later he was glued to the Renegade's ass.

Had to be them; description fits. He had work to do, investigate the fire, no real need to follow . . . except to satisfy a vague sense of curiosity.

One of the few pleasures he still had left in this job was the quiet satisfaction of knowing everything that happened on his turf. He was as familiar with these twelve hick burgs as he was with his hemorrhoids. And although they were just as much a pain in the butt, Williams managed to get a handle on the pulse of the towns quite a while ago. It had paid off lately. He intended to keep the advantage.

And the game was fun. He knew about the woman and boy. They didn't know about him.

Nearing the town of Chesborough, the two vehicles passed the Donaldsons' farm on the left. What was left of it. Unplowed fields overgrown with weeds. Set in their midst were two buildings in charred ruins. Last night, just after sunset, the barn went up in flames fast and the fieldstone house had been gutted. Now it was just a reeking blackened shell. The crematorium for the Donaldson child.

Three wood frame houses went by on the right. Landmarks in the region, they were homesteads built around the turn of the twentieth century. Tall, weatherbeaten, severe, each stood like a defiant spinster determined to outlive the entire town.

God, he hated this place. But he could remember feeling differently. In the beginning, the first year . . . the first two . . . Chesborough seemed friendly, vibrant. Williams still had his dreams then.

It had been a mistake letting Mary Ellen talk him into accepting this posting. He could see that now. They'd been happy in the city, at least *he'd* been. Twenty-five years old, full of spit and fire ambition, he saw a promotion to Detective Inspector with the Criminal Investigations Bureau in his future. From there it would have been easy to move to a top position in the Ontario Provincial Police ranks. That wasn't just ego talking, the fantasy of a cocky young officer full of himself. His fellow cadets confirmed that assessment. And his instructors. Even Mary Ellen.

He lighted a cigar, Cuban, from the box brought back by his in-laws last winter when they went on vacation. The Renegade slowed to within the town's speed limit; he eased up on the gas.

They'd met fifteen years ago, he and Mary Ellen, his last year at the OPP College in Alymer, Ontario. He lived in Toronto. Commuted. Talked to her at a party. Slept with her a week later. Got her pregnant. The day after he graduated they married. At the end of that month they drove the U-haul to Chesborough. It was only supposed to be for a year or so.

She said she hated the city. Too crowded. Noisy. Polluted, even then. Bad for her allergies. Complaining the way people do. He didn't know it was more than that. Even before the move here she was always down with something or other and, at least at first, he took her symptoms seriously, hoping a brief stay in her home town would settle her. It didn't. She lost the baby and the possibility of having any more.

They'd been in Chesborough a year and a half when he started making noises about a transfer. He wanted to go back to Toronto—the fastest way to move up. She claimed the stress at the thought of returning to the city made her sick. Besides, this was her hometown. Her parents were old. She owed it to them to stay a while. They wouldn't live forever. Wasn't he being selfish? Only another year or two, at most. They were young, had plenty of time.

Four more years down the road and just when he'd decided that, dammit-all, it was time, her allergies worsened and she developed asthma. Then the headaches started, bad ones, migraines that kept her in bed alone for days on end, drapes drawn, the bedroom dark and quiet. Their medicine cabinet bulged with codeine, Advil, Furinol, Valium. His sex life was a joke. How can you make love to a wheezing corpse? he thought bitterly. He abandoned his wife to her shadowy, bedroom world, but he wasn't callous enough to leave her altogether.

Another year went by and he was just about fed up when Mrs. Van de Vooren, his mother-in-law, suffered a stroke. Mary Ellen accused him of being heartless when he squawked about the transfer. His father-in-law sweetened the bitter pie by making him a silent partner in the business, on condition they stay in Chesborough.

The Jeep signaled, slowed and pulled into the gas station. Williams kept going. In the rear-view, he watched Earl Gwinski come out of the garage. Williams radioed in the license number of the Renegade for a computer check. Damn if it wasn't taking forever to get those VDTs installed in the cruisers up here!

Left elbow out the window, right hand on the top of the wheel, he drove slowly to the other end of town, beyond Nirvana's billboard, past open fields gone to seed, then some farmhouses. Half the homes were abandoned. At one time he would have resented them. Alive but dead. Too much like him.

Somewhere along the way the town lost its energy. Maybe it was the free trade agreement with the States and Mexico, maybe not. Half a dozen years ago Benson's Furniture Factory relocated to Buffalo. Then, this spring, dammit all to hell, Van de Vooren's Brewery, the other industry in Chesborough, not to mention the rest of the region, had to shut down when the natural spring got contaminated. The money, any hope of a future was dead.

Twenty years and all he had to show for it was a Sergeant's badge and partnership in a bankrupt brewery in one desolate region of Ontario. His dreams, once so solid, so close he could almost squeeze them, were as empty as these houses. It was too late. Or had been.

Ahead, a blackbird, wing broken, flopped at the edge of the road's shoulder. Fucking bird! He hated birds. Always had. They shit everywhere. Make a racket at dawn. Try to peck your hands open when you feed them. Alfred Hitchcock had it right. If he had to tell the truth, Williams had always been a bit spooked by flying creatures. And Mary Ellen had to keep two of them right in the house!

He felt a familiar urge well up. He could tromp on the

gas. Turn the wheel. Squish! Yeah. Easy. Who would know? Or care?

He listened to the swoosh as he passed on by. Williams had just surprised himself.

It wasn't that the cauldron of bitterness didn't still gnaw at him. His life was wasted time. Lost chances. He'd been run over by goddamn fate.

Chesborough had become a monster in his mind. Sucking his energy. Slowly draining him of life. Just last year he might've given in to the impulse to crush the bird. Hell, he *had* given in. Regularly. Groundhogs, Squirrels. One night a goddamn red fox, startled by the headlights. Splat! Right onto the fender. Felt *good*. Eased the frustration that chewed his insides.

But now—he still couldn't believe it fully—maybe all that had changed. He had hope again. In fact, wouldn't it be a laugh if he was responsible for helping breathe new energy into the town that had swallowed his for so long. Life was still possible.

He turned the cruiser. When he reached the gas station, the Jeep was gone. Williams pulled up to the garage door. Earl came out wiping his hands on a greasy rag. When he saw who it was, he hurried over reluctantly. The kid wasn't bright—the result of inbreeding—but he was smart enough to remember the couple of run-ins they'd had.

"Hey, Sergeant. How ya doin'?" His voice was wary.

Williams climbed out without answering. He adjusted his belt, aware of a gut whose spread had finally been arrested and was now shrinking. "The lady in the Jeep, and the kid. Seen them before?"

"No, sir."

"What'd they want?"

He saw the kid struggling about whether or not to mouth

off, and gave him a hard stare. "Gas." Earl played it straight. "Checked the oil—it was okay. Cleaned the windshield."

"You talk about anything else with them? Like town business, anything like that?"

Earl looked scared. "No, sir. We never talked about nothin' like that. Just gas and oil. And I give 'em directions."

"That's good, Earl," Williams said, clamping a hand onto the boy's shoulder. "Our business is our own, not meant for strangers."

"Yes, sir."

"Where'd they go when they left here?"

"Into Emerson's. When they come out they headed down to the lake."

"Good boy." Williams squeezed the shoulder until Earl winced.

Inside Emerson's, he walked behind the counter and brushed past the faded curtain to the back room. The stench made his stomach turn. Body odor. Body excretions. Decay.

Burt Emerson sat on the edge of a pullout bed staring at a fourteen-inch color TV screen. A soap opera played out. In one corner, an old enamel stove, half wood burner, half electric, had a cast iron frying pan full of grease sitting on top waiting to catch fire. In another corner, a small refrigerator, the door encrusted with years of grime. Between them a sink crammed with dirty dishes.

Williams switched off the TV. Emerson, who was hard of hearing, jumped. "What'n tarnation . . . ?"

Williams stalked towards him.

Emerson recovered his crustiness.

"Trying to scare me to death? Ain't you cops never heard of knocking?"

"The woman and boy who were in the store. What'd they want?"

"Groceries. That's what I sell, ain't it?"

"What else?"

"Nothin'."

"Didn't go shooting off your mouth, did you, Burt? Talking about things that aren't the business of outsiders?"

"You know me better," the old man said, but his left eyelid twitched nervously.

"Anybody else in here?"

"Gord Roberts."

"He talk to them?"

"Yep."

Williams sighed. "What about?"

"Don't know. She didn't take to him, though. They had a row."

There was no use pursuing this. The woman and boy didn't know anything and wouldn't likely be here long enough to make trouble anyway. Roberts likely spouted his usual paranoid bullshit, but nobody in their right mind took him seriously.

When Williams returned to the cruiser, he reached through the window and called the station. The computer check on the Renegade's plates confirmed what he already knew—the owner was Claire Mowatt, Lillian Palmer's niece.

Before he headed for the Donaldsons', he sauntered across the road to the pay phone outside the theater and placed a local call. When he got an answer, he smiled and announced, "We've got visitors."

# Four

"Man, lookit that car!" David yelled.

Claire turned onto the bare earth driveway and pulled up behind Lillian's 1959 Chevrolet, the same one she'd owned for over forty years. An immense feeling of loss hit.

David jumped out of the Jeep. He circled the Chevy, trying the doors, opening the trunk. "I'm keeping this!"

Claire made her way along the narrow flagstone path, nearly overgrown with grass. Dandelions had invaded the flower beds; Lillian had always kept them neatly mulched. Wild red roses and orange day lilies looked under siege. The petunias and impatiens, which should still be blooming, had been suffocated; only their brown-edged leaves remained. Claire suspected she'd find the vegetable and herb gardens out back in similar condition.

The maroon paint was badly peeling from Lillian's A-frame. The mesh on the screen door had been nearly ripped out. The birch door was locked—Lillian had never locked it—and Claire used the key that had been sent to her. The moment they entered the stuffy cottage the odor of mold engulfed them.

Dust covered the old-fashioned love seat's wildflower upholstery, the rustic tables and chairs, the large, shiny mahogany radio from the forties that Lillian loved and had always kept in good repair. Claire opened windows to air the place out.

"There's no TV. Or microwave," David said petulantly.

She crossed her arms and sighed impatiently.

"TV must be upstairs," he said, heading up.

The mantle over the fireplace was crowded with photographs, rocks, pieces of wood, shells, things that had been important to Lillian. Claire picked up a framed black and white photograph—the picture of her with Lillian at Witch Rock on the island. Memory tinted the photo: silver hair, blue eyes fired with immense warmth and wisdom, the mauve pendant dangling at her aunt's throat. Lillian had always worn that rough, unpolished chunk of amethyst, a natural cross. She claimed she'd been led to it when she was a girl and it was more than a lucky charm. "It's my ally," she'd said. "Someday it will save your life."

"There's a loft up here," David called.

Next to that photo was one Claire sent her aunt two Christmases ago, just before Bill's accident. She, Bill and David had been on holiday in Tampa. Pink flamingos dotted the bay in the background and Claire had written, "Hope to see you soon." Things hadn't worked out that way.

"I can't find the TV."

"David, I don't think you'll find a TV. Or a microwave. Or even a telephone."

"Man, that sucks! At least I've got my cell. If I had anybody to phone."

Claire climbed the ladder, the steps rounded on the edges from decades of wear. On the antique brass bed lay a lilac down comforter that covered what Claire remembered as the softest mattress in the world. A cherrywood dresser and matching chest of drawers, mammoth pieces of furniture by today's standards, stood under one side of the sloped ceiling. At the other side stood Lillian's easel, and a small table with her paints. And everywhere bundles of herbs hung upside down from beams, drying in the attic's drier air.

Claire opened the window to let some fresh air flow through the screen.

"Yuck!" She turned to see David squatting, examining canvases stacked against the wall. Lillian embraced nature in her artwork. Plants, the detail impressive, woodsy scenes, animals, the lake surrounded by sky and bush. All bright, alive, colors she used to call Peruvian, "Because," Claire recalled her saying, "South Americans live in this world. They're not ethereal, like the pastel people. Or reptilian, the way most North Americans dress."

But when Claire looked over her son's shoulder, she was startled. Every canvas was thick with browns, blacks and grays, the reptilian colors, the ones Lillian said symbolized death. Harsh, matte finishes made with flat haphazard brush strokes, not the fine work Lillian favored. Ugly, rabid animals, burnt out forests, dangerously jagged rocks, a blood red lake filled with garbage and bloated, decaying fish. One winter scene showed grey-tinged snow and another, of spring, had the new bright green leaves on a maple tree already decaying.

Lillian knew she was going to die, Claire thought. A shiver ran the length of her spine. Neither she nor David needed this right now. "Let's unpack the Jeep," she said, starting back down the stairs.

They were just lifting out the bags when a battered green pickup truck pulled up behind the Jeep. An Irish setter had its head stuck out the open window and looked to be the driver. Claire saw Gord Roberts behind the setter and felt her jaw clench.

He turned off the ignition, climbed out, and tried to close the door to keep the dog in. "Stay Mouche!" he ordered sternly. Mouche, however, ignored him and scrambled out. Tail wagging, rump wiggling, the dog went straight to David.

Claire folded her arms across her chest. "I hope you didn't drop by to harass me further."

Roberts' sheepish look amused her but she wouldn't show it.

"I came to apologize." He removed the big hat. "I was out of line."

Claire waited.

"Look. Maybe we can start over. I'm Gord Roberts, your basically friendly neighbor." He put out his hand, which Claire left hanging in the air for an extra couple of seconds. But the vulnerable, boyish expression on his face caused her to reach out and shake his hand.

"Claire Mowatt. My son, David."

David, who'd been playing with the dog, nodded. Gord reached down and scratched the setter behind the ears. "And this is Scaramouche, my master and owner."

Claire admitted the guy had a nice smile. And when he looked back at her, pale brown eyes so intense, she was aware of blushing for the third time in his presence. My God, she thought, I'm acting like a teenager. To hide her embarrassment she looked across the water. "It's a beautiful day."

"Yes," he said. "Weather's been decent. Hot but not as humid as last year. Smell off the lake's not too bad today."

"Did you just come up for the summer?"

"I live here year round."

"Must be cold in the winter," David said.

Trust a man who likes kids and dogs, Claire thought, noticing the way Gord looked at her son. And then, but what do I care? He's just a neighbor.

"You get used to the cold," Gord was saying. "But there are only five of us on this road, Lillian included, who stay the whole year. We call ourselves 'the locals', although the townies have never quite accepted us into the small-town fold. Almost everybody else along this part of the lake is just a summer cottager—back to the city after Labor Day. At least up until last year."

"What happened?" Claire asked.

He gave her his full attention again and once more she felt those eyes, as though they were recording details about her body and soul. "Nirvana began buying up the land. They own this whole strip of Skeleton Lake Road now, except for me, Bailie Rankin, Colette and Gilles Robineau, and Lillian. You now. That's why I went a little crazy in Emerson's. Nirvana's been pressuring us to sell. The others won't. Lillian refused. I overreacted when you said you would."

"I said I was *considering* selling. David and I live in Florida. I'd love to keep this land, but owning property in Canada isn't too practical."

"Probably not." His eyes turned the color of hard-packed sand. Claire hoped there wouldn't be another outburst.

"The thing is, sometimes issues are bigger than personal convenience. Or even economics. Sometimes they concern values."

Claire felt her jaw tighten again. Who the hell was this guy? Ralph Nader of the woods? The world isn't perfect; you have to live your life. And what did selling a couple of acres in Canada have to do with values?

She didn't want to argue. Not with him or with anyone. The stress of traveling, of being at Lillian's again, the paintings that brought home her aunt's horrible death, it was all piling up. "Look, Gord, maybe we can talk about this later." She knew her voice wasn't encouraging. The attraction she'd felt only moments before had dissolved into irritation.

"All right," he said, the sheepish look back on his face. "We won't talk about it now."

"Good," Claire said.

"It's just that I really would like to tell you some of what's been going on around here."

Her hands clenched into fists.

Gord must have noticed. He raised both palms. "Hey, we won't talk about it right now. Honest. And when we do, I promise to keep it simple and as short as possible. But you're a land owner here. Before you sell, to whoever you decide to sell to, you probably want to have all the facts so you can make the best decisions."

"Are we talking about it now?" Claire felt herself slip a little out of control. She didn't know whether to laugh or scream. "It seems to me we *are* talking about it."

"We *aren't* talking about it," he insisted, his voice low, oh-so-reasonable.

"I don't want to talk about it right now."

"Fine."

"Good!"

They stood glaring at each other.

Claire began to feel that maybe she was being too defensive. She sighed. "Okay, look, you've convinced me. We'll talk about it. But not today. David and I have been on the road for five days. I just want a swim in that lake."

"I wouldn't do that."

"Why not?"

"People around here have been getting skin rashes and sore throats this summer. Local health department posted warning signs recently. Your indoor water's from a ground well and Lillian put in a chlorine filter. Should be safe. There's a water sampler—Lillian kept it by the sink. You can do a quick test."

"Well, I'll have a shower, then. I'm hungry and exhausted. All I want to do is unpack and unwind."

"Come to our place for supper. We're right next door."

"Let me take a rain check. I've got a lot of memories I want to sort out tonight."

He looked a little fearful she was just trying to get rid of him. It made Claire feel she had to offer something concrete. "Tell you what. Why don't you and, what's your son's name?"

"Jerry. My stepson. His mother and I are divorced."

The information sent a thrill through Claire and she reprimanded herself severely. "You and Jerry come to dinner here tomorrow night. About seven."

"Sure. If it's no trouble."

"None. And you can tell me about all the skeletons in the Skeleton Lake real estate closet then."

He smiled but then turned serious. "It might not be healthy dinner conversation."

"Well, after dinner then. I'll take my chances."

He nodded and looked relieved. "I'll bring the wine. Home-made. And I really am sorry. All of us on this road have been through a lot the last year. I . . . well, we won't talk about it."

Scaramouche barked sharply, then growled. He moved away from a suddenly scared David and slunk over to Rob-

Eternal City

erts, who said, "What's wrong, boy?"

Coming up the road, silent but for the crackle of pebbles under wheels, was a silver stretch limousine. It looked completely out of place here on a dirt road.

"Wow!" David said.

The driveway was full and the long vehicle pulled onto the overgrown lawn and stopped right beside them. The rear window eased down smoothly, noiselessly, and a woman wearing a stylish blue-grey summer business suit and designer sunglasses leaned forward and turned to face them.

"Mrs. Mowatt?"

"Yes," Claire answered, happy to have found her voice. She looked at David, whose mouth had dropped open, and then at Gord. His face had become as hard as the granite boulders that dotted the terrain.

"Brenda Lawrence." The woman in the limo smiled with thirty-two even, white teeth. She extended a hand through the open window. "Head of Public Relations. From Nirvana. I'm here on behalf of Mr. Varik, CEO of the corporation." Her handshake felt pretentiously firm to Claire.

Claire said, "Mr. Varik made the offer for this land."

"On behalf of Nirvana Corporation, yes. Now that you're here, the company hopes we can do business."

Claire felt a little dazed. "Ms. Lawrence—"

"It's Brenda."

"Brenda, we just arrived, less than an hour ago. I haven't had time to consider anything yet, even dinner."

The glossy smile seemed fixed. Brenda's unlined skin, the precision cut of her hair, the expensive clothes made her look like a mannequin. Claire suspected that at the hint of a wrinkle in that suit, and Brenda would chuck it.

"Claire, would you be my guest for dinner in the Eternal

43

City? We have several haute cuisine restaurants which serve some of the finest food in North America. Our saucier is French and our pastry chef from Switzerland."

Claire laughed, thinking, I've had more offers for dinner in one day than I've had in two years. "Not tonight. Maybe another time."

"Lunch tomorrow, then. The car will pick you up at eleven-thirty. Our launch is at the dock a mile down the road. The ride to the island is thirteen minutes and twenty seconds. I'll show you the City and we can discuss the offer then." It sounded like a command and Claire felt her resistance rising.

"I'm not sure about tomorrow—"

"Why don't you take yourself and your ostentatious car back to your Kevlar world and leave her the hell alone! You're poisoning the air!" Gord's tone reeked of venom. In Claire's opinion, he was way out of line and now she felt resistant towards him too.

Brenda seemed unperturbed. "Mr. Roberts, I understand your reluctance to part with your property, despite a generous offer, but Mrs. Mowatt may feel differently. She's obviously a woman of intelligence, which I hope you can appreciate. Surely she's capable of acting on her own behalf. Unless, of course, I've misperceived and you officially represent Mrs. Mowatt's interests and—"

"What you misperceive could fill that dome ten times over. Mrs. Mowatt isn't interested in having lunch with a cyborg. And if she wants to sell her land, there are other buyers, most of whom aren't interested in turning the earth into an exclusive playground for rich plastic bitches like you."

"Just a minute!" Claire said. "I'm perfectly capable of speaking for myself."

"You are, when you have all the facts."

"Well then, I'll get all the facts from both sides, if you don't mind. Brenda, eleven-thirty sounds fine."

Gord snorted in disgust. He called, "Mouche!" and jumped into his pickup. The dog leaped through the passenger window. The vehicle backed out quickly and, tires spraying stones and gravel, and tore up the road.

Claire gritted her teeth, furious at Gord, not only for taking off like that, but also for getting her into a situation—the lunch—which she didn't really want to be part of. The damage was done, though.

Brenda was already saying, "Eleven-thirty it is. Looking forward to it. Til then, Claire." The smoky window rose and the limo pulled away.

When she and David were finally alone, Claire shook her head rapidly, hoping to get enough oxygen circulating in her brain cells so she could think clearly.

"Something tells me Gord won't be coming to dinner tomorrow night," David said.

"I already knew that," Claire said.

"That Brenda's a Styrofoam junkie."

"I knew that, too," she said.

"I think Gord likes you."

Claire glanced sharply at her son, who stared back at her all innocence. "I *didn't* know that," she said, feeling a blush rise up her face, thinking, so much for ESP.

# Five

Just after sunset, Earl stalked the lake half nude. Stinging nettles gouged his bare feet and pine branches whipped his exposed back and chest. He tripped over jagged rocks that cut his flesh. Disinterred tree roots seemed determined to force him down to the ground. They would not stop him, though. He had to get there in time. He had to be ready.

As the full moon hung rigid at the top of the sky, Earl reached the cottage shaped like an A. Almighty. Ascendance. Always. He scrambled up the knoll. The air felt heavy; crickets and night creatures made racket but otherwise, silence.

THEY would come here. He always knew where THEY would be. Where he should go. It was like a short wave radio in his head. He had a direct link to THE FATHER and THE MOTHER. THEY *knew* he was tuning in. He overheard things, secret things, every night. Who was good. Who was bad and needed chastisement. Who was going to heaven. Or to hell.

Like last night. He knew THEY were going to the stone farm house. He'd got there first, and watched and waited and grew so tired he almost fell asleep. It was just after midnight. THE FATHER and THE MOTHER and all their angels descended from heaven in a burst of glory. The fever eyes of THE FATHER spotted him. THE MOTHER'S benevolent eyes. THEY blessed him for coming. For obeying.

That night he had been witness to terrible things. THEIR majesty and glory unfolded before his eyes. Great apocalyptic powers sprayed the night and lit the sky brilliant as day. Wasn't that a miracle? Bringing the fires of hell to earth for all to see so that they may atone while there was still time?

He cried when THE FATHER took the boy. Not for the boy but for himself. He begged THE FATHER, "Take me too! I'm ready. I'm a good boy. Don't I deserve life everlasting?"

THE FATHER and THE MOTHER spoke in unison. Evil lived in him. He must prove himself. The evil must be purged from his body before his soul could attain the innocence worthy of dwelling with them in their realm. Forever.

He felt his heart fracture.

But that was then. By morning he had been purged. Tonight THEY would see how much he had changed.

But he grew bored waiting. He tried the cottage door; it was unlocked so he let himself in. Darkness filled the inside, but he'd been here before.

He stopped and listened. Someone on the couch snored deeply. The boy from the Jeep the woman called David. He lay on his side, facing the back, one arm clamping a pillow over his ear. He wouldn't hear a thing.

Earl climbed to the second floor, where he had been before, when the old witch lived here. A body lay in the crone's big bed. As he approached he saw it was the woman who drove the Jeep. Blonde hair. Younger than the wrinkly witch. Pretty. He lifted the comforter. A gauzy white nightdress covered her slim body. Fleshy rounded breasts swelled and fell with each breath. He peeled down the sheer

fabric and blew lightly on a pink nipple. The nipple hard-
ened. The woman's mouth opened and a low moan escaped. Her body shifted towards him. Slut! he thought. Just
like the old whore of the Devil. The one THE FATHER
relegated to hell fire for eternity.

The young witch seemed dead to the world, but he knew
it was a trick. They always tried to trick him. If the witch's
malevolent eyes popped open, he would be plunged into
damnation. He had to avoid that at all costs.

He took the little bottle he'd stolen from his father's
shop out of his pant pocket, unscrewed the cap and poured
clear liquid onto his handkerchief. The air turned sickly
sweet. He held the hanky near her mouth. She breathed in
and out. He moved it a little closer. Breathe in, out. Closer.
He had to do it gradually, not like his father did with the
animals. After six breaths the cloth touched her nose and
lips. He lay the handkerchief on the table and returned the
bottle to his pocket.

He unzipped his pants and his bad thing sprang out. It
had already grown and gotten hard. So hard there was no
way to stop it now. It was the witch's fault. If she wasn't
evil, he wouldn't be doing this. He lifted the skirt of her
nightdress. Blonde hairs curled in an upside down triangle
that taunted him—Satan's sign.

A word branded into his brain flared as if the letters were
on fire: SINNER! This was the devil's work. He better run
before THE FATHER discovered him weakening. But he
couldn't move. Maybe THE FATHER would never find
out.

He crawled onto the bed, careful not to touch his flesh to
hers. It was enough to defile this bad part, which was already wicked. No use contaminating the rest. He shoved
her white legs wide apart and got between them. The smell

of her Venus trap swirled up like smoke from perdition to fill his nostrils and set his brain smoldering. He was the fly she was trying to snare in her web. Knowing this did not make the slightest bit of difference. He held his bad thing in one hand and rubbed it and aimed it at her evil trap.

A noise! THEY were coming.

His bad thing shrank to its right size. Panicked, he raced to the window.

A wind had blown up, churning the lake. He heard THEM calling, as if from a great distance, the eerie cry cutting the night air. The creatures of the earth fell silent in adulation. Suddenly the sky filled with the power and the glory. He watched THEM descend, bringing heaven to earth. His heart quickened in joyful fear and awe; that and the heat of the night made his body leak sticky sweat.

THE FATHER led, as always, eyes terrifying, cleansing as white fire. A blaze that could purge sins and manifest righteousness. THE MOTHER was right behind, supportive and nurturing.

The angels descended onto the A-frame like a flock of birds. The structure creaked as he heard them perch across the sharp line of the roof, along the eaves; he watched others float to the lawn. THE FATHER hovered in mid-air at the upstairs window, a miracle. HIS massive body gleamed and quivered. Liquid fire sparked from HIS eyes, an accusation!

THE FATHER struck out in rage. Earl jumped back. Metal scraped as if the doorway to hell was being torn open when the window screen ripped apart. A shriek of condemnation cracked the air like a whip. THE FATHER told him that he had no business here, and ordered him to leave the woman alone.

Earl ran downstairs as quickly and quietly as he could,

pulling his pants up, hiding his bad thing from HIM. He dashed into the yard and cried: "Am I not your son? Take me with you now. I am ready."

THE FATHER pierced him with those terrible eyes. Earl knew what that meant. Despair ate through him.

"Take this cup away!" he pleaded.

THE FATHER, displeased, barely controlling himself, turned away.

THE MOTHER interjected, *You are not ready. Do what must be done.*

He knew what that meant too. He needed further purging. The impurities must be burned out of him until he shone clear as star fire.

THE FATHER and THE MOTHER were going away. THEIR angels followed. Their heaven scent, their other-worldly voices drifted and lifted until he stood in the yard alone in the black silent night, tears of shame and loss streaming down his cheeks. There was nothing to do but obey.

At dawn, exhausted, he returned to the sickly sweet world of silver pain.

His dad's towering body blocked the work trailer's doorway. Earl eased by him. His mom, bloody knife in hand, quivered in fury.

"Obey thy parents!" The annihilating voice of his father packed the clotted air with a pronouncement of doom.

"I was called. By HIM," he tried to explain.

"Blasphemer!" his father yelled, and slapped him hard. "Liar! Prepare yourself, in His name," his mother commanded.

He undid his pants. The unnaturally bright eyes of the dead things cluttering shelves and attached to the walls stared accusingly. His bad thing had been the cause of his trouble. It had always kept him from his reward. If only he could get rid of it, but that was not possible, at least he didn't know how. He pushed his pants down to his knees and bent over the rusted oil drum. Immediately hard leather cracked against still-tender flesh, first from one side, then the other. Pain seared his backside as the two flesh-colored straps struck him again and again, so fast he could hardly catch his breath.

Pain would purge him. It was the only way. This time he would be clean. Clear as water. Pure enough to lighten and ascend. He strained to concentrate, to listen above the cracking for THE FATHER'S words. And although HE said nothing, there was a feeling that THE FATHER and THE MOTHER looked favorably upon this penance.

"I'm a sinner!" Earl cried.

"In His name . . ." Leather tore across his backside.

"Punish me."

". . . forever . . ." Crack!

"Purify the spirit through the body!"

". . . and ever . . ." Crack! Crack!

"Don't pity me."

"Amen." Crack! Crack! Crack!

"Show me no mercy!"

His father and mother complied. THE FATHER and THE MOTHER were pleased.

# Six

*Gnarled hands reach out for her. Hands not human. She shrinks back into a corner. The walls emit a sickeningly sweet stench. They collapse inward, creating a vertical stone coffin, suffocating her. She clutches at her clothes, ripping them away from her throat, from her body, but still the air thins. She is dying.*

*Suddenly she is a girl again. She lies alone in the grisly forest Aunt Lillian painted. Naked. The trees, the grass and bush, everything is enlarged, engorged. Distorted sounds sift through the decaying plants. Metal scrapes metal, and a whirring, like the wind turbine spinning on the roof, but inflated and dulled, as if she is listening underwater.*

*Lillian springs from the blood-filled lake. Her bloated corpse, rises straight up. Arms extend for a hideous embrace.*

*Claire screams. She tries to run but her body feels leaden. When she looks down, it has withered and turned mold green. Lillian's eyes glitter mauve, as if the amethyst she always wears has split in two and replaced her eyes. The stones are fixed in death. Her aunt's body is livid and stiff. Words stream from between her lips without the rotting flesh even moving. "You've been chosen. My death won't be in vain!"*

*Ripples appear in the crimson water. Ripples that quickly churn to tidal waves. From behind Lillian a pale shadow expands to fill the sky. The silhouette shape-shifts into something*

*Claire knows she should recognize but wants desperately to turn away from. It writhes erotically, and Claire feels caught in a ring of fire. A rancid odor presses in. The density surrounding her grows malignant. Evil.*

Claire jolted awake.

Sunlight splashed the room. In the distance the faint sound of water licked the shore. The air was dense with the smell of bacon frying, and freshly brewed coffee. Sweat covered her body, exposed by the nightgown bunched at her waist. She felt confused, and tried to focus her eyes but could not.

The scent of herbs. Was her aunt up already, making breakfast?

She trembled, trying to clear her head of the haze. Then she remembered: it was David downstairs.

Through the open bedroom window the sun just lit the tree tops. Surrounding it, a sky of crystal-blue.

She noticed the screen and gasped. The mesh had been forced outward and shredded. The gap was the shape of the indecipherable form in her dream, the darkness about to engulf Lillian. Good God! she thought, jumping out of bed. She stumbled and her head spun. She felt nauseous and panicked. Was she coming down with something? She reached the screen and fingered the jagged edges; she didn't remember it being ripped yesterday. She didn't remember that shape. But there'd been so much going on . . .

She found her watch on the table. Next to it lay a filthy man's handkerchief. This had not been here last night, she was sure of it. She picked the cloth up by a corner. A vague smell, sickly sweet. Nothing she could identify. She tossed it into the trash can, meaning to ask David about it later.

Her watch said eight a.m. Couldn't be! Since the summer holidays began she'd been intentionally sleeping in until nine. She'd been so exhausted last night she wouldn't have been surprised if her eyes opened today at noon.

As she washed, Claire's head began to clear and her stomach settle. But remnants of the nightmare clung to her. Being here, the stress of the trip, Lillian's death paintings, all of it had infected her sleep. The screen had been like that yesterday and she hadn't noticed; she'd transferred the image to her dream. But the handkerchief. Why couldn't she remember? She splashed more cold water on her face.

By the time she joined her son in the kitchen, daylight had nudged her into the here and now. "I hate early risers," she grumped, sitting down at the table.

"Good Day, eh!" David said, mimicking Canadian speech he'd heard en route, waving a spatula at her.

"Especially cheerful ones."

"Couldn't make pancakes. We forgot to buy syrup. I'm scrambling eggs. Want some?"

"Whatever." She poured herself a mug of coffee. "Just add syrup to the list on the counter. We'll have to go back to Bracebridge today or tomorrow."

David lifted the short, wide strips of Canadian back bacon out of the frying pan, and tucked the slices between paper towels. He drained most of the grease into a tin can and poured the mixture of eggs into the pan.

"My young chef," Claire said, as he served her breakfast.

"Chef Boy Ar Dee!"

The airy bright kitchen lifted her spirits. They ate at the big scarred oak table that took up most of the room to the sound of the old refrigerator purring like a cat. Claire looked at the gas stove and stainless steel double-sectioned sink, which were new since her last visit, both of which needed cleaning. But the butcher's block her aunt had found years before they were trendy still stood proudly in the corner. The knotty pine cupboards were crammed with boxes of staples and preserves and some canned goods. And jars and tins of unknown roots and herbs. Old fashioned, practical, and entirely Lillian.

"There's a root cellar out back," Claire said, "near the garden. We'll probably find it stocked with vegetables and maybe last year's apples, if I know Lillian."

The fresh country air and conventional breakfast worked magic. Her brain unclogged and other than being tired she felt almost normal. She noticed David had only taken a bite out of his bacon. She reached for a strip. It tasted meaty, low fat but packed with salt. "We always had this when I came up."

"It's awful," he said.

"It's an acquired taste."

"You said that about brussels sprouts."

Claire had planned to clean the cottage right after breakfast until all of a sudden David said, "I don't hafta go to lunch with that woman, do I?"

"Oh-my-God!" The Eternal City's car would be here in a couple of hours. "Honey, could you clean up a bit? You know, just sweep the floor and vacuum the oval rug down here. I'll do the rest when I get back."

He looked horrified. "Mom, this is supposed to be a *vacation.*"

"I'm just asking you to help me out. The place has been locked up since spring. It's pretty dirty."

"Why do we have to clean now? I mean, we just got here."

"David, please. I'm not in the mood. Like your t-shirt says, *Just Do It.*"

He got up and threw his plate into the sink angrily. "I'm so glad I made breakfast. If I knew I had to spend the day cleaning the whole house, I wouldn't've bothered."

"Just the downstairs," she said. "The kitchen and living room floor." This struggle of wills had been increasing in the last year or so. Maybe it was Bill's death or just the fact that David was at that age when boys rebel. Whatever, Claire found herself getting more and more annoyed with him and the sour note that too often seemed to permeate their relationship now.

She ran a bath and by the time she got out, the air had turned humid, and already she felt sticky. She had brought only one dress along, a red shift with short sleeves and tie belt. Her sandals would have to do. Claire felt self-conscious and irritated from the humidity and resented dressing up.

By eleven-ten she was at the window waiting for the car.

David had gotten around to doing what she asked; he was just pulling out the old carpet sweeper. "Honey," she said, "don't go swimming."

"Aw, Mom!"

"You read the warning signs. And don't take the canoe out until I show you how to use it."

"I was in a boat before, with Dad, if you remember."

"That was a while ago. And it was a rowboat. Canoes can be dangerous. Promise me, David."

His face became a mask of youthful angst. She could envision battles in a not-too-far-off future when she wouldn't let him have the Jeep whenever he wanted it.

"I guess I have to promise, don't I?"

"You're being unfair, David."

"Right!" He pushed the sweeper angrily across the braided rug and slammed out the back door.

At precisely eleven-thirty the silver limo pulled off the road into the driveway.

Aunt Lillian's home-made chamomile shampoo had left Claire's short hair a bit dried out, and she hadn't been able to blow dry it properly. Rebellious strands stuck up here and there. Leaving the cottage, she struggled to pat them down.

The uniformed driver, an older Tom Cruise, stood smiling. He opened the gull wing. She looked inside. Brenda was not in the back. Neither was Donald Trump.

Claire slipped into dark, air conditioned comfort, delighted by the luxurious salmon-velvet seats. There was a deep thud as the chauffeur closed the door.

The only other limousine rides she'd taken had been on the occasion of her wedding, and Bill's funeral. Those cars were basic. In this one, sprays of fresh orange and yellow daisies had been artfully arranged in vases attached to the mahogany side-panels. Before her, a panel holding a small television, a compact disc player, a DVD player, and a cabinet of movie and music discs. She slid open the door below the entertainment equipment and found a well-stocked bar. Claire was tempted to pour herself something to boost her confidence, but getting a clear head had been work today.

Through the tinted window she watched the woods pass by on the right and the lake on the left. Out in the water sat the island that housed the Eternal City, covered by the metallic bubble.

The incredibly smooth and silent ride made it seem as if they weren't moving at all. Claire realized that she couldn't hear the engine beneath the soft New Agey music drifting from the sound system. Harps and flutes; lofty, ethereal sounds that she found half comforting and half annoying. A devilish impulse prompted her to pick through the CDs in search of the Rolling Stones. Nothing even remotely like it.

The car tilted to the sky as it climbed a low grade. Claire sensed the engine's power beneath her and let herself be pushed back against the plush upholstery. Decadence! she grinned. I'd love to get used to this!

Within ten minutes they arrived at the dock, concrete, modern and permanent, not one of the ramshackle floating jobs dotting the lake. Beside it, bobbing up and down against tire bumpers, sat a two-tiered cabin cruiser with the name *Heaven Sent* inscribed in gold letters across the bow. International flags fluttered above the mahogany cabin. Claire couldn't even begin to guess how much the white fiberglass craft cost.

A white-suited crew member helped her onto the gleaming deck. The air stank of fish and gasoline and the rancid smell coming from the water itself; her stomach turned over. As she looked over the bow, she noticed a massive iridescent oil slick, floating in the water like an abstract painting. The waves pushed dozens of dead fish against the bank and then out again.

Powerful engines growled to life. Water churned, destroying the painting. As the boat slowly backed up, Claire was offered a comfortable deck chair and a drink. Throwing caution to the wind, she chose Dubonnet on ice and sat back to watch the captain on the fly bridge turn the vessel; the throb of the engines deepened and the bow lifted.

The green geodesic dome grew larger and larger, the glass panels reflecting like mirrors the surrounding environment: clouds, soaring birds, trees. Its size and—she had to admit it—splendor amazed her. Approaching the island, she remembered this place; Witch Rock on the north other side of the island had been the backdrop in the photograph of her and Lillian. The two of them canoed over and picnicked on this very island. They foraged for wild foods, gathering milkweed buds—when Lillian cooked them, they tasted like asparagus—and daylily tubers—baby potatoes. She remembered the island as at least two miles across. Lots of room for a small city.

As they glided into port, the dome turned opaque. Photosensitive, she realized. Nice touch. Probably almost clear at night.

They moved into an open marina at the entrance, roofed against the elements further in. A catamaran, sails furled, drifted by. The shirtless man at the tiller gave Claire a grin and a sailor's wave, which she returned.

Traffic in and out of the marina was heavy. There were all kinds of craft; large ones, small ones, motorboats and sailboats. The only common feature seemed to be the obvious quality of each vessel. A moneyed crowd, Claire thought, feeling pangs of jealousy.

The other commonality was the people; some on the decks of their boats, reading or sunning, drinks in hand, others preparing for departure. Claire had never seen a healthier, more beautiful crowd. Slim, tanned, smiling, dressed in trendy, casual clothing, not a frump to be seen. An advertisement for the good life. She wondered if you had to be part of the glitterati to live in the Eternal City.

The scene irritated her. Perfection always had. A little humanity, one or two warts, a crooked nose, a few mistakes here and there were comforting. She looked down at her simple dress.

This perfection left her feeling inadequate. But she wasn't inadequate. Her clothes might not be chic enough for this classy yacht club, but she looked pretty good. She still wore the same size dress as she had at university, and, apart from slightly unruly hair, she knew she could hold her own, here, anywhere, if she wanted to. She wasn't sure she wanted to.

Brenda, a bronzed Barbie doll in a white cotton short-sleeved dress with shoulder pads, approached the moment Claire stepped ashore. The woman's perfectly coiffed hair glowed auburn, the red strands highlighted by the sun. She wore white, fashionable sunglasses and expensive-looking high heels and walked quickly, with precise movements. Smiling as brilliantly as an actress in a toothpaste ad, she extended a hand. "Claire. So good to see you again. Did you have a pleasant ride over?"

"Yes," Claire said, shaking the cool hand. She had an outrageously juvenile thought: the next beautiful person I see I'm going to toss in the lake. Brenda, cool as an iceberg, made Claire wonder if the woman didn't sweat like an ordinary mortal. Instead of feeling conspicuous about her simple dress and shoes, the beginnings of a stubbornly haughty attitude surfaced.

They entered the city by a double airlock system. A golf cart with a fringed, canvas roof waited in the parking lot on the other side. Brenda got behind the wheel, Claire beside her, and they started up a road so new it looked like it had been paved yesterday.

From inside the dome, Claire could see outside clearly. A fence of pruned trees circled the perimeter of the island. Most of the interior birches and cedars had been cut away to accommodate the buildings and massive dome itself, the walls of which looked sturdy enough to withstand a nuclear blast.

"What's the dome for?" Claire asked.

When Brenda smiled, Claire got the feeling that her facial muscles moved automatically. "It's just one of the things that makes the Eternal City unique."

Here comes the pitch, Claire thought, as Brenda continued.

"Have you seen our ads?"

"Many times. I heard them on the radio coming up here. And I think I read an article on one of your Cities in the Caribbean."

Brenda laughed. "I guess you'd have to be a hermit to not have run across an Eternal City. The dome's part of our plan to keep the City environmentally pure. The technology is based on the Biosphere projects, NASA's self-sustaining environments they hope to build in space—of course, they had a few bugs, we're ironing them out. Our heating and cooling systems are solar generated. We grow three-quarters of our own food hydroponically or in greenhouses. The air is carbon purified and a careful balance between all the natural gases is maintained, the way it was before the earth's atmosphere became so damaged. The pollutants are filtered out and the solex glass acts like a sunscreen, blocking some ultraviolet and infrared rays of the sun. If we blocked all ultraviolet light, we'd risk nitrous oxide poisoning, as they did at Biosphere 2. This is a near total healthy living space, except for boating on the lake, and we're working on that. The environment's one hundred percent controlled. Marvelous, isn't it?"

Claire didn't answer, but she wondered where the expelled pollutants ended up. Back into the air for us plebs to breathe, no doubt.

The temperature-controlled air did seem easier to breathe. And from every direction the delightful scent of flowers slid through her. Suddenly, startlingly, Bill's funeral flashed to mind. Claire struggled to focus on what surrounded her, and on what Brenda was saying.

The buildings were modern versions of Swiss chalets,

German and French provincial styles and even the odd mock-Tudor manor, composed of wood, some fieldstone, some red brick. They drove down a street called Lancelot Lane. Spacious lawns, a park at every corner—most conspicuous was the absence of cars.

"Each square block has its own recreation facility. With aerobics classes, swimming pool, tracks, weight rooms, squash and racquetball and lots more," Brenda recited. "There's also sailing and waterskiing on the lake, with a wet suit, of course, because there's no swimming until they clean it up. Oh, and windsurfing too. Instructional classes run regularly throughout the day for every level."

Claire looked right and left. Every street they turned down became a new surprise. Homes now were in pastels, with gilded or silvered window and door frames, white or wrought iron terraces and balconies and latticed trellises up the sides with climbing rose bushes.

"We entered through Phase I," Brenda explained. "We've designed the periphery of the city with young adults in mind. The section you're seeing now is Phase II, mainly for families with older children, and middle-aged residents. We have another area at the center for retirees. You probably know the Eternal City functions on several levels. We're a time-sharing resort as well as a year-round mini-city."

"Everything to everyone," Claire said brightly.

"Exactly."

Brenda apparently missed the sarcasm.

It wasn't that Claire felt unimpressed. On the contrary, she found herself bowled over. Someone had a universal plan and the foresight and ability, not to mention the funds, to execute it.

But something felt wrong with this life in a Hallmark

card. Only the wealthy could escape to the Eternal City. This corporate wonderland was a fantasy, blocking out the real problems that the real world, the one she lived in, had to face.

Obviously the dome kept the rain out; Claire guessed plants and lawns were automatically watered. A sudden realization struck that she had not seen any animals, neither pets nor wild creatures, even birds and squirrels. She was about to ask about that when Brenda distracted her.

"Our residents usually fly into Bracebridge airport. We send the limo. We also have a heliport. You probably didn't notice, but panels at the top of the dome are retractable."

"I'm not surprised," Claire said, looking upward, beginning to feel claustrophobic. She wondered if she could live in a place like this, even if she had the money. Life must be predictable. The people she saw were all the same. Happy, healthy, wealthy and wise. And probably vacuous. At least, Claire sincerely hoped so. She'd hate to find out these people have depth too! I'm being so petty, she thought. After all, Brenda's been nice enough. If these people want to live here, this way, what's it to me? But regardless of the open-minded policy her brain insisted on, feelings of resentment persisted.

About the center of the city they headed towards a structure that resembled a small castle—grey stone, with turrets and towers and a little drawbridge across what was meant to resemble a moat. If I were in Disneyland, this would make sense, Claire thought. The building looked so preposterous she laughed.

"Lunch," Brenda said, pulling the cart to a halt by the bridge. Claire followed her up the path to a door opened by a liveried doorman. A small brass plaque overhead announced the obvious: *The Castle*.

Once in the vast hallway, Claire realized, to her relief, that this was only a restaurant, fancy, but one she could cope with. The maitre d' hurried to them, welcomed Brenda, bowed to Claire. He escorted the women through the dining area, lit only by candles on the tables and electric torches held in sconces along the walls. There were few diners at the white linened tables but they were, as expected, chicly dressed.

Two men waited at a table in a secluded alcove. Both stood, the younger bounding to his feet as if springing from a trampoline. "Isaac Sullivan," Brenda said, "Assistant Public Relations."

"A pleasure to meet you, Claire," he said as they shook hands.

But it was the other man that caught Claire's attention. Brenda's voice became deferential. "Claire Mowatt, I'd like to present Varik, CEO of Nirvana Corporation."

A gloved hand extended towards her. Beyond the thin grey leather a paler grey silk cuff pinned with a black pearl cufflink peeked out, on top of which rested the sleeve of a smoky business suit of expensive light wool.

The suit was Paris or Milan, the lapels the latest cut. The tie fashionably conservative, yet another shade of grey. Like a Gorey sketch, a single rose stood out as the only color this man wore, if such a dark purple could even be called a color. The outfit of a designer undertaker, Claire thought uneasily.

But the clothing suited him. For all the health and vigor enjoyed by the Eternal City residents, Varik hadn't, apparently, benefited. Taut skin on his face and neck seemed the result of too much cosmetic rearrangement. If the light had been better, Claire might have been able to confirm that his skin was as pale as she suspected. Veins protruded in his neck and forehead up to his black hairline. He wore grey-framed sunglasses and she couldn't see his eyes but felt the impact of his stare, as if, like Superman, he had x-ray vision. The man definitely had presence.

"Mrs. Mowatt," he said in well-modulated tones. Maybe he has a skin condition, she thought, excusing the gloves. Claire found herself taking his hand. Power and energy radiated through the leather and crawled up her arm, as if his body emitted a low-grade charge that was determined to spread through her body.

The hand felt cool, even through the smooth calfskin. He held her hand in his firm grip a fraction of a second longer than was necessary. Long enough, she realized, for him to be certain she felt his power.

For some reasons she found herself staring at his well-defined lips. Sexy, she thought, especially the straight line where they joined, as though he was incapable of either smiling or frowning. That made her want to elicit one reaction or the other. She couldn't get a sense of his age. Certainly over forty. Overall she found him intriguing, in a corporate way, but sensed there was a lot more to this man than business intrigue.

The four sat down and immediately a cadre of waiters appeared, like insects emerging from the woodwork. Sullivan asked what she would like to drink and Claire ordered another Dubonnet. Brenda had a vodka martini, dry, straight up with a twist and an olive. Sullivan ordered a bottle of Chardonnay. Varik was the only one not drinking, nor eating either; when the others ordered, he did not.

Brenda and Sullivan asked Claire about Florida, the drive up, her son, they understood she was a potter and taught classes and wasn't that interesting. The usual chit chat. They carefully avoided any mention of the property, which, Claire knew, was the sole reason for this lunch. All the while Varik said nothing but it was clear he paid careful attention, particularly to her—his head was turned slightly in her direction and she felt his concentration like a laser beam. He sat nearly immobile and if he hadn't exuded such a strong presence, Claire would have forgotten he was at the table.

The meals arrived. Both Brenda and Sullivan had ordered the quiche. Claire had opted for fusili with chicken and pesto sauce, not so much because she wanted it, more because she needed to keep a distance from these people, even if it meant ordering different food. One bite and she had to admit the chef was five star.

It wasn't until they had almost finished that Brenda brought up the subject of Lillian's property. "You know, Claire, we're anxious to acquire your land. In my opinion, Varik's offer is extremely generous."

Claire patted her lips and laid her napkin on the table.

She glanced at Brenda, then Sullivan, and finally Varik. She felt enticed yet repelled when she looked at him, like staring down into the hypnotic center of a pot spinning on the wheel. "It's a fair offer. And I'm not averse to selling," she admitted.

"Good!" Sullivan tossed his napkin on top of his plate in a decisive movement. "I'll see that an option to purchase is drawn up before you leave." He motioned for a waiter and asked for a phone.

"Of course, you'll want the document faxed to your attorney," Brenda added. "We'll arrange that."

They were pushing a little too hard, and Claire felt herself digging in her heels. "I'm confused."

An indulgent smile from Brenda. A look of consternation from Sullivan. From Varik . . . the inscrutable face she somehow did and did not want to read.

"In what way, Claire?" Brenda asked.

"Why are you so interested in my land?"

Sullivan's smile stayed plastered to his face. "The concept of every Eternal City is self-containment. Up here we are truly a city unto ourselves. The environment, the lifestyle, they're the best, the healthiest money can buy."

"Brenda gave me the tour. But what does this island have to do with as few acres of mainland property?"

Brenda explained. "In order to insure our exclusiveness, we need private access to the portion of Skeleton Lake Road where our dock is located, for our time-sharers. The Government of Ontario is more than willing to give us sole use of the road, provided we own all the properties. You see, each deed, including yours, has a clause regarding the road. What's known in legal terms as 'joint limited and/or exclusive access'—it allows for exclusive access to all other Skeleton Lake Road deed holders."

"You want the land for a private driveway? Or is it a parking lot?"

Brenda's smile shifted slightly. Sullivan seemed agitated.

Varik still sat, almost immobile, but very much present.

Brenda said patiently, "Naturally residents who wish to drive up need a place for their vehicles since, as you saw, gas driven cars aren't permitted in the City. They pollute the air."

"So you're going to pollute the town's air?"

"That's not our plan," Sullivan said. His tone had a distinct edge to it that made Claire feel even more obstinate.

"We're simply interested in exclusivity, Mrs. Mowatt," Brenda said.

"For those who can afford it."

Brenda didn't respond. Sullivan began to fidget.

Varik spoke. His voice resembled a computer voice, smooth, lacking the inflections normal human beings use. Still, as Claire grew accustomed to it, she could discern a vague New York accent.

"Brenda, Isaac, I'm afraid you've both inadvertently insulted Mrs. Mowatt. She is obviously an intelligent woman, concerned with the environment, with the quality of all life forms. Concerns I share."

Right, Claire thought. If a micro chip can share my concerns, you do. She was embarrassed by her thought, partly because she had the strange feeling he could read her mind, and it occurred to her that, if she tried, she might be able to read his. Give the man a chance.

An unnatural silence followed. Sullivan looked afraid to speak. Brenda interjected nervously, "We're not a heartless corporation, Claire. Each week we bring deprived children, indigent seniors, and patients recovering from drug and alcohol abuse up for weekends. We have a special clinic where we provide treatment. And they get a taste of the good life."

Claire could feel one side of her mouth twist into a smirk.

Varik's somber gloved hand resting against the virgin white linen created a stark contrast. He lifted his index finger, a minimal gesture, but Brenda stopped talking. He started. "It would distress me if you reached the wrong conclusions, Mrs. Mowatt. Therefore, I'm prepared to offer, in addition to monetary compensation for your land, ownership in the Eternal City for both you and your son.

"I'll provide a condominium for two weeks per year, on the same basis as other time-sharers, with the exception that the annual fee will be waived. You'll own the apartment for the duration of your natural life. And your son's."

Brenda looked startled. "In that case, there are no other costs involved. You and your son can come up each summer, or sell the time, with the usual restrictions. All our recreation facilities, boating, dining, housekeeping, it's all-inclusive. Of course, we have a screening process—"

"It will not be necessary for Mrs. Mowatt or her son to undergo processing."

"Why?" Claire asked Varik. It was the head honcho she wanted answers from, not his lackeys.

If his mouth could have lifted to a smile, the slight movement she saw must have been it. "You're an artist, Mrs. Mowatt. Intuitive. A rebel by nature. An animal not afraid to stray from the pack. Therefore you're unpredictable, as was your aunt."

The reference to Lillian unnerved Claire. She wondered what her aunt had thought of this man. Lillian would never have considered selling her land, especially to a corporation. Claire felt guilty that she was here for that very purpose.

"I'm not unlike you," Varik continued. "It was my foresight, my concerns, that created this dream, the Eternal City. We are in the vanguard of a trend. Frequently I've been forced to stand alone while others resisted what, to them, seemed at first preposterous. But eventually they appreciated the wisdom and were swayed to my way of thinking. Under the skin we're all basically animals and survival is of paramount importance, don't you agree?"

Before she could answer he continued. "You are suspicious of authority, especially those who get in the way of the natural order, making survival more complicated than is necessary. I understand that. Believe me, Mrs. Mowatt, you deserve respect."

He leaned forward until he was close to her cheek. His

lips parted, revealing a row of very straight, gleaming white teeth. His "smile," combined with the scent of floral cologne nearly overwhelmed her and Claire had to stop herself from falling either against the back of her chair or into him.

"Claire, I find you bewitching," he whispered.

The air warmed and the room faded so that Varik's face came sharply into focus. Claire had the startling thought: his cells have mutated. Is he human or more than human? His skin was as solid as fired porcelain, and yet at the same time seemed fluid, like wet clay. The result mesmerized her, the way an insect is fascinating to watch and, at the same time, slightly repulsive. She recognized both her fear and attraction as immature but that didn't stop Claire from warning herself: if he takes off those sunglasses, close your eyes. Quick.

# Seven

David hung around the cottage for a while after his mom left. Boy, she could piss him off!

He sprawled the length of the sofa on his back, head on one armrest, bare feet dangling over the other, leafing through a graphic *Batman* he'd bought somewhere on the trip up.

This place was *boring!* He felt like going for a swim, or taking the canoe out, but figured it wasn't worth the grief. His mother could be so paranoid. And not only that, she seemed to have the uncanny ability to read his mind. He remembered his dad winking at him, saying, "She's got a different way of knowing, Dave, and you're just like her."

"How's that, Dad?"

"Intuition. ESP. Call it having a hunch. It's not logical. We've all got it, but some people have more of it. The thing is, it works."

Sudden emotion flooded David. He let the book fall to the floor, and flung an arm over his eyes. He missed his dad. Sometimes he ached for him.

Outside, he heard a dog bark, and thought of Mouche. Maybe he should go over to Jerry's place.

He slipped on his Nikes and headed to the back of the cottage, where he'd seen a path up in the woods that more or less paralleled the road out front. He turned right towards Jerry's cottage.

At first he thought he was completely alone in the woods. Twigs snapped under his feet. He had to push tree branches out of his way. Then he heard a kind of soft whirr, and looked up. A tiny hummingbird hovered in the air, wings a cellophane blur of motion. Up above the trees he saw black birds circling—crows maybe—and then a seagull climbing and dipping and heading for the lake, a wild squawk floating down from the tree tops. Suddenly, he realized the forest lived all around him. Chirps and tweets and buzzes, scurryings in the underbrush. He stopped and inhaled the smell of earth. Behind that pleasantness a nasty fishy odor drifted off the lake, strong, with a sour undercurrent. That was crappy. It should smell good too.

Still, all the activity going on around amazed him. A whole world existed out here. The trick, he figured, was knowing it was here, so you could find it again.

A slight clearing on his right gave him a good view of the water, and the dome. The green glass bubble reflected trees and sky and birds soaring. He wondered how much Windex they needed to clean it. And how many people it would take, and if they needed a crane. Then he wondered what kind of mind would wonder about that. Sometimes he felt like an alien, the way his brain worked.

He took his time to Jerry's. Gord might not be so thrilled to see Claire's son showing up at his door.

Suddenly, a loud crack of wood nearby. Then, "Mouche! Don't eat that! It's dead!"

"Hey!" David called.

"Hey, man. What's up?" Jerry said as he came into view.

"Nothing much. You?"

"Nothing. Taking Mouche for a walk."

The big red setter's tail wagged frantically, and he leapt at David, up on his hind legs, paws on David's chest so he could lick his face.

"Mouche, the attack dog!" Jerry said.

"Yeah, I can see that," David laughed.

"We trained him to gum people to death."

"It's working!"

"Mouche, chill!"

The dog got back on all fours, his enthusiasm hardly diminished.

Jerry had on a great t-shirt, with LIFESTYLES OF THE BROKE AND OBSCURE! silkscreened across it. "Wicked shirt," David said.

"My mom brought it back from L.A."

"Cool."

They walked down to the water's edge, Mouche bounding ahead of them. Lake water rippled and lapped lazily against the rocky shore. The day had gotten pretty hot, and David felt like taking off his clothes and going for a swim. "Like, you really can't swim in here?"

"Nope. You get sores and stuff. Makes your dick fall off!"

David and Jerry giggled over that one.

They watched Mouche's jaw snapping as he jumped up after the green and yellow iridescent flies that buzzed everywhere. David noticed a delicate blue dragonfly, then another, their wings moving as fast as the blades of a helicopter, poised above the surface of the lake. Then they took off really fast. "What's that noise?"

"Cicadas."

"Man! Sounds like the attack of the killer insects!"

"Yeah, they're pretty loud. Your Aunt Lillian used to say they make that noise when it's gonna be hot out. My dad says they're mating. Whatever."

David picked up a stone and threw it far out into the water. Plop.

"Hey. Try this!" Jerry said. He found a flat stone and, sidearm, sent it skipping across the surface of the lake, counting aloud the six touches.

"Cool!" David said, impressed. He hunted for a flat stone and tried it and got three skips out of the first stone, and five out of the second.

They sent stones skipping for a while, until they got bored, and ended up sitting up against a wide tree, Mouche at their feet.

"You here the rest of the summer?" David asked.

"Til Labor Day. Then I gotta go back to school."

"Me too."

"Sucks, huh?"

"Greatly. And you know what's worse? My mom's a teacher at my school!"

"Oh man! No way!"

"Way!"

"My mom owns a store. She sells junk for the bathroom."

"How come she doesn't live with your stepdad?"

"Uh, 'cause they're divorced."

"Oh."

"Gord's not my real dad, but he's *like* my real dad, except my real dad's long gone. I live with my mom but come up here with Gord in the summers. It's okay up here. I like it. It's boring and all, but it's okay too. There used to be families with kids, but not this year. You like it here?"

"It's okay. Except my aunt's place doesn't have a TV. Or even a phone. I got my cell, though," he said, patting the phone hooked to his belt.

"Call me on my Fido!" they said in unison, and laughed.

"Hey, look, you can come over to our place anytime. We got a TV and VCR. No DVD up here, but they don't have any in the town anyways, just, like three videos or something."

"Great, thanks! And yeah, I noticed. You seen *Tramphire?*"

"No, but man, that would be sooooo cool! We should rent it, sometime when Gord's going to Bracebridge or Huntsville or someplace for the day."

They had walked all the way to the Nirvana dock. Ahead they saw the silver stretch limousine. Nobody around. "That dome is soooo weird," Jerry said.

"Yeah, it's pretty creepy, out here in the woods and everything. Like it's from space or something."

"Gord says they probably do experiments over there."

"Like what?"

"I don't know. Like, maybe turning people into cyborgs!"

"Sounds paranoid."

"Yeah, well Gord's paranoid, I guess. Everybody thinks so but Lillian."

"Do you?"

"I don't know. Maybe a little. I mean, he's a great guy and everything but sometimes he gets cranked up about stuff."

"A radical dude!" David said, and they both laughed.

"Mom calls him the oldest-living-hippy. He hates corporations, government, Mom, the Eternal City . . . I'm just glad he likes me."

They stood watching the dome for a while, until David said, "Ever been there?"

"Once, but don't tell Gord. I went there last summer, with Lillian."

"Really?"

"Yeah. I used to go out in the canoe with her sometimes and help her pick wild food and stuff. She was a real nice lady."

"So, you got inside the dome?"

"Not quite. They were still building it then. Lillian and I went early, when there were no workers around. There's a natural cave on the other side, past where the last boats dock. The opening's small and you gotta swim underwater to get in. Lillian said we shouldn't go in, but I wanted to. She said she was sure it would lead to the City, because they'd need an escape route."

"Escape route? To get out of the city? Why'd she think that?"

"Man, I don't know. She used to say a lot of strange things. Anyway, I want to go back there. I could find that cave again, I know it. Gord would hit the roof if he knew and—"

"Hey, I'll go with you!"

"You wanna go?"

"Do you?"

"Yeah!"

"Me too!"

"Alright! We'll make a pact. Before the summer ends, we go! Agreed?"

"Agreed!"

They slapped palms together, hooked thumbs together, grabbed each other's wrist, then slapped palms in the other direction.

"Hey look!" David said. They watched the Eternal City's yacht streaming across the lake towards the dock. The engines slackened off as the boat sidled up to the dock. A young man in whites jumped out and secured a thick rope to a wood bollard. The gangway lowered with a loud clank and David's mom was helped down the stairs.

"Hi boys!" she called out when she saw them. "I see you two found each other."

Man, she always had to make everything so obvious! David thought.

Mouche jumped up at her and she tried to pet him but he was too enthusiastic.

A chauffeur got out of the limo. David hadn't even seen the guy through the tinted glass. "Wow, a gullwing!" he said, as the chauffeur lifted up the side of the car.

"Want to ride back in style?" his mom asked him and Jerry.

"Can Mouche come?" Jerry asked.

Claire lifted a questioning eyebrow to the chauffeur. He grinned. "No problem, ma'am."

"Mouche's first ride in a limo," Jerry said. "Mine too. Come, boy!"

The dog hesitated. He pulled back, tail between his legs, ears flattened against his head.

"C'mon!" Jerry tried to pull him by the collar, but the animal dug in its paws.

The chauffeur reached down to help and Mouche snapped at him. The hand quickly drew back and the driver's friendly smile died.

Mouche danced away from the car, then sat on his haunches in the middle of the road, a low growl coming from him.

"He *never* bites," Jerry said, obviously upset by Mouche's behavior.

"Never mind," Claire said. "Dogs are like people. They have their moods."

Jerry turned sharply to her. "Lillian said the same thing once."

David's mother looked startled for a moment, then said, "Well, whoever is riding with me, get in!"

David got in after his mom, then Jerry, who looked at Mouche and said, "Okay, walk home if that's what you want, you dumb dog!"

Mouche waited until the car started up, then ran and disappeared into the woods.

David looked around the inside of the limo. "Wow! They got a DVD player, a CD player, a computer . . ." He and Jerry picked through the stack of CDs looking for anything alternative, but only found New Age music. "Whale music," David said.

"You guys had lunch?" Claire asked.

Both shook their heads.

"How about I make some sandwiches? Want to stay for lunch, Jerry?"

"Uh, no thanks, Mrs. Mowatt. My dad's waiting. We have to go to Huntsville today and get some food and stuff."

"Maybe another time, then."

"Hey, do you think your dad would mind if I came along?" David asked.

"Nah, he wouldn't mind. That would be awesome!"

"David, I mind. You have to eat lunch, and—"

"Mom, I'm not a kid. I can skip a meal and not die of starvation."

"It's not just lunch, David. We just got here. And there are things we need to do to make the cottage livable, and—"

"Forget it!" he snapped. His life sucked! She didn't want him to go anywhere or do anything that was fun!

The limo stopped before the cottage and the chauffeur had the gull wing open before his mother could reply. David leapt out with Jerry right behind him.

"The car can take you home, Jerry," Claire said.

"It's okay. I'll walk. It's not far." David figured Jerry didn't want Gord to know he'd been in the Eternal City car.

"Hey man, see you soon!"

"Yeah," David said. "Soon!" He went into the cottage and banged the door, just to let her know how pissed he felt.

She came in warily, half prepared for a fight, half for retreat, he could tell. "How's peanut butter and jelly sound? Or would you like tuna?"

"Whatever," he said in a surly tone.

"Look, David, I know you wanted to go with Jerry, and you can another time, but today—"

"Sure. Another time. When will that be, Mom? Ever since Dad died I feel like a dog on a leash!"

The minute he mentioned his dad, he felt sorry he had. The look on her face was awful, and he had caused it. "I . . . I didn't mean to bring Dad up."

"It's okay, David. You don't have to tiptoe around about your father. And you're probably right. I am overprotective. It's just a little hard for me being here, with Lillian gone, in her house, having to cope with all this—"

Now he felt *really* bad.

She looked at him for a moment. "I'm sorry, David. I don't want to lay all this on you. And I'm sorry about you not going with Jerry. I wanted you to stay here so I could tell you about Eternal City, what happened there, and the offer they made. This affects you too."

He sat down while she made him a sandwich, and ate it while she told him about the Eternal City.

"Sounds alright," he said between mouthfuls.

"The concept is. Milk or juice?"

"Coke." He grinned. She frowned, shook her head, then pulled out the big bottle of Coke. He poured himself a glass while she sat down.

"I don't know, David, it *sounds* good. Clean air, water, healthy lifestyle. They grow as much of their own food as possible, and the rest is organically grown and shipped in. They even have a section for retired people, and try to help the disadvantaged." She paused.

"But, it's not perfect, right?"

"No, on the contrary, it's *too* perfect. And I get the feeling they'd just as soon let the majority of us out here rot."

"But they're letting us *in,* Mom. We get to live there too."

She pulled in her lower lip and chewed on it a bit, but said nothing.

"You gonna sell?"

"It seems like the best thing, don't you think? I mean, the price is right. And the two weeks a year free condo—"

"They got tennis, right?"

"*Have* tennis, yes."

"Excellent! When we movin' in?"

"Not so fast, buster. I haven't signed on the dotted line yet." She reached across the table and pulled a large envelope out of her purse and extracted long legal-sized sheets. "I want Mr. Bennett to have a look. Varik is faxing a copy down to him."

"Who's Varik?"

He thought she blushed a little. She got up quickly and pulled his plate away and he wasn't even finished eating. "He's the head of the corporation. A very powerful man."

He watched her, not having a clue what she was thinking. He noticed that same look on girls his own age. Females were a total mystery, like a different species, but he wasn't used to thinking of his mom as a female.

Finally he said, "So, are you gonna sell it to them, if the papers check out?"

"I don't know, David. There's so much to consider—"

"Like what?"

"Like the fact that I'm just not sure Nirvana is a good company. I'm not sure of their motives—"

"Mom, you're just selling some land! I mean, it's not the end of the world."

"I hope not, David."

"I'm going down to look at the lake," he said. "If that's okay with you."

"Of course. Just don't go in the water. And be careful around the rocks down there. They—"

But he was out the door and trying to ignore the rest of what she said.

He just had to get away from her for a while. She made everything so complicated, like she was afraid to make a decision about anything, as if everything would be snatched away from her in a second. He knew it was all because of his dad dying, but it made it hard for him to live. More and more he felt stifled, like he just had to get away some times. God how he wished his dad was still alive!

# Eight

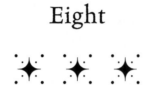

Gord hopped out of his pickup and glanced at his watch. Six-forty-five. Early.

He reached into his shirt pocket and pulled out a pack of Players Light, noticed the grisly picture of rotting gums, took out a cigarette, then tucked it back into the pack, which he returned to his pocket. Cutting down was hell.

He took several deep breaths, then rapped on the frame of the screen door. Claire answered almost at once. Her blue eyes widened and her lips parted in surprise.

"I'm a little early," he said.

"Early?" The dawning of memory. "Dinner. You came."

"I was invited."

"But the way you left, I thought—"

"You don't have a phone. I would have called."

Claire stood in the doorway as if blocking it. He could tell she didn't know which way to blow, so he made his pitch. "I suspected you'd think I wasn't coming so I took a chance and made dinner for four."

When she started to protest, he put up his hands. "Nothing fancy. Lasagna. Salad. I'm not a bad cook."

When Claire hesitated, he added, "If you don't want to, I understand."

She stood aside. "Come in for a minute." As he entered,

his smile must have been sheepish because Claire gave him a look—part exasperation, part amusement. He found it comical. He also thought, she's a beautiful woman, the kind that gets sexier with age.

"To tell the truth," she said, "we'd love dinner. Have a seat while I change my clothes. I've been out in the garden most of the afternoon, doing some heavy weeding."

Gord took a seat opposite David on the couch. Lillian's A-frame had always been warm and homey. Yellows, greens, golden browns. Woodsy colors. As Claire climbed upstairs, he found himself watching her rear end sway. He caught David watching him. "Good comic?" he asked.

"Not bad."

The main room was exactly the same as Lillian had left it and, for some reason, Gord felt relieved. He'd spent many evenings here, pleasant evenings full of camaraderie and understanding, especially important for both of them during the long winters when six-foot drifts and plummeting temperatures held them prisoner. Even getting to Lillian's had been a tough snowshoeing trek through half a mile of powdery snow.

"How's it going?" Gord asked the boy.

"Okay."

"Not like Miami, is it?"

"Not much."

"The forest has its own rhythm. Once you find it, you're plugged in."

"Yeah," David said, in the uninterested way kids have.

"Jerry instructed me to invite you over to watch the tube. Come by any time you want. We get movies on weekends. If you like, c'mon into Bracebridge with us this Friday and pick one."

David brightened. "That'd be great!"

Claire descended backwards. Again Gord noticed her body and thought, I've gotta cut this out!

Automatically he reached for a cigarette but stopped his hand in mid-air.

"I'm ready," she said. "David?"

The boy nodded.

"What shall we bring?" she asked.

"Just your appetites."

They piled into the front seat of the pickup. Claire took the middle and he was foolishly aware of her body beside his.

Within minutes they were at his place. Gord winced at the condition of the yard. What a mess! The grass needed mowing. The rusted bumper of a car lay at the end of the driveway. An old tire Jerry used to swing on hung from a rope tied to the maple tree, half the rubber shredded. Thirty wooden lawn chairs in various stages on construction. Ordinarily Gord didn't care what people thought of him, but for some reason he did tonight. At least they'll see the real me, he reassured himself. He led everybody including Mouche inside.

"Hmmmm," Claire said from the doorway. She stood there a minute, taking everything in. "Nice."

"Hi!" Jerry said, and everybody exchanged hellos. Gord offered Claire a glass of dandelion wine.

"I'll try anything once," she said. "Even twice."

"My kinda woman," he said, then realized what an idiot he was to have said it. Rust had set in; his libido creaked.

Gord went to the kitchen and poured a couple of Cokes with ice for the kids and two glasses of wine. When he returned, Claire had seated herself on the corduroy couch. Jerry took David up to his room.

Gord handed Claire the wine glass.

"Thanks. You have a nice place. Comfortable. Rustic."

"Rustic or rusty?"

"It's very beautiful," she said. "And wonderful to be in a place that's natural."

Again she looked at him with those pale blue eyes and he felt like a teenager. "So," he said, trying to distract her, "how's life in the woods?"

"Great." She sipped the yellow wine and he was aware of her lips on the glass. "This is okay. Dry, but I like it. Make it yourself?"

"Every year. I need three bushel baskets of dandelion flowers. Jerry and I take a day and go out and pick and pick and the weight of the flowers packs down so you feel like the basket's always half full. I make wild grape wine too."

"A man of many talents. Lillian must have loved you."

"I loved *her!*" Gord blurted out, the vehemence in his voice surprising him.

Lillian, of course, was their connection. If he hadn't known Lillian, if Claire hadn't been her niece, if Lillian hadn't disappeared, they wouldn't be sitting here together. The link upset him. "We spent a lot of winters by her fireplace or mine, reading together, talking, drinking this." He lifted his glass. "Your aunt understood what's important in life and didn't waste time on passing disturbances."

As soon as he said it, he regretted the remark—Claire's eyes misted a little and he thought, *for God's sake, you're making her cry. Surely she's cried enough over Lillian. Haven't we all?*

They ate dinner in the kitchen at the old pine table.

Claire had a large helping of lasagna and two servings of salad, both of which she praised. Gord liked to see women eat. So many of them—Grace, at least when he'd been married to her—nibbled at food as though it was poison. They treat sex the same way, he thought, wondering if he'd just made an astute observation or a chauvinistic generalization. Whatever, the thought was probably politically incorrect.

After dinner, Jerry and David stayed in the kitchen making ice cream flavored with fresh blueberries, taking turns cranking the ice-cream maker and laughing a lot. He and Claire had coffee laced with Cointreau in the living room, side by side on the couch, but not quite close enough to touch.

Conversation felt easy. She told him about her life in Miami, the joys and frustrations of being a potter by trade, what it was like teaching the craft. Eventually she got to her husband's death.

"It was such a shock. He'd been touring the Tampa plant. Bill was an accountant, no reason to even visit the manufacturing end, but there was this special promotion, to show off state-of-the-art equipment to a couple of executives from Japan. It was a freak accident. They started up one of the front-end loaders and a part wasn't hooked up properly. It struck Bill on the head. He died before they could get him to a hospital. The doctors told me even if he had lived, he would have been a vegetable. The worse part is, I knew." She paused. "I had a premonition that something had happened to him." She took a big sip of wine and he refilled her glass.

"You never think death can strike someone you love," she continued. "I *still* can't believe it. The hurt is bad enough but you know what's worse? I'm furious at Bill for dying. How could he leave me? How could he leave David? I loved that man, and it wasn't his fault, but I can't forgive him for dying. Isn't that awful?"

She looked vulnerable and Gord felt a strong urge to put an arm around her shoulder, at least touch her hand. But the relationship was too new. She might misinterpret the sympathy for something else. *He* might misinterpret it.

"I'm just getting my life back on track now. Starting to feel more alive again. Coming up here was the right thing to do, but it's painful. Lillian meant a lot to me."

"I know," he said. "She mentioned you often."

Claire looked both pleased and shy, and touched with sadness. "I regret so much not seeing her for so long. It's funny how we let day-to-day things get in the way of what we really want to do. It's some kind of naive belief that we'll live forever. Well," she shifted towards him, "I guess you know my secrets. But I don't know yours. Yet."

The "yet" thrilled him. There was an implication in it, a promise of a future. Watch you don't drift out to sea, he warned himself, wanting a cigarette badly.

Jerry, David and Mouche came noisily into the living room. Jerry said, "We're gonna take Mouche for a run."

Gord looked at Claire. She nodded. "Sure thing," he said. "Stay in sight!" he shouted as the door slammed.

"I guess you want to talk about Eternal City," she said.

"Do you want to hear it?"

"I'd rather hear about you."

"Right now, in my life, who I am is bound up with the Nirvana people."

"Well, let's hear about both of you."

Gord got two fresh cups of coffee, partly because he didn't know where to begin and wanted time to think. She was asking him to open the door to his soul. And, although he needed to, the hinges were corroded. Besides, it was risky. Behind the door were ugly wounds and God knew what would spill out.

But when he sat down again and looked into her eyes, he saw something familiar that loosened him up.

"You remind me of Lillian," he admitted.

"They always said I looked like her."

"I came up here for good four years ago, just after the divorce. Jerry's my stepson. He was two when Grace and I married. His father took off before he was born. Our marriage was a disaster from the start, but I found the divorce one of the most painful things I've ever gone through. It was really strange. I don't think I even loved Grace but separating from her felt like having my heart gouged out. Most of the time we're civil now, and she accepts the fact that Jerry thinks of me as his dad. He couldn't be more of a son if I'd been his natural father. He likes coming here summers, so it's worked out."

Claire put her feet up on the footstool and inexplicably the gesture of comfort and familiarity touched him.

"You push and shove and try to make the pieces fit, but they won't because you're playing with two different puzzles. I worked as a documentary film producer with the Canadian Broadcasting Corporation. Grace wanted more money and I guess she needed to do her own thing so she opened a store. It got so we never saw each other. We fought about it and both of us could see what it was doing to Jerry. We tried counseling, but—" He didn't know what else to say. It all felt too complicated.

"Do you still make documentaries?" Claire asked.

"Sucked the life out of me. Finally I dried out for good. It was an action-packed life, though, let me tell you. Up at dawn, thirty cups of coffee an hour, the requisite schmooze parties every other night. Cocaine. That's part of that world. I felt chopped in pieces and everybody had a wedge but me. I took a leave of absence that turned into early retirement." He was aware of skipping details. No use boring her to death this early in the relationship. Relationship?

God, he was delusional!

"So, what do you do with your time?"

"I'm pretty good with my hands, carpentry, and got into making those chairs you probably noticed all over the lawn. Cottage furniture, they call it."

"That's a far cry from the glamorous fast-paced world of the media."

"Building chairs is a snail's pace, but it suits me. They buys them groceries. Anyway, it's enough—at least for now. The land's paid for. I bought it when I was young, on the spur of the moment, one of the few smart moves I've made. I built the cottage ten years ago. My needs are pretty basic and I saved a lot over the years, invested, and guess I was more lucky than smart. When Grace and I split, she took the house in the trendy end of town and the BMW, and I got this place and enough money to buy a pickup. You could say it all worked out nicely, except I got a better deal."

"Do you miss her?"

He laughed then grimaced. "Let me correct myself. Divorcing Grace was painful. Less painful than living with her. Another cup?"

Claire shook her head. "I'll be up all night." Her face glowed from the food and wine and caffeine. The top two buttons of her shirt were undone—just enough to reveal her collar bone—but he could imagine her breasts. Rolled up sleeves exposed slim, muscled arms, tan as her face.

"Don't you get lonely? This is close to being wilderness here."

"I miss having a partner," Gord said. "But I'd rather be alone than with someone I don't love."

"Why have you stayed here? It's so isolated. Why not just come up in the summers, with Jerry?"

He hesitated. "Used to. But then I wanted to be here year round. Things were pretty good up here, at least until two years ago." It wasn't a complete answer, evasive at best, but it would do for now.

"Is that when the Eternal City came?"

Gord shifted. "You sure you want to hear this?"

"Yes. Just don't jump to conclusions about my intentions. Hear me out."

"I'm sorry," he said, again aware of how poorly he'd treated her. Maybe it was too long since he'd been around a woman his own age. An attractive, intelligent, vital woman.

"And no more apologies," she laughed.

He nodded, feeling sober all of a sudden. "They scouted the area three years ago. Then they bought the island and as much of the mainland property along Skeleton Lake Road as they could get their paws on. The dome went up last summer, people started moving in early spring. Most landowners around the lake are cottagers, city folk. They come up for a couple of weeks during the good weather and annoy the locals, then leave by Labor Day. Nirvana offered a fair price and a lot of them on this part of the road sold outright. This summer more sold. The water's getting bad, that swayed people."

Gord took a deep breath and went on. "The townies are another story. Despite Nirvana's hype, I don't think their plans include the town, but the people in Chesborough can't see it. They still hope they'll get something out of the Eternal City being here. So far it's worked against them. Nirvana's a world unto itself, and an expensive one. Condo owners pay more than they'd pay for a house plus a hefty yearly fee.

"There's just a few holdouts left along this stretch of the Road. The Robineaus, down past Nirvana's dock, Bailie

Rankin around the bend in the road. Me. You. And the Gwinskis, but they're another story. You don't have to avoid them, they'll avoid you. Anyway, if Nirvana could get our land, they'd have this whole section to themselves, private access to the highway. There's been a lot of pressure on us."

"Will the others sell?"

"They say no, but the Robineaus are getting on. He's pushing eighty and she's early seventies. The winters are hard on them and their children all live in Quebec. Bailie's retired, grew up here, a loner, as stubborn as I am. The Gwinskis nobody knows; they're not talking. I've felt pretty alone with this, except for them. Your aunt was solid. Had no intention of selling, no matter what they did to her."

Claire sat upright and frowned. "What do you mean, 'what they did to her'?"

Gord reached for the pack of cigarettes. "You're not going to believe this."

"Tell me."

He started to take a cigarette from the pack when Claire said, "I'm allergic to smoke," so he returned it. But he felt nervous.

"They're slick. Corporate harassment. Letters from lawyers. Constant visits. Pressure from the town council—the council's in the palm of Varik's hand and we think the federal environmental department is too. At least the local health people are. You met Varik, I take it, when you went for lunch?"

"Yes."

Gord sighed and licked his lower lip. He could really use a cigarette. "Varik's a self-made over-achiever, pulled himself up by his designer bootstraps, took the high road, ivy-league school, a Mensa vampire, the best. His background's sketchy but once he got enough dough together to play the market full-time, he hit it big before the semi-crashes in '82. A low-key Donald Trump clone. Made money selling junk bonds in the eighties, gutting companies, juggling subsidiaries. Profits from his mega-empire financed the cities, with the help of big-name corporate and private backers. He's probably in hock up to his sunglasses."

"How come you know so much about him?"

"I did a documentary on him in 1989, just after the free trade agreement between Canada and the U.S. came into effect. Varik was up here the next day, buying out the Canadian Oil Corporation, one of our largest oil companies. It was in trouble financially and he got a controlling interest cheap. Everybody thought he was nuts. But COC no longer exists. He nearly drained the wells, ripped the guts out of the company until it was only a skeleton. Thousands of people lost their jobs, stocks plunged and COC went bankrupt. Of course, before Varik finished, he'd managed to gouge out a huge profit for himself and then write off the loss. It's a pattern he's repeated before and since all over the U.S., in Canada, in Mexico, but he came out clean when the U.S. government witch-hunted the corporate sector. But the man's a predator and Nirvana's ravenous.

"And make no mistake. Varik *is* Nirvana, and vice versa. But Lillian could handle him. As you know, she could handle anything and anybody. She was a fighter."

"Yes, she was."

"Her body was never found."

Claire paused. "I know that. She was presumed drowned."

Just then the door opened. Jerry stuck his head in. "Did Mouche come back?"

"No. You're supposed to be taking him for a walk," Gord said.

"We were but he ran off and we can't find him. Thought maybe he came home. We'll look a little more."

When Jerry shut the door, Gord turned back to Claire. "Don't you think it's a little odd? I mean, in the first place, Lillian was an Olympic-caliber swimmer."

"Gord, Lillian was over sixty-five years old. She stopped swimming competitively when she was twenty-five."

"She was in good shape," he protested. "Spring, summer, fall, she swam every morning, until this spring, when the warnings went up about the lake. Then she went to the quarry. She walked everywhere. She handled a canoe like a native. You didn't see her in the last few years of her life, I did. She was still a great swimmer."

Claire accidentally knocked the spoon off the edge of her saucer onto the coffee table. "Come on! You're implying that Lillian was murdered. By a giant corporation. To get her land. That's preposterous."

"Is it?" He stood and pulled a cigarette out of his pack, walked to the door, opened it, and struck a match. After he lit the cigarette he inhaled deeply. The nicotine felt good. He blew smoke out into the night.

Claire looked both horrified and frightened. He couldn't tell whether it was what he said that scared her or if she thought he was crazy.

"All I'm saying, Claire, is that it's odd. She was a good swimmer. Her body was never found. The OPP came to the conclusion she drowned."

"But you don't buy that."

"No, I don't. It's just too damn convenient for Eternal City." He looked at her closely. She was even more frightened. "Claire, if you stick around long enough, get to know what's inside Varik and the other pseudo-humans over there, you probably won't buy it either."

She stared at him but he couldn't read what she was thinking. "Look," he said. "I'm not crazy. Angry, yes. Scared, definitely. Foolish, well, there's not much doubt about that. But not crazy." He took a drag on the cigarette but it had burned down to the filter. He flicked the butt out the door. It landed on the gravel path and he watched until the embers faded. He turned back to Claire. "There's no way that woman could have drowned. Not without help!"

# Nine

Jack Williams leaned back from his desk and glanced out the side window. The Jeep pulled into the Ontario Provincial Police parking lot. Well, whaddaya know?

Seconds later the Mowatt woman came through the door. Yellow tank top. Cute cutoffs. Nice legs. She walked to the counter and waited.

Williams took his time getting up. "G'morning."

"Morning." She looked ill-at-ease. Must have been talking to Roberts.

He tapped his ballpoint on top of the mound of papers. "Something I can help you with?"

She smiled but he didn't return it. No use encouraging familiarity.

"I hope so. I'm Claire Mowatt."

"Sergeant Williams."

"I'm Lillian Palmer's niece. She died recently and I've come up for a few weeks to look after some land she owned along Skeleton Lake." She paused.

"What can I do for you, Miss Mowatt?"

"Mrs."

He nodded brusquely.

"I'm hoping you can give me some information about my aunt's death."

Williams folded his arms across his chest. "What kind of information?" His eyes narrowed into a guarded, hooded stare.

"The details," she said, not intimidated. Disconcerted, maybe. Moving towards irritation. Well, she had a right to know some of it. And it was his job to tell her. Couldn't hurt.

"I was one of the investigating officers," he said. "The other was Sergeant Fine, but he's been transferred to Sault Ste. Marie. If you like, I'll check the file."

"I'd appreciate that."

"Come inside." He pressed a hidden button beneath the counter then made his way to the swinging gate which he held open for her to enter.

She stepped into the main office, pausing to look through the door that led to the holding cell. It was ajar. She could likely see the bars.

Williams pointed to a chair under a 1955 portrait of Queen Elizabeth. Ugly then too. The Mowatt woman sat and he went to his swivel chair. Besides papers, the desk was cluttered with memos, ledgers, *Wanted* posters and file folders. The coffee mug that Mary Ellen had given him one Christmas with Jumpin' Jack Flash written across it rested precariously close to the edge of the desk. Its contents had turned an unappetizing grey. "Like some coffee?"

"No thanks."

He swiveled his chair to the right, to the vertical filing cabinet, and opened the bottom drawer. Under 'P' he found *Palmer, Lillian* and pulled the blue file. He turned back to her and read aloud a paraphrased version of the reports.

"We received a call the morning of Friday, May 2$^{nd}$, from Gord Roberts, neighbor of your aunt's. He went to her place, found she wasn't in, got worried."

He looked up briefly. "It's standard policy to allow at least twelve hours to elapse before we investigate a missing person report. Except for children." She nodded, and he looked down at the papers again.

"Let's see. Me and Fine drove out next morning. We met Gord on your aunt's property. Had to send Fine to Huntsville to get a court order to search the house."

"Why?"

"Illegal to enter without the owner being present. Besides, the door was locked."

"My aunt never locked her door," the Mowatt woman said.

Williams just shrugged. "While Fine was gone, and I was on the radio, Roberts broke the back window and went in illegally. Says he was thinking heart attack or stroke or something, but she wasn't inside.

"We searched the woods, Skeleton Lake Road and the shrubbery on the bank. Roberts had found Lillian's canoe day before, overturned and floating in the lake not far from the dock. He also found a running shoe, may have been hers, in the water.

"When Fine got back, we spent the day doing a more thorough search of the area but did not locate the body. We don't usually drag the lake unless a relative requests it but in this case we did. Nothing. Our conclusion, your aunt drowned." He looked up.

"Wouldn't her body surface, though?" Mowatt asked. Her voice quivered a bit and Williams knew the cold, straightforward way he'd passed the information had probably upset her. For some reason, that reached him. He was aware that a year ago he wouldn't have been moved. He tried to soften his tone.

"Not necessarily. It's a big lake. Full of underwater rocks and tree roots, especially near the shore. Body could have been trapped. Or floated to the other side. Could be it'll never surface or maybe just as bones, like the Indians."

"The Indians?"

"Land used to belong to the Ojibway. Hundred years or so ago, when the government started to develop it, workers discovered the bones of a native woman and her child. Winters are pretty harsh here. Probably lived in a cave—area's full of caves, some submerged in the lake. Anyway, they either froze or starved to death. Likely both. Skeletons washed up in the spring, when the ice thawed. That's how Skeleton Lake got it's name."

"That poor woman and child . . ." She had a look on her face that told Williams she could picture herself and her son starving and freezing to death, their flesh shrinking, contracting, until there was nothing more. Suddenly Varik's face flashed to mind.

"Sergeant, despite what you've said, I don't understand why my aunt's body hasn't been found."

"It still may be, but by now there wouldn't be much left. This is a tricky lake. Water's deep and, like I said, underwater roots and caves. The two Indians surfaced in spring. We're brushing autumn, Mrs. Mowatt."

She looked a little sick and he closed the file. "Your address was listed in Lillian's address book and Roberts knew you were her niece. I notified the Miami police. You know the rest."

He tossed the folder to the side of his desk farthest from her reach. "That's about all I can tell you."

"Sergeant, there are a couple of things that seem strange to me, about my aunt's death."

"Such as?"

"I don't know if you're aware of it, but she was an excellent swimmer. She nearly made it into the Olympics when she was seventeen."

"Yes, ma'am, I'm aware of that. I also know that was nearly fifty years ago. Your aunt was old. She could have been in the canoe, had a heart attack or hey, even a dizzy spell, and fallen in."

She shifted to another tack. "Regardless of her abilities, and putting aside just for a moment the idea that she had a fainting spell or heart attack, it seems a bit odd to me that she would have gone out on the lake after dark."

"Not odd at all. Locals boat all hours. Especially Lillian. She was quite a character. Roamed the woods day and night. Besides, she could have been out in the day. We don't know when the boat capsized."

"But in May? When the ice has hardly thawed? And it's so chilly?"

She didn't know what she was talking about, stabbing in the dark, and he was beginning to feel annoyed. His time was being wasted. "In all my years with the OPP, Mrs. Mowatt, I've learned that it's normal for people to do strange things, especially if they're strange to begin with."

"But what about the shoe?"

"We don't know that it was hers. And if it was, well, we don't know how long it'd been there. Mrs. Mowatt, I can't tell you exactly what happened. Her canoe capsized. Looks to me like she went over with it. Every year we have four or five boating or hunting accidents up here."

"But Lillian was an excellent swimmer. Even a poor swimmer could have floated to shore or just grabbed hold of the boat and kicked."

Williams sighed, and stood. "Look, Mrs. Mowatt, I'm sorry for your loss. Lillian was a nice lady, wacky but nice.

Accepting death is always hard. All I can tell you is that we didn't find a body and your aunt hasn't returned. There's only one conclusion. If you're interested in having the lake dragged again, I can get in touch with the proper department. May take a while, though. Been three months, they won't see the need to hurry to repeat what's already been done. And chances are good you'll have to pay for it yourself this time. In my opinion, you likely won't find anything."

"Did you check the Eternal City?" The question caught him off guard and, from the look on her face, it showed. He dropped his eyelids so the fleshy hoods shielded his eyes again.

"What are you getting at, Mrs. Mowatt?"

"Maybe they saw something."

He was silent, studying her. Finally he said, "As a matter of fact, I checked with Mr. Varik, who's in charge over there. He didn't know anything about it."

"What about the people who live there? Maybe a resident knows something."

"This is the first year they've been open. At that time the only people moved in were two dozen retirees brought in over the winter."

"What about them? And the staff? That must be a fair number of people."

"Everybody was questioned. Nobody saw or heard anything."

"Why does that not surprise me?" She looked both angry and on the verge of hysteria. "Well, thanks for your time. And for passing along the information, what little there is."

She turned to the gate but he didn't buzz her through right away.

"Mrs. Mowatt, it sounds to me as if you've been listening to Gord Roberts and his grumblings."

Claire turned to face him. Her features were attractive, lush in a way, but firm. She looked a lot like her aunt. The kind of woman that challenges a man. "I've met Mr. Roberts, yes."

"Every town has its crank, Roberts is ours. He doesn't want to sell his land and doesn't want anybody else to either. He's got some crazy ideas about the Nirvana people, but his ideas are just that. Crazy. Most of the folks around Chesborough have lived here all their lives and their parents before them. But they've accepted the changes and don't feel the way Roberts does."

"I suppose the Eternal City has benefited the area, Sergeant Williams."

"Nirvana's paid good prices for the land they've bought."

"I guess that's important to some people."

"This is a depressed area. Around here it is."

She turned back to the gate and this time he smacked the buzzer.

Just before she left the office, he told her, "Living in a town and vacationing in it are two different things. I'd bear that in mind if I were you, Mrs. Mowatt. If you don't intend living here, I'd say there's no use going out of your way to make enemies. It could ruin your holiday."

"Thanks for the advice." She slammed the screen door on her way out.

Williams dialed the Eternal City. "Brenda, Jack. I need to talk to Varik. Now."

He was put through immediately.

"I thought you'd be interested to know that Claire Mowatt, Lillian Palmer's niece, was just in here."

"And?"

"And she was asking questions about her aunt's death. Seems she was talking to Gord Roberts."

"I'm well aware of that, Sergeant. I fail to see how this concerns me?"

Williams hesitated. His gut feeling was that Varik *should* know why it concerns him. But, if Varik felt it wasn't a problem, maybe it wasn't. On the other hand, Williams had a few concerns of his own.

"While I've got you on the line, Mrs. Mowatt asked me to double check."

There was a pause.

"The morning her aunt went missing and was presumed drowned. I told her your people were questioned."

"As I told you, Sergeant."

"Nobody saw anything unusual? Heard anything?"

"Again, as I informed you that day, no. Ms. Palmer's unfortunate accident went unobserved."

"What about the yacht captain and crew? They have a good view of the water between her dock and yours."

Varik's voice grew impatient. "What's your point?"

"No point. Just double checking. Mrs. Mowatt asked."

"And you have your answer. It doesn't pay to antagonize the hand that feeds you."

"Sounds like a threat."

"Not a threat, Sergeant, simply a statement of the politics of business."

Varik hung up on him.

When Williams got off the phone, he realized he was sweating. Besides being angry, he was surprised to feel fear.

He'd laid a lot of solid groundwork to pry himself out of the rut that had been his life over the last decade and now, thanks to Roberts, suddenly that ground felt damned shaky.

# Ten

He knows he is dreaming. They call to him the way they always call. It is personal. As if their whispers flow through his body with the blood in his veins.

The air weighs him down and he moves through it slowly. The light guides him, and the sense of them waiting. It is as though he is returning to a home he has never known, a place of peace.

*Join with us.*

THE MOTHER, serene in her exquisite beauty. Her embrace soft and comforting as the clouds. Her promise eternal.

THE FATHER looks on, approving of this intimacy.

THEY surround him with love, both conditional and unconditional. Love without end. He would do anything for them, anything.

THE FATHER makes HIS wishes known. THE MOTHER smiles radiantly.

The air thins and as he opens his eyes the scent of flowers clings to him. He looks around the room. He is alone. He knows exactly what to do.

# Eleven

Claire left the OPP station feeling uneasy. She liked to err on the side of questioning authority and was glad she had with Williams.

As she climbed into the Renegade, her mind replayed the conversation. What Williams said was all very logical. It was the *way* he said it. Patronizing towards her, and about her aunt. Secretive. She couldn't figure out whether that was just a cop thing, if it was Williams, or if he knew something that he wasn't telling.

Claire hated not being taken seriously. Gord's inferences might be loopy as hell, but the concerns he raised were legitimate and deserved to be addressed. Williams hadn't addressed them. On the other hand, she didn't really buy it that the Eternal City killed her aunt to get the land. They were a large, multinational corporation. Respectable. It didn't make sense. Why kill just Lillian? There were other holdouts.

Driving through Chesborough, Claire looked at the town with eyes unclouded by the rose-colored glasses of nostalgia. Buildings *are* dilapidated, she thought. Nobody's making money here, that's obvious. Emerson's had a *Closed* sign on the door. Shutting a grocery in the middle of the day didn't seem like a good way to stay in business. She wondered if the old man was ill.

She woke this morning with a lot of questions. About Chesborough. The Eternal City. About Lillian's death. Now she had more.

When Claire arrived home she found Gord, David and Jerry in the kitchen making fruit pies.

She stood in the doorway for a second before they noticed her: Gord leaned over the scarred oak table, rolling out a whole wheat crust onto waxed paper with Lillian's heavy marble rolling pin. David cored apples at the sink from the bushel basket they'd found in the root cellar. Jerry stood in front of the stove stirring a puree in the top of a double boiler. If she hadn't seen this with her own eyes, she wouldn't have believed it.

"What an industrious group!" she said. "I hope you're going to clean up after yourselves."

"Don't worry," Gord assured her. "Organization R Us."

He flipped the waxed paper into a glass pie plate. Crust hung over the edges by two inches. He peeled away the paper then patted the dough down into the shape of the dish. Once that was done, he lifted the pie plate and balanced the bottom of it on his fingertips. Deftly he began to trim the edge. Obvious he knew his way around a kitchen. Absently she wondered if he knew his way around a bedroom too.

"Watch out, Mom," David said. "Gord's a serious delegator. I think he has his eye on *you* for cleanup."

"Where do you think Mouche is?" Jerry said.

"Don't know," Gord said, still trimming crust. "He's stayed out overnight before. Probably chasing rabbits in the woods."

"Why don't we all go for a walk when you're through

and look for him?" Claire suggested.

"Sounds good," Gord said.

"What's this?" Claire reached for a white envelope on the corner of the table, shaking off pale brown flour.

"An invitation," David said. "To a party at Eternal City Friday night. Can we go?"

She opened the envelope. "The whole town's invited?" she asked, astonished.

"Yet another sleight of hand. One more attempt to bowl over the local yokel holdouts," Gord said bitterly, fitting the second crust into another pie tin.

"I take it you're not going."

"You take it right." He crumpled the waxed paper into a ball and hand-grenaded it across the room into the trash bin. He threw the utensils into the bowl and took the bowl to the sink.

No one said a word for a moment. Gord turned to look at her. He was still angry but his eyes seemed to plead for understanding. Is this man sane? she wondered. He's so hostile towards the Eternal City, maybe he's infecting me with his views.

Claire realized she no longer knew what to think. Was everything as complicated as she was making it? Williams had been a jerk, that was clear enough. But he was also a policeman, trained to investigate. Lillian *could* have drowned. Odds were she had. Claire wondered why she felt so skeptical. Finally she said, "I think David and I should go to this party. I want to get a better idea of what Nirvana's all about, how the townspeople feel about things. If you'd reconsider, I'd like both you and Jerry to be there. With us."

Jerry turned to look at Gord. Gord's face metamorphosed into a mask of worried relief.

"All right, Claire, we'll go. We'll *all* check the place out. But I'd like you to meet the Robineaus and Bailie Rankin first, so you have their views, too. I also have to warn you—"

Resistance must have shown on her face. He raised a hand for her to allow him a moment's grace. "I'll just say this much. Things aren't what they seem. And I don't even know exactly what I mean by that. I just want to make sure everybody has their eyes wide open and nobody's been lulled into dreamland by the flashing of dollar signs or Nirvana's glamorous lifestyle and wealthy CEO."

"Or rigid with fixed opinions," Claire added, irritated he'd brought up Varik, not sure why.

"Fair enough."

It occurred to her that the four would probably be spending the rest of the day together. She felt delighted by the idea and laughed. The three turned to look at her. "Well," she said, "you aren't just making dessert, are you? How about stuffed roast chicken? And vegetables from the garden? If we work together, it should only take about three hours to pick and wash the veggies, cook the food and eat."

David and Jerry looked trapped. Gord's face curled into a grin, catching her drift. "Or," he said, "we could rustle up a batch of Gord Robert's World Famous Ixtapa Chili, complete with corn bread. Twenty minutes to make, two hours to simmer, and all night to digest!"

"Yeah!" David yelled.

"Let's do it!" Jerry added.

"Guess I'm outvoted," Claire said, then blurted, "I love anything that's hot!"

Gord smiled, and Claire blushed, wondering why she was always embarrassed by this man.

★ ★ ★ ★ ★

Tuesday evening, Claire went with Gord to the Robineaus'. Their cottage, more modern than either Lillian's or Gord's, spread out on one level. From their front door she could see the Eternal City's dock. The limo was not parked there tonight.

Colette and Gilles Robineau were definitely senior citizens, she the more spry, but not by much. Both were short and round, with weathered skin and white hair, although he was mostly bald. They were warm people, with sparkling eyes and ready smiles. She could envision them on a postcard from one of the wine-growing provinces in France. They spoke in accented English, his smooth enough to remind her of old Louis Jordan movies.

Bailie Rankin was also there, an outgoing Scot, red-faced, feisty but well-meaning. Claire found him straightforward, a veritable open book. She liked him immediately, although he seemed to love playing devil's advocate.

It suddenly occurred to her that, Lillian included, all the year-round residents on this stretch of the lake were elderly. All but Gord. That made her wonder about why he chose to spend his time with . . .

"So, Claire," Bailie cut into her thoughts, "how are our woods treating you?"

"Pretty well, so far, except for the black flies. But I'm only beginning to relax. By the time I'm comfortable I'll have to go home."

"Being a cottager's like being a lake bass—you let yourself have a nibble and before you know it you're hooked."

"I wish I had the luxury of spending more time."

"We do what we must," Gilles Robineau interjected diplomatically. His wife cupped a hand over her ear. He repeated what he'd said louder, and in French.

Gord poured coffee and passed around little sugary cakes that Colette had baked. Claire had the feeling they all treated him like a son and he not only enjoyed the role but acted his part. Once everyone had been served, he said, "I wanted Claire to meet all of you. Now, with Lillian gone, and so few of us resisters left, we need to stick together."

Bailie asked Claire directly, "You're not planning to sell Lillian's land?"

"I'm still thinking about it," she said evasively, although secretly she felt there was little choice. "Gord suggested there may be other buyers besides Nirvana. If anybody here's interested, please let me know."

"None of us can compete with Nirvana's price," Gord said.

"Money's important—for David's schooling," she clarified. "I mean, I won't *give* the land away but it doesn't necessarily have to go to the highest bidder."

"That's very humanistic, Claire," Bailie said, biting into a second cake. He chewed a bit then added, "Course, there's a possibility we could buy collectively." He turned to the others.

Gord shrugged but the Robineaus stayed quiet. Claire suspected they weren't in that good a position financially. She was beginning to feel guilty. Lillian would not want her to sell to a corporation, no matter how nice a face they turn to the world. "Maybe someone in Chesborough's interested. Or in Bracebridge or Huntsville?"

"Two years ago maybe, not anymore," Bailie said. "This town's halfway through death's door."

"Well, I don't understand it. With the Eternal City up here, and offering so much for land, real estate values must have skyrocketed."

"That they have. The problem lies in the fact nobody

wants to buy land here *except* Nirvana. You see, Georgian Bay, to the southwest and the Lake of Bays to the east, that's really prime cottage country. Where everybody wants to own. We're too far north and not north enough. Most people just drive through this area on their way up to Algonquin Park to camp. This lake never had many cottagers to begin with and now, what with the state the water's in . . ."

"Nirvana's been buying the town," Gord added. "But they don't have it yet. Their first interest is collecting all the properties surrounding the lake."

Claire couldn't quite get a grip on the situation, although she had seen for herself that this whole area was closing in on itself. "But isn't Nirvana's interest attracting other resorts, if not individuals? And surely local business should flourish."

Gord, who was about to sip his coffee, paused. "Local business? What local business?"

"Well," Claire said hesitantly, "Emerson's. The gas station. I don't know."

"Facades," Gord said. "Since Nirvana began acquiring land, the town's population has dwindled to eighty. There are only three businesses left in Chesborough and they're fading fast, or hadn't you noticed?"

"Four, counting the Gwinskis' taxidermy up the road. Another problem," Bailie added, "is Skeleton Lake's isolated. Not appealing to boaters. Now, take Huntsville—you've got Fairy Lake, Vernon Lake and Mary Lake. They're all connected by the Brunel Locks."

"But I can't understand this," Claire said. "A corporation like Nirvana usually causes an area to prosper. I know they're self-contained, but still, some jobs must have spilled over—"

"That's usually the case. Take Lagoon City, a resort down in Brechin, near Orillia. Why, money's turned hand over fist since they opened a few years back, even if the locals ain't too crazy about the way they're polluting the lake and dumping sewage into the fields. But Nirvana doesn't hire locals—they bring in their own people. And they don't buy local either. Even from Bracebridge or Huntsville."

"They're destroying the area," Gord said, adding, "and they don't give a damn."

"It's very strange." Claire couldn't get over the feeling that this didn't make sense. "The people at Nirvana told me their goal is to create a healthy environment and yet the town near them is dying."

"It's a healthy environment, all right," Bailie said, "for the upper crust. But it's not just the town. Skeleton Lake's become more polluted since they arrived. We noticed the fish dying when the lake thawed this spring. Over the summer it's gotten worse, so bad we can't swim in the water. The government won't do bugger all about it but put up signs so there's a payoff somewhere. Gilles here's a naturalist. He's kept a diary of all the wildlife that's died since Nirvana moved in. Believe me, there's plenty. The lake's badly polluted, that's for sure."

"A lot of lakes are polluted. How can you blame the Eternal City? Doesn't it take years to change the chemical balance?" She felt annoyed, suddenly, forced to become a defender of Nirvana. But there had to be a dissenting voice. Gord and Bailie, if not the quiet Robineaus, seemed to be on some vendetta. She didn't especially want to argue for Nirvana, yet everything she was hearing was so one-sided.

"Sure they're polluted. Acid rain," Bailie said. "Sulfur dioxide drifts up from manufacturing plants, mainly in the U.S., but some from Canada too. But our problem's not the pH balance. We got bacteria in our water and we don't even know what it is, let alone where it comes from."

"We've tried to find out," Gord added. "The local health department is hopeless. Besides the signs, they advised us all to buy chlorine filters last April. They tell us the bacteria count is up but they don't know why. Typical government stall. We've sent samples directly to the Ministry of the Environment in Ottawa several times. Gilles just sent another last week. Nothing."

"But how could Nirvana be polluting the water? They have their own sewage system, their own air, for God's sake. They don't manufacture anything. What could they be dumping?"

"That's what we're hoping to find out," Gord said. "Maybe we can get them into court. Or, better yet, get the government to take them to court."

"My wife and I, we are not young." It was only the second time Gilles Robineau had spoken, and everyone paid attention. "We live here since twenty years. Not so long even as Lillian or Bailie. When we move from Québec, this house, we build it from the trees on our land. We grow food. Together we watch many times the sun rise and set. You understand? We cannot leave. We live here and, when we die, it is here. I do not know how to say . . . the land, we have become the land."

The old man's words made more sense than any arguments Claire had heard so far. This is how Lillian would have felt, Claire was sure of it. The idea that Nirvana would put pressure on such people made her furious. Why couldn't the Eternal City tolerate neighbors, especially people as innocuous as the Robineaus?

The meeting continued another half hour until the Robineaus showed signs of tiring. As she and Gord were leaving, Bailie agreed to attend the party at the Eternal City Friday night. The Robineaus wouldn't commit themselves, and Claire understood. The trip would be arduous for them, especially so late at night. A strange voice in her head suddenly said, *especially that night.* Suddenly she felt chilly and wanted to go home.

But as soon as they got out of Gord's pickup, he took her arm. "There's the moon . . . Let's meet it."

They went out back behind Lillian's cottage, past the vegetable garden, the opening to the root cellar and a small tool shed. They climbed the hill through the trees along a narrow dirt path cut in the bush. There were plenty of mosquitoes and both Claire and Gord rolled down their sleeves and buttoned their shirts to the neck. But as they ascended the bloodsuckers didn't follow, much to Claire's relief.

The high-pitched cries she'd heard every night carried along the air in the distance. Wildly eerie, those cries made her think of something primitive and unknowable, yet she found them intriguing at the same time. Suddenly she remembered her nightmare, and shivered.

At the top of the knoll they found a small clearing. Through the birches and jackpines half a white-silver moon dangled in black space. Up here, the stars were many and bright. To the north, light flickered across the sky, luminous radiant bands of it, like magical, electrical clouds.

"Aurora Borealis," Gord said, quietly taking her hand. "The northern lights. Electrical solar particles pulled along the earth's magnetic energy field."

Claire felt her heart beat quicken. The shock of his hand grabbing hers rivaled the excitement of the waving patterns of light and the haunting cries. A ripple of sensation rode her body. She felt afraid to look at him.

"You go a hundred miles further north and the lights are

113

brighter and clearer," he said. "One summer I went to Ellesmere Island, the most northern point in Ontario, right at the edge of the Arctic Ocean. It's not like any other place on earth. There's nothing between you and the Arctic but wild dark blue water and pale green icebergs the size of small mountains. But up there the whole sky blazes blue, red, green. You feel like you're on another planet. Or dreaming."

The lights, the ancient cries, altered her perceptions. For a moment their eyes locked and Claire felt a primitive charge surge through her body. She held her breath. Something ancient and primal could happen between them.

Overhead, an ear-shattering, unearthly shriek split the night. Her body jerked. "My God! What—?"

"Let's get out of here." Gord's tone had altered. He dropped her hand abruptly and started down the rise.

Confused and more than a little frightened, Claire followed close on his heels, thinking about that sound. Wondering why, when it had been far away, it had felt comforting, and now, close, terrifying. And entirely familiar. As though someone called to her in a language she had not heard in a long long time. A forgotten language that, if she just had enough time and if she heard it often enough, she might remember what it all meant.

# Twelve

"A castle! Unreal!" David said to Jerry. It didn't even matter that the high grey-stone walls, turrets, battlements and even the moat and drawbridge were just parts of a restaurant.

So far, he was having a great time. The Eternal City boat had sliced into the darkness like a shuttle moving deep into space. The dome, a distant emerald planet, expanded as they approached. And the closer they got, the more he could make out shapes inside the dome. Then, just as they docked, a chopper floated down onto the heliport.

As David and Jerry followed their respective parents across the wooden bridge, their footsteps echoed faintly.

"There're sharks in the moat," David said. He and Jerry paused to look over the railing.

"Ferocious yuppies," Jerry flung back.

"Worse than that," Gord said. "It's stocked with a rare species of cuppies."

"Cuppies?" David and Jerry said in unison.

"Carnivorous urban professionals. Don't fall in. They'll network you to death."

Jerry laughed and groaned.

Security guards wearing helmets and tunics stood on either side of the arched door.

"Think those are real swords?" David whispered to Jerry.

"Yeah, right. That's, like, illegal."

They entered a dimly-lit hall. Pillars disappeared into the shadowy ceiling. A curved balcony bulged from the wall. Flames from torches lit the room and tossed shadows around. Well, maybe they were light bulbs, but they looked pretty good.

"Surprise, surprise," he heard Gord tell his mom. "All the political parties are represented, both locally and federally. Looks like Varik's multi-partisan."

"This must be David," a tall, important-looking guy wearing sunglasses said. He held out his hand and David had to take it. Geez, he hated it when adults did this.

"Yes," Claire said. "David, this is Mr. Varik. He runs the Eternal City."

"Hello, son." The sunglasses looked like two black holes floating in a pale universe.

"You've changed the decor." His mother smiled.

"Less intimate than the restaurant but more suitable for our needs tonight. I hope it meets with your approval."

"It's delightful! I feel as if I'm in a banquet hall in ancient Rome."

"A goddess in her temple." Varik took his mother's hand and kissed it.

David knew he'd never say anything so stupid to a girl. He didn't like this guy. For one thing, his mom seemed attracted to him. For another, the guy was negative-charged. Frozen electricity.

They all went down some concrete steps and into the main room, only half full of people, but tons of people were coming in behind them. Musicians dressed in bright minstrel outfits strolled around playing weird stringed instruments. David hated the tinkly music. Jerry did too, by the face he made.

Jerry elbowed him in the side and grinned. David looked to where he was looking. The walls were filled with tapestries and enormous paintings of nudes and entwined lovers.

They stopped at a curved table in one corner of the room. Huge gold platters with roasts ready to be carved. All kinds of salads, as well as bowls of peas, carrots, corn, broccoli and vegetables David couldn't identify and didn't care about anyway. "The royal feast," he said.

"Yeah," Jerry said. "Let's eat."

They got into the short line. The woman ahead of them was saying something about the desserts and how the cake with green icing that looked like the dome was "both a culinary and architectural triumph."

Behind the table, three white-capped chefs served everything and two more were cooking at a walk-in fireplace.

"Man, do you believe this? A whole pig with an apple in its mouth!" Jerry said. David, too, was impressed. They loaded up their plates.

At the end of the table sat goblets half full of red or white wine. He and Jerry looked at each other with a Why not? look. Who would know?

No sooner did he get his fingers around the stem of one than his mother—she was on the other side of the room!—took it out of his hands. "When in Rome," he explained.

Jerry snickered, but he put down his wine glass.

"The Coke," she said pointing, "is over there."

"Thanks. We were afraid we'd have to drink this."

"Don't mention it."

After he and Jerry got drinks, they parked themselves on a couch and dug in.

"This place is excellent, eh?" Jerry said. "Disneyland."

"*Better* than Disneyland."

It was true. The City enchanted David. The boats, the tennis courts he'd seen on the way in. Everything. "They offered us a place here," he said, munching on a chicken leg. "You could come over and visit, play tennis n' stuff."

"I could handle that," Jerry said. "It'd be rough, though. I'd have to give up my exciting days."

As the room filled, the decibel level moved up a few notches. The minstrels disappeared. A band started to play old sixties music. Some people danced, if you could call their movements that. A haze of smoke drifted towards the ceiling.

Jerry pointed out local residents. "Sergeant Williams, the OPP's finest, out of uniform. Mr. and Mrs. Van de Vooren, they're related to him or something." He pointed in another direction. A faded crowd, looking uncomfortable, in dull, washed-out clothing, long out-of-style.

"Definitely Chesborough."

"Definitely," Jerry confirmed.

"You can tell the City people from the townies," David shouted in Jerry's ear. He pointed to a well-dressed couple who stood chatting. Next to them his mother and Gord were talking to an old guy in a Scottish kilt.

"So, like do the men in Canada wear skirts or something?"

"Just Bailie. He lives on the road."

"How come he's dressed like that?"

"He was in the Scottish army or something."

David thought he looked like a goofy salesman on Saturday Night Live.

After he and Jerry threw away the food they didn't like the taste of and helped themselves to seconds and ate those,

David said, "Wanna go outside?"

"Sure."

They stopped to tell their parents where they were going.

"I don't want to have to come looking for you two," David's mother said.

"We're in a dome," David reminded her. "How far can we go?"

But the second they were outside, a Roman-clad soldier at the end of the drawbridge stopped them. "Sorry kids. The City's off-limits."

"How come?" Jerry asked.

The guard's laugh seemed forced. "First of all, it's the rules."

"And second?"

"Second, I got the spear and sword."

"Good point," David acknowledged." He gave a significant look to the man's weapons. "Two good points, in fact."

They turned and, on their way back in, Jerry laughed. "Pretty smooth, Mowatt."

"That was short," Gord said.

"The security guy wouldn't let us out."

"Well, you two do look like a couple of subversives," Claire laughed.

They wandered around for a while. There were no girls. Nobody even near their age. The stupid music went on and on.

David felt bored.

"This place is so slow," he said.

"Hey. What do you think's back here?" Jerry parted the heavy curtain behind them.

"A factory where they build bionic people, of course," David said.

"Yeah, grade A cyborgs."

"And they're force-fed special drugs—"

"Steroids—"

" 'Cause without them—"

"They'll rot right before your eyes."

"And turn into maggots."

"Martian pond scum."

"That they make cakes out of. Like that one that looks like the dome."

They couldn't stop laughing.

"Let's check it out," Jerry said.

They ducked behind the curtain. Along the wall they found a door and, in the dim light, looked at each other. With almost one mind they nodded agreement. "If we get caught, just say we're looking for the bathroom," Jerry suggested, trying the knob. "It's open," he whispered.

"Go!" David hissed. They slipped inside and closed the door after them.

It was a pretty good-sized room, but the place made David's skin go clammy, and it wasn't the temperature either. A fire snapped in the fireplace. Grey wallpaper and dark wood paneling. In the middle of the room stood a long, highly polished, wood table with three fancy high-back chairs that faced the door.

"What is this, a flower shop?" Jerry said. The room reeked. Vases full of flowers; on the marble mantle, at both ends of the table, two tall stands in the corners.

David wrinkled his nose. Underneath the perfumey smell he caught a different odor, a stink, really, one he knew, like, like . . . "Like a funeral," he whispered.

A large dark painting hung above the mantle. David went to look at it. A naked woman petting a swan. No, more than that. The swan's head was between her legs!

"Man, this was bizarre!" He felt embarrassed and glanced around.

Jerry was busy looking at two sketches on another wall. Old-fashioned ones, from some other century. In each, a guy with a cane and a long, black coat was kissing a lady in a dress with a bustle. The weird thing was the guy had these big wings growing out of his back. "Stupid!" Jerry whispered.

"Yeah," David agreed, although he found them intriguing.

There was a vent on one wall up near the ceiling, and across from it and down the far wall a bit, a pebbled glass door. Jerry opened the door and they saw a long brightly-lit corridor, white, smelling like a hospital. But underneath was that same funereal odor. The corridor was so long they couldn't see the end. "Wanna see where it goes?"

David hesitated. "Well . . ." He turned slightly and jolted.

"What?" Jerry looked where he pointed. Over the door they'd come in by hung another oil painting. An image ripped out of a nightmare. A woman in a flimsy dress lay sprawled, half on, half off a bed, her arms flung over her head. But it was the creature squatting on her chest that got to David. Naked, short, part-human, part-beast. A dwarf with bat ears and a hideous face. The eyes looked crazy and the way they were painted, the monster seemed to stare back at them.

Suddenly, from somewhere down the white corridor, an ear-splitting screech exploded. High-pitched. Echoing.

"I'm outta here!" Jerry said.

"Tell me about it!" David agreed.

They ran to the other door, shoving each other out.

No sooner had they rounded the curtain than they saw

Mr. Varik coming towards them with three people dressed in white and wearing sunglasses. Varik scowled as he passed, like he knew they'd been in the room. David put on an innocent face, and noticed that Jerry had too.

The blaring band music, tinkling glasses and laughing chatting people brought him back to earth. His courage returned. He turned to Jerry. "Know what I'm thinking?"

"Yeah, I know what you're thinking."

"What am I thinking?"

"You're thinking about that room."

"What else?"

"You're thinking about the corridor."

"And?"

"You wanna know what's in there."

"You got it!"

# Thirteen

*"Vas souper maintenance!"* Colette called from the kitchen.

Gilles closed his journal but left it on top of the desk. Outside the window only the green light from the dome lit the dark night sky. So many changes in the last year. It made him feel old and that his time had passed.

He glanced at his watch. An hour to eat, another to set up. Then the wait.

He joined Colette at the kitchen table. Mmmmmmmm, tortiere! His favorite meal. She slipped the spatula under a slice and lifted it out of the glass dish then slid the spicy meat pie onto his plate. Such a wonderful cook! She had always prepared food he enjoyed . . . except when she was angry at him.

Early on in their forty-eight years of marriage, Gilles had noticed that a disappointing meal invariably followed an argument. For the sake of gastronomy, he had learned long ago to settle disputes before Colette went into the kitchen.

"What are you smiling about?" she said.

"Nothing," he answered affectionately. "I'm thinking of my love for you."

She waved an impatient hand at him but he caught her grinning. "They go to the dock?" she asked, nodding towards the screen door as she poured the homemade wine.

He nodded, picked up his wine glass and went to the door. Dozens of vehicles cluttered the Eternal City dock. Tonight the air stank of exhaust fumes.

"Would you prefer to attend?" he asked Colette, returning to his chair.

She gave a loose Gallic shrug. "It is for the young. I need my beauty sleep," she said. But he knew that what she really meant was she would feel uncomfortable with so many strangers. Not the people of Chesborough, but the Eternal City residents. She had been a shy girl when they married so many years ago in the Cathédrale Saint Jean-Baptiste in Québec City. She was still shy. And although they had both aged—considerably—even today he found her attractive. Especially her eyes. On impulse he caught her hand and kissed it.

*"Mon petit chou,"* he growled.

She blushed and giggled like a girl and said, *"T'es fou fou."* He knew she did not really think him a fool.

After the meal, as they sat drinking coffee, Colette turned on the kitchen light. Gilles looked at the cat clock over the stove. "Will you come to see these noisy creatures?" As he stood his knees ached. How he wished for youth again!

Colette was running water for the dishes. "Perhaps later," she said. "Now I watch a program on the cinema from France. Would you like me to tape it?"

*"Mais, oui,"* he said, kissing her on the cheek and patting her bottom.

Gilles hung the camera with the long clumsy lens around his neck and took a thin brown jacket from the peg beside the door.

He felt the front right pocket of the jacket to make sure the pen and small notebook were still there.

"Once they pass, I will return," he told her.

*"Au revoir. Je t'aime,"* she said, the same words and tone she had used every time he left the house for over three decades.

*"Et moi, je t'adore,"* he replied as always, and, as always, meant it.

# Fourteen

"More Nectar-of-the-Gods? The price is right."

Claire smiled. Gord intercepted a passing waiter and lifted two glasses of champagne off the silver tray.

She felt like Cinderella at the ball and silently thanked whoever had chosen to cast her in this delightful role.

Sure, every once in a while, somewhere down inside, a disapproving voice cut through the pleasure: This is frivolous. What about the sick? The homeless? The millions of starving people in the world? Thankfully that voice stayed a whisper in her head. Claire just couldn't help it. She was having a fabulous time.

She and Gord clinked glasses. While sipping, he stared at her with those sand-colored eyes of his, those *gorgeous* eyes. He grinned. "Fun, eh?"

"Fun," she admitted, laughing.

"Claire Mowatt," he said, in a lightly taunting voice.

"Yes, Gord Roberts."

"I do believe I detect guilt."

"It shows?" she giggled and sipped champagne.

"Ditch the 'shoulds' and 'oughts' and 'supposed tos'. For tonight anyway." He stopped. A funny expression played on his face. "Isn't this the speech *you're* supposed to give *me?*"

"This place is insidious."

"We're strangers in a very strange land."

"That's the problem. I feel right at home."

He smiled indulgently. "I hate to hear you say that."

The band took a break and the minstrels returned. Dressed in pastel robes, they played lyre and lute, and a musical object she couldn't identify. Claire recognized the mellow Bach sonata and closed her eyes for a moment to listen.

Candle smoke, incense, and the fragrance of cut flowers saturated the air. She took a deep, luxurious breath. Yes, she just might be able to indulge in this once in a while. It would be tough but Gord was here to save her. What a handsome guy! No question. The bush hat and safari jacket, ridiculous on most men, looked great on him. And tonight—mentally she crossed her fingers—he seemed to be on his best behavior.

"You appreciate Bach." She opened her eyes.

Varik. White suit and shoes. Charcoal silk shirt. That same darker-than-night rose in the lapel. And those sunglasses!

"One of my favorite composers," she said. "He lifts my spirit."

"A woman very close to my own heart."

Claire felt herself blush. The man certainly exudes charm and sophistication, she thought. And nobody carries off wearing sunglasses at night the way he does.

He must have just come back from wherever he'd taken those people. The Eternal City denizens were attractive, but the trio that made an entrance a few minutes ago left the others looking like rabble. The woman possessed the type of skin the romantic poets would have described as alabaster. Pale but luminous. She wore an evening gown, the floor length white sequined skirt slit to the thigh. She also wore a white fur stole that covered her shoulder to waist. *Haute courtier,* no doubt. Her hair glowed pure white, and although Claire hadn't been close enough to see her facial features, she had the feeling the hair color was premature.

Both of the two men accompanying her wore summer suits like Varik's, with lightweight, floor length white leather coats draped over their shoulders. Although one was much older than the other—they appeared to be father and son—*their* hair was white too. Maybe, Claire thought, the latest fad is an Andy Warhol revival.

All three were fashionably slim and tall. And each wore sunglasses. She wondered if they wore them to bed, too.

Most of the guests stopped what they'd been doing to stare. The trio moved gracefully, economically. Peculiarly. Haughty, they scanned the room. At one point Claire felt the woman focused on her, as though an invisible beam connected them. But almost the moment Claire became aware of that, the woman turned away.

"And who are They, Themselves?" Bailie had asked, taking a sip of the scotch he had gotten from the bar.

Brenda, nearby, said reverently, "Our charter members," her tone obsequious.

Claire looked at her, waiting for some further explanation, but none came.

Varik had rushed to them. He kissed the gloved hand of the woman and, after a few moments, led them across the room. They disappeared behind a curtain.

Claire had wondered if the three were entertainers. Or heads of state. Maybe even discrete billionaires. Whoever they were, they certainly were gorgeous. And reeked of power and wealth. They had also exuded an arrogance that annoyed her.

"Nice bash," Gord said to Varik, bringing her back to the present. "But don't you think you need a few noses pressed to the outside of the dome to complete the ambience?"

One side of Varik's face lifted, the hint of a tolerant smile. "You find our little thank-you to the residents of Chesborough offensive, don't you Mr. Roberts? That's unfortunate. I like to think of your opinion as a dissenting view."

"And I like to think your city won't be eternal. In fact, it may not even last the decade."

Varik raised a dark eyebrow above the top of the sunglasses. "And why is that?"

"The masses are more aggressive than you give them credit for. Come the revolution—"

"Ah, the revolution. A quaint concept. Yes, the peasants can be revolting. But even Marx seems to have gone to his final resting place. It's tragic to watch someone trapped in another era, don't you agree, Claire?"

Claire, listening to them spar, had the uncomfortable feeling of being the trophy. She resented being cast in silver. Gord had done it again! Why the hell couldn't he leave it alone for one night?

She glanced around the room, looking for the kids. Last she'd seen them they'd been helping themselves to more food.

She'd watched David throw away most of what was on his plate. She'd have to have a talk with her son. This place positively *inspired* decadence.

Suddenly she realized Gord and Varik were waiting for her to answer. She looked at one, then the other. This called for feminine wiles. A change of subject would do the trick. "Is Varik your first or second name?" she asked, pretending his question had never been asked.

"Neither."

"Well, then, what was the name you were born with?"

His face softened a touch. "One that did not suit me."

Out of the corner of her eye, Claire saw Gord open his mouth. She tensed, imagining what he was about to do with a straight line like that, and prepared to step on his foot.

"Quite the shindig, Mr. V," commented Bailie, inadvertently diverting World War III.

"Thank you, Mr. Rankin. Your colleague-in-arms here does not share your view."

"Well, he takes things more to heart than me. Your Glen Deveron is good. I'm having a fine old time, although I feel a bit like a condemned man struggling to enjoy his last meal."

Gord gave a malicious chuckle.

Varik smiled thinly.

At least Bailie shifts into low gear, Claire thought. Gord, on the other hand, needs a complete overhaul. The other night, for instance, when he should have kissed her and hadn't . . . She wondered if it's a cultural thing, but she couldn't believe Canadians were *that* reserved.

Of course, she and David were leaving soon. Maybe Gord just didn't want to get involved. Understandable. Neither did she. Still, he might've brought the subject up. He *did* hold her hand.

But there was something odd about Gord—a man in his forties, living alone all winter with a bunch of senior citizens. He was hiding but she didn't know from what. His failed marriage, maybe, but she sensed that wasn't all of it. Also, his mood swings frightened her. She wasn't used to it. Bill had been even-tempered. Emotionally dependable and upbeat. Gord, on the other hand, went from warm one minute to an out-of-control firestorm the next.

She and Bill had survived ten years of marriage without having to deal with any major catastrophes. Right! Claire thought bitterly. Other than the minor disaster of his death, but then only she and David had been left to deal with that.

But their life *had* been blessed. Maybe it had lulled her. And now, out in the real world again, she certainly felt unprepared for someone like Gord. Hell, she wasn't sure *she* wanted involvement. It would be letting herself in for upheaval, just when she was feeling stable for the first time in two years. And where did all this come from, anyway? Nothing moved from Gord's end, so why should she even think about it? The only man showing any interest in her as a woman was Varik. He wasn't her type, or was he? Such intensity focused on her felt flattering, to say the least. He seemed to like her—clearly he was giving her special treatment. And something hid within the man that attracted her as much as it frightened her. He might be different than any man she'd met but that didn't mean she shouldn't give him a chance.

Bailie, probably sensing that he couldn't crack Varik's armor, aimed his next provocation at Brenda. "Tell us then, Ms. Lawrence, what's the real purpose of this bash?" Although slightly barbed, the tone reeked of good-naturedness.

Brenda took an equally good-natured stance. "Why, how else can we seduce you into selling your property, Mr. Rankin? We've tried money. We thought wine, women and song might do the trick."

Everybody but Gord and Varik laughed.

Claire looked around the room. The City's residents were gathered in clusters of three or four. Relaxed. Happy. Of course they could smile and be cheerful, they had none of the worries of ordinary mortals. Who the hell do these Eternal City people think they are?

"Excuse me," Claire said, and hurried to the ladies' room. Fortunately it was empty. She looked in a mirror.

What's going on? she wondered. She had never felt this resentful and vindictive in her life. Suddenly a wave of grief hit. She missed Bill terribly. Nothing could have prepared her for the loss.

She thought she was over it. Two years had passed. She was getting her life in order. And now Lillian. Being here, she felt so close to her aunt's spirit. A horrible image of Lillian's body being eroded by water, her flesh eaten . . .

Claire hurried into one of the stalls and locked the door. Alone at last, she allowed herself the luxury of a good cry.

# Fifteen

Gilles followed the well-worn path up into the forest. Deer had used this trail for hundreds of years. Until recently, he and Colette had often spotted stags and does, sometimes with gangly, knobby-kneed fawns, wandering down past the lawn to the lake to drink.

This year again in May, his wife put out salt licks. For the first time, no deer turned up.

He waved a hand in front of his face. Mosquitoes. He hated the whine of these high-pitched blood suckers. Unlike other species, *their* population did not seem in any danger of extinction. Gilles entertained a sobering if common thought, one that often came to him: First the dinosaurs, not intelligent enough to prevent their own extinction. Was man next? Secretly he suspected the mosquito would do a better job of surviving.

One of the most astonishing aspects of nature—his rational mind *still* couldn't accept it—was that humanity had evolved so far ahead of other creatures, at least in the mental department. It did not seem logical. He could see how one species might be dominant. He had no problem with that. But the incredible gap between *homo sapiens* and the most intelligent animals . . . What a mystery. But then, nature held many mysteries.

At the top of the path, just out of sight from the house, he stepped into the clearing. In the middle stood his Kowa spotting scope, used for observing wildlife. He had affixed to the lens a brand new eye-piece that would magnify forty-five times. And now that the light amplifier, borrowed from a former colleague at the University of Toronto, had finally arrived, nothing would stop his study. Gord had helped him move it up the hill, and attach it to the lens. It could increase whatever light there might be this night by one hundred times.

He sat on the tree stump behind the terrestrial scope, resting from the climb uphill. Excitement suddenly swept over him. Flying species had always been his favorites. And now, to discover one new to this region! He was fortunate indeed. He had read once the Zen theory of becoming one with the animal. The concept appealed to him and on several occasions he had managed to still his inquisitive mind enough that for a moment, here and there, he had merged; he had a sense of what it must be like to be a bird; to cut through the air and experience wind caressing his body; to look down on the earth from great heights and view the loveliness of green and blue and brown; to be blissfully unaware of impending death.

Gilles coughed long and deeply and spit onto the ground. Blood again. How long could he conceal this from Colette?

When he caught his breath he reached into the breast pocket of his jacket and pulled out a pipe and a pouch of *Coeur de Bois* tobacco. Leisurely filling the bowl, he clamped the stem between his teeth and, with his forefinger, tapped down the dried, shredded leaves.

After his heart attack three years ago, both Colette and Dr. Milton worked diligently at him until finally he agreed to cut back to a pipe a day. Gilles had laughed at them. "Smoking won't kill me," he reassured the two worried faces from his hospital bed. "I've just contracted a mild case of old age." He had not let them know of his fear, that it was more than his heart that was giving out. Since that time he had struggled to come to terms with death. He had made progress. Accepting mortality was the most difficult task of his life. And yet, still, he longed to be free of the awareness that one day life as he knew it would cease. He longed to be free in the way animals are free.

The deep black of the sky surrounded him like a womb. The amplified light would work fine. He would see these elusive creatures close up, not the blur of wings jetting up near the clouds through the darkness.

Gilles set about attaching the camera behind the amplifier, to shoot through the spotting scope's viewfinder. He had charted the regular route the birds took just after sunset and before sunrise each night. Anyway, if necessary, he could adjust the angle easily.

He leaned over to light the Coleman lamp he'd brought along and began to make a few routine notations in his outdoor notebook that later would be transferred to his large journal.

*Skreeee! Skreeee! Skreeee!*

Adrenalin rushed through him. *Calm down, calm down,* he told himself.

He jotted a hurried final entry and looked up. Nighthawks? Great Horned Owls? No, he had long ago dismissed the possibility. Those species traveled alone or in pairs. Bats? Not likely. The fruit and insect eating bats native to this region liked to fly alone or in very small groups. There must be dozens of these creatures.

Whatever was crossing the sky came from the north, as

usual. Their routine never varied. They flew very high and fast over the water, circled the domed city, then continued on over his cottage and beyond his land and further south, towards the more populated cottage areas where, presumably, their food supply was more abundant.

Gilles imagined his birds, as he liked to think of them, rising up as a dark flock from their nesting grounds. He peered through the viewer of the Nikon, focused to infinity. The camera was loaded with 800 ASA recording film, the type used by news photographers for night photos. The pictures would be grainy but for this first glimpse they would do.

*Skreeee! Skreeee!*

He saw them in his mind, a cloud of wings, gathering, circling. Finally, instinctively, if they were birds rather than bats, which of course are mammals, they would move into formation as they ascended. Life is extraordinary, Gilles thought. So mysterious!

*SkreeeEEEEE! SKREEEEEEE!*

Louder. Closer. As the sounds grew, so did his excitement.

He rested his finger on the shutter. They must be overhead.

He peered through the viewfinder.

*Merde!* Nothing to see!

The path to the stars was perfectly illuminated, as brilliant as mid-day, but empty.

A flicker. Movement at the edge of his field of vision.

Gilles swiveled the telescope to the right.

Ah! Caught one. There! Luck was with him. Something drifted into the center of his viewfinder and grew in size as it neared.

Gilles' mind suddenly stopped its endless thought processing. His jaw dropped. The pipe fell from his fingers onto the grass.

The wingspan! Wide. Iridescent. Incredible! The most beautiful, alluring creature he had ever come across!

The bird—it *had* to be a bird, what else could it be?—hung above the clearing like a bee hovering in mid-air. Graceful. Oddly albino. Enormous. Its pinions, nearly transparent, infracted the entire spectrum. Amazing!

Gilles felt entranced by the creature. The beauty of its precise movements mesmerized him. What an honor, to be the one to witness this! Lovely. Beyond lovely, the creature was . . .

Another part of his mind, the logical side, revived and now operated on automatic, independent of the awe-struck part of him. Surely this species has been recorded before? The files stored in his head opened and he scanned bits and pieces of information: ancient China, a bird so elaborate and dynamic that the Chinese called it *Chen,* meaning "like thunder"; late 1400s during the Ottoman reign, sporadic sightings in Turkey and what was then Transylvania; early 1950s, obscure references by anthropologists of a pale night bird worshipped by Indians along the Oronoco River in Venezuela; two sightings in the Nevada Desert a few years ago . . . But here? Now? Why?

Suddenly Gilles realized that the creature had slipped lower, closer. He noticed other things. The air filled with the scent of flowers. He could make out wisps of white around the creature's head, like angels' hair, blowing in the wind. Eyes, immaculate clouds, or fresh snow. Pure.

He felt attracted as a man is to a woman. To look into those innocent eyes! A curiosity? No, he saw something eternal. For only a moment. He let himself look deeper.

*Gilles!* A seductive voice. Intimate.

He felt drugged, but pleasantly so. He sensed the creature's need. It wanted him in some way. Hungered for contact. He understood that, and more. Its movements became a dance, perfectly in tune with his energy, a dance meant for him alone.

*Join with us, Gilles.* The whisper urged him to action, the whisper of hundreds, a chorus of desire that stroked his body like fingers of fire that burned deliciously.

Tears of longing rolled down his cheeks. One arm reached up. He wanted to touch this life form. To meld.

Accidentally the shutter button depressed. In that instant the telescope jerked left. Contact severed, pain shot through Gilles' head as if the disconnection had been physical.

Confusion hit. Then shock.

He'd seen something strange. But what? He could not remember. He prayed the camera hadn't caught black sky, leaving the negative without an image.

Until a moment ago, he'd been in touch with two parts of himself. The fascinated, erotically-charged Gilles, and the efficient, calculating scientific man. Below both, a deeper consciousness had been on guard all along. Right from the moment he'd spotted them.

Gilles felt his heart pound far too quickly. His autonomic nervous system *knew* what he had seen, and his cells were reacting. Rapid breathing. Icy skin, though the temperature must be in the eighties. A stench hit, nearly knocking him off his feet.

Putrefaction. *Rotting* flowers. Gilles gagged, nearly throwing up. Suddenly he became aware mentally of the threat his body had known about all along. "This cannot be," he said, falling back from the telescope.

*SKREEEEEE! SKREEEEEEE! SKREEEEEE!* Harsh

calls cut the night, at different octaves, one after another, as if they were signaling each other with a verbal sonar. The sweet-tart odor enveloped him, as repulsive as sniffing ammonia.

Wings rustled above and behind him. More of them. At least eighteen.

They hovered close, at the outer edges of the Coleman's glow. Hideous. Prehistoric. No longer transparent, but solid, Gilles noticed in sudden confusion. Pale, solid shadows. Opaque predators. All albinos. Freaks of nature that should have died out long ago. Those iris-less eyes that had entranced him were, in reality, cunningly malevolent. Whatever species they might be, they were blind, that was clear, and perceived him by other, stronger senses. And now they were diving. Towards him!

Gilles scrambled to his feet, accidentally kicking over the storm lantern.

Fluttering. Whooshing. *SKREEEEE! SKREEEEE!*

He clapped his hands over his ears. The dense air became a wall of stink.

Gilles staggered to the path and started down, his stiff arthritic limbs struggling to obey his command to "Hurry!" Incredibly, they followed. Swooping. Diving close, like a swarm of angry wasps. His left foot caught on a root and he fell with a whomp, then tumbled partway down the knoll.

Bushes clawed his face. His temple smacked a rock. He could no longer catch his breath.

Rolling to his hands and knees, he half stood, but something rammed his back, sending him sprawling face-down in the dirt.

He turned to find a large one suspended above him. Wings spread astonishingly wide, it waited with easy confidence and sinister patience, enjoying the terror of its prey.

Gilles felt sickened by the smell, horrified by the sight. Up close its body glistened with a sheen of mucus, like a newborn. But this was no infant of the species, that was clear! Its harsh, angular facial features identified it in his mind, a pterodactyl, and yet at the same time the features were strangely, distortedly humanoid.

Its mouth opened and Gilles screamed. Two rows of jagged teeth glistened with saliva. The eyes, dead white, unearthly, glinted with a light of their own. Inches from him, the thing stretched out its talons, and Gilles shrank back from that lethal touch. He covered his face and screamed again.

The pressure behind his ribs increased dramatically, refusing to be ignored any longer. Heavy sweat covered his body, the moisture soaking his clothes. White hot pain stabbed him in the chest. It spread to his left shoulder and arm.

The creature above him waited. Gilles struggled to turn towards the cottage. In the bushes he saw a familiar face watching. He tried to reach out, but pain sizzled down to his fingers. He couldn't catch his breath enough to make a word form. He couldn't move.

The thing *knew* he was having a heart seizure. Had known all along. And Gilles finally understood. It would keep vigil until he, until he . . .

Pain locked his throat and jaw, paralyzing his liquid-filled lungs. He tried to hold on. But the creature called to him.

*Gilles. Gilles. Join with us now. You have no choice.*

No! He refused to listen. Or to look into those blanched sockets again. But he wanted to. He really wanted to.

# Sixteen

"So, where's Mary Ellen tonight?" Gord asked, as Williams and Brenda joined the small group waiting for the Eternal City vessel to return and take them back to the mainland. Williams scowled. A direct hit. Good! The asshole deserved it! Gord thought. Williams had been instrumental in convincing a lot of people to sell out to Nirvana.

But Claire turned away from him. Ouch.

Brenda's shit-eating smile remained in place. "Have a good time?" she said brightly to Claire, who answered "Yes." Brenda's insincerity seemed obvious to Gord. He wondered why he was the only one to notice.

But the way Williams acted around Brenda—attentive, sheepish, happy—made it clear: He'd been in Eternal City's pocket all along. Corporate pocket, her skirt.

"Wife's sick. You might remember, she's an invalid." Williams glanced at Claire. Gord watched her eyes soften with sympathy. Naturally. And of course she was already shooting *him* daggers. He felt annoyed. She could use a history lesson.

"Lighten up, Gord," Bailie laid a hand on his shoulder and whispered covertly in his ear. "It's late. Not the time nor the place."

But Gord couldn't stop himself. "I've often wondered

what you get out of Eternal City. Now I know."

"They're good corporate citizens," Williams said toler-antly, ignoring the innuendo.

"Why don't you tell us their hidden agenda?"

"You've had too much to drink," Williams said.

"Sergeant Williams, I was going to show you my sail-boat." Brenda took Williams' arm. They turned.

"Touch a nerve, Sergeant?" Gord shot.

Williams spun back. "You always touch a nerve, Rob-erts. Quit trying to make it personal."

"It *is* personal. You're helping Nirvana destroy my home."

"You don't know a good deal when you see one."

"Obviously you do. That's why you busted your ass to make sure this town crumbled under the pressure of big bucks."

"This town," Williams spat, "has always been a washed out rabbit-hole with small-minded ideas that haven't changed since the first settlers moved in."

Gord smiled triumphantly. "Ah! Out in the open. Finally."

"Bullshit! I'm just amazed so many people did see the light and take the money. Just goes to show they aren't as dumb as some others."

"Meaning me?"

"Meaning anybody who's afraid of taking risks to get something out of life. If the shoe fits, Roberts, that's not my problem."

"What *is* your problem?"

"Gord," Claire said, "cut it out!"

"Unlike you, *my* problems are minor." Williams started across the dock with Brenda. "I'm doing just fine." He slid his arm around her waist.

Gord knew the old Williams would have stayed to fight. This one walked away. "Must be some hefty sums passing hands," he called, but Williams didn't take the bait.

Claire just shook her head. "You're impossible," she said, exasperated. "I'm going to check on the kids."

Gord finished off the glass of wine he'd brought with him from the party. He felt shaky, his legs wobbly. He wondered if he was becoming an alcoholic. His anger scared him. And puzzled him slightly. He couldn't understand why he felt so much animosity towards Williams. Maybe it was even more personal than he cared to admit. Maybe he was jealous.

Gord remembered the OPP officer when they first met several years back. A real surly son-of-a-bitch. Mean. A walking stereotype of a small town cop. It was obvious he hated Chesborough, hated his life. There were stories, rumors. Gord wasn't surprised to hear now and then that Williams took the law into his own hands. He had a reputation.

But last summer when things started changing, Williams changed. He lost weight. The hard edges of his personality were blunted a bit. He started doing out-of-character things, things he'd never done before; he became active at the town council meetings; actually began dropping in on people socially. Gord, always the skeptic, figured he had plans to run for office.

He'd never liked Williams. Didn't trust him. It all made sense when, even before they finished building the dome, Williams turned into a one-man sales team for Nirvana.

Everywhere Gord went last summer he found Williams talking up the advantages of selling. Even recommending other areas to move to. "You moonlighting?" Gord had asked. "Police work slow these days?" Williams didn't bother answering.

It hadn't taken long for the people on Skeleton Lake
Road to get suspicious. Now he knew for sure—Williams
was being cut in somehow. Gord realized he resented the
policeman even more than Varik. At least Varik was a vulture from a distant shore, one who showed his talons
openly. Williams, damn it, lived here. Residents of
Chesborough, if not his friends, were his neighbors.

"The boat's here," Claire said. "You're not going to
continue your private war onboard, are you? The enemy has
retreated." Her tone was still exasperated, but tinged with
humor. Gord wasn't sure if he enjoyed not being taken seriously, but at least she didn't seem totally pissed at him.

"I think they've merely withdrawn to regroup. They'll
fight to the death." God! he couldn't shut up. He wondered
what made him so volatile tonight. Probably because he
liked this woman too much. But they were certainly different people when it came to partying. His idea of a good
time was a few close friends sharing a meal, some laughs,
maybe an evening together. Claire, while not a life-of-the-
party type, seemed attracted to the glamorous world. He
didn't mind that. What he minded was the interest she
showed in the Eternal City. It was— Wait a minute, Roberts, he thought. If he wanted to be honest with himself—
and that was always in question—what upset him was the
fascination she held for Varik.

Great. Just great. Will it never end? he thought. First I'm
jealous of Williams for being able to change his life. And
now it's live-off-the-fat-of-others Varik, because Claire
finds his cadaver sexy!

At that moment, as if on cue, Varik stepped out of a cart
and approached them, ostensibly to see his guests off, but
Gord knew it was to see Claire. Varik took her hand and
kissed it, mumbling about seeing her soon. Suave. Real

suave. And Claire gave the bastard an enigmatic smile! Whatever *that* meant.

Varik exuded power, wealth, and sophistication. He was smart and good-looking, in a dollars and cents way. While not athletic, he moved smoothly, with grace and control. So, Gord asked himself, other than those vapid qualities *and* not counting the small cities he owns, what's Varik got that I don't?

"What's so funny?" Claire asked as they stepped on board.

"Just planning strategies to get an invite to your place for coffee."

"Hmmmmm," she laughed, eyes sparkling mischievously. "The question is, can you make coffee?"

"Lady, I am the world's foremost coffee brew-master."

"There also happens to be a bottle of Remy Martin lurking around the cottage."

"Unopened?"

"Unopened."

"Isn't that coincidental? I am a certified opener of brandy bottles, specializing in Remy Martin."

"Amazing," Claire said. "I've been wishing someone would volunteer to come over and make coffee and open the Remy Martin for me."

Gord lifted his eyebrows and raised his hands palm up. "At your service!"

Once the boat launched, he began to relax. Williams stood alone at the railing at the bow, which was just as well. Gord and Claire stood at the aft rail, watching the dome recede. "Strange," he told her, "how my body goes into warrior mode around Eternal City. I wasn't completely aware of it while we were there, but now, leaving, the armor feels heavy."

145

"Those are some pretty sharp weapons you carry," she said. Her laser eyes went right into him, even in the darkness.

Gord, disconcerted, realized her tone hadn't been judgmental. "Yeah," he acknowledged. What else could he say? He watched the wake spread out behind the cruiser.

Moments later, as they docked, he noticed the Robineaus' lights still on. He checked his watch. One a.m. Strange. He mentioned it to Claire.

"Is that unusual? Don't they ever stay up late?" she asked.

"Maybe I'm still in defense mode. Mind if we stop there for a minute? It won't take long. Just want to check everything's okay."

Claire surprised him by reaching up and kissing his cheek. "You're very caring," she whispered.

"Me? The original thorn in everybody's side? Can't-take-me-anywhere Roberts. I'm rude, crude and obsessed."

"Yes," she said, "you're all those things. But not only. Here you are, stopping in to make sure the Robineaus are okay just because you see their light on. That's incredibly sweet."

High above them loud screeches cut the night. The crowd disembarking stopped in their tracks and listened. Silence, like a pall, hung over the dock.

Suddenly, despite the humidity, Gord felt chilly.

Claire was looking straight ahead, her eyes focused on nothing. Her voice sounded strange and faraway. "It's Gilles. Something's wrong." She turned her face and stared at him as if she hypnotized.

He hurried her and the boys into the pickup and raced to the Robineaus'.

# Seventeen

Jack Williams pulled into his driveway. He switched off the ignition, punched the button for the lights, then just sat staring out the windshield at nothing. Suddenly his fist slammed the steering wheel. Damn Roberts! He's asking for it! Somebody would shut his mouth for good.

He climbed out of the patrol car. Up on the veranda, he fumbled for the right key, found it, and quietly unlocked the front door.

As he stepped inside, his mood sank even further. Jeez, before Eternal City and Brenda, he hadn't even been able to face how unhappy he'd become. They'd both given him something. A new lease on life. He didn't want to lose that. He *wouldn't* lose it.

Coming home lately felt like visiting a cemetery on a daily basis. Nothing here for me, Williams thought. A well-kept lawn. A mausoleum. And inside? A living corpse for a wife.

Only a corner lamp lit the living room. Mary Ellen always left it on for him. He switched it off and walked quietly down the hall to the bedroom. He pushed open the door a crack and peered in.

Pitch-black. Drapes drawn. His wife had had a bad day. As usual. Rustling sounds from the bed. "That you, Jack?"

"Yeah."

"What time's it?"

"Almost two."

"Umm."

"How ya feelin'?" He hadn't cared in a long time, just asked by rote.

"Headache's bad. Since lunch." Her voice was heavy, from sleep, but also the antidepressants. Williams couldn't help comparing her dull voice to Brenda's lilting, sensuous one.

"Need anything?"

"Nothing helps. You know that."

"Wanna see Doc Wagner tomorrow?"

"We'll see."

"Go back to sleep," he urged, already closing the door.

He used the basement shower, not so much to keep from disturbing his wife further, but because he didn't want to talk to her. He'd been avoiding Mary Ellen a lot these days. Actually, it surprised him how easy it was to do.

Hot water cascaded down. Williams adjusted the showerhead. Needle spray stabbed his shoulders and back, easing some of the muscle tension. He exhaled and let the water do its job.

Something felt wrong. The situation at Eternal City was beginning to smell. Like milk that's started to turn. Jeez! He hated to admit it but Roberts might actually be on to something. Williams didn't like the notion of being tangled up in more than he bargained for. Sure, he profited, Brenda saw to that. But that didn't mean he was stupid. He could look the other way, but he still saw things out of the corner of his eye.

What the hell was Varik really into? The land purchases seemed on the up-and-up. Drugs? Ridiculous! Couldn't be.

Well, maybe. There'd been talk about pollution—water, soil, air—but that couldn't be it. Besides, those rumors had been circulating a long time now, even before the City had been built. He hadn't noticed less wildlife in the area, although fishing seemed to have dropped off. Still, that went in cycles. One thing *was* true. Since Nirvana moved in, the number of violent deaths had doubled, a big increase for such a small place. Not that he thought the City had anything to do with that.

He went over some of what had happened in the last couple of years, starting with the most recent: the Donaldsons' farm burning down (possibly arson), their kid killed; Lillian Palmer (probable drowning); Hilda Emerson dropping dead outside the store (hit-and-run); the disappearance of Cindy Peer, five-year-old daughter of Randy and Agnes (lost in the woods, remains never found); Harry Francis (suicide by shotgun); the Jackson twins' disappearance (probable runaways). Something went click, that same little satisfying click as when you hit the last number in a combination lock.

*Every* family affected had been holdouts; they'd refused to sell their land to Nirvana.

That's crazy, he told himself. Other people haven't sold but they're alive and kicking; Lillian's niece, the Robineaus, Bailie Rankin, the Gwinskis, that asshole, Roberts, not to mention the people left in the town proper.

He picked up the soap and lathered his chest, arms and back, scrubbing hard. But Williams couldn't wash away the worry that nagged at him like an itch. He was a small town cop who knew all about itches. The more you scratch, the worse they get.

He turned off the spray and stepped out of the shower. He was toweling off when the phone rang. He caught it before the second ring on the basement extension.

"What the hell! Look, Roberts, it's the middle of the goddamn night. If you want to argue—"

"Better get over here to the Robineaus'."

"Call the station. I'm off duty."

"Gilles has been murdered."

When Williams arrived at the scene, chaos reigned. He set about restoring order.

Colette Robineau, too distraught to question, kept babbling in French. Obviously out of it; in shock. He asked the Mowatt woman and the two kids to stay in the house with her while Roberts took him to the body.

They crossed the backyard, Williams lighting the way with his heavy-duty flashlight. Gilles Robineau lay at the foot of a steep path on his side, curled in a fetal position. His clothes were torn, his face and hands scratched. Some blood, not much. All of it consistent with a fall.

Williams had seen death often enough. He was always struck by how ordinary a corpse looked, like you could just wake the person up and things would be fine.

"He died out here alone," Roberts said.

Williams felt a little sorry for Roberts, and that surprised him. After all, Roberts was a friend and neighbor of the Robineaus, like a son to them. Had been with Lillian, too. Williams didn't miss the connection. "Touch anything?" he asked.

"Just his eyelids. They were open, I closed them."

Williams nodded. "Looks like he tripped and fell." He knelt down and felt with two fingers in the groove between the windpipe and the large muscles in the neck. No pulse. He listened at the chest for a heartbeat. Without moving the body, he also checked for head injuries that

150

might have caused death. Nada.

"Could have been pushed," Roberts said.

Christ! Was he going to start that paranoid crap again? Williams kept his temper in check. It would be a long night. Too long to start with an argument. "Either way, the fall didn't kill him. Looks like a stroke or heart attack. He had a heart condition, didn't he?"

"Yes," Gord said reluctantly.

Williams stood and flashed his light uphill along the packed earth of the path. He pulled a notebook from his shirt pocket and began jotting down routine information about the body and the surrounding area.

He walked up the hill, Roberts on his heels. In the clearing at the top he found a telescope. "What the hell's this for?"

"I helped Gilles set it up so he could photograph the birds. That's what he was out here doing."

"What birds?"

Roberts faced him. "You must have heard them. Everybody has. They're around every night, after sunset, before sunrise, sometimes around midnight. Gilles thought they're a species new to our area. Night-hawks. Maybe even bats."

Williams snorted but jotted a note. He picked up the camera, flashed the light on it, rewound the film and pocketed it.

Footprints on the ground showed a lot of movement but the heel marks were apparently from the same shoes. There was, however, a pipe on the ground and a small notebook and kerosene lamp on a stump behind the telescope. Williams picked the book up and flipped through it. The last notation read: "They're coming. Must get a decent picture." Obviously didn't have time to make further entries.

As they walked back down the path, Williams played the

beam of the flashlight over the ground. Broken branches, leaves yanked off. Gilles had fallen. If something or somebody had been chasing him, there were no tracks. Williams did, however, find prints of bare feet behind some bushes closer to the house. Could be Robineau's or his wife's. On the other hand, Earl Gwinski had a bad habit of snooping around people's houses barefoot. Williams had picked him up a couple of times. He'd have to question the kid.

"What's it look like to you?" Roberts asked.

"He was taking pictures of birds and on his way home he fell down the hill. Why? No way to tell. Maybe he was having a heart attack."

"That's about what I'd expect you to say."

Williams had doubts but had no intention of sharing them with Roberts. "Hey! I don't want to hear your bullshit."

"Giles knew these woods and this path. He wouldn't fall unless he was running and he wouldn't run unless something was chasing him."

"For christsake, the man was in his late seventies. People his age die, especially when they have heart problems. I don't see signs of a struggle, do you?"

"If you mean with a sloppy murderer, no."

"I mean *any* kind of a struggle, other than an old man having a heart attack and trying to get back to his wife." Williams snapped his notebook closed. Talking to Roberts was worse than talking to a jackpine. "Doctor Wagner should be here soon. Why don't you ask him what happened?"

"I intend to."

"Good."

But Roberts kept pushing. "Don't you think it's strange Chesborough's had more unexplained deaths and missing persons in the last year and a half than in the past ten?"

"What I think is unexplained is how come you're always around whenever there's trouble."

"I could say the same about you."

"I don't have time for this," Williams said. What a prick, he thought. He turned his back on Roberts and went into the house.

Colette was still in a state. Sobbing. Screaming. Out-of-control. Poor woman. The two kids looked scared. The Mowatt woman had her hands full. It wasn't a situation he wanted to deal with so he put it off.

The ambulance arrived, no siren, but a red light whirled on the roof. Doc Wagner's blue Toyota followed behind. While Wagner examined the body, Williams wandered into Gilles' study. He noticed a ledger-sized book on the desk and flipped through the entries, scanning the latest and going backwards in time.

What he read disturbed him. It was obvious Gilles thought something was going on with the environment. Of course, it was common knowledge that a lot of the lakes were dying from acid rain. And it wasn't unusual for a lake to register a high bacteria count. Still, the changes on this one and the notations looked like they happened unnaturally fast. He'd have to read the notes when he had more time.

Stifling a yawn, Williams jammed a cigar into his mouth but didn't light it. He took the journal with him and headed into the living room to try to find out from Colette what had happened. This wasn't a part of the job he felt comfortable with.

Williams walked through his front door again at five a.m. Beat. All he could get out of Colette was the phrase, *la grand oiseau de la nuit,* which Roberts said meant large birds of the night.

Doctor Wagner made an instant diagnosis: myocardial infarction. Heart attack. But an autopsy would confirm that.

There wasn't anything more to be done at this point, but Williams decided to have a quick read of Robineau's journal before hitting the sack. An hour and a half later he placed a call to Varik.

When the CEO of the Eternal City came on the line, Williams hit him with the news of Gilles Robineau's death. He paid careful attention to the reaction.

"Very unfortunate. But, why call me, especially at this hour?"

"Thought you might be interested."

"I am. Marginally. I suppose Mrs. Robineau will be more inclined to sell her land now."

At one time, Varik's coldness wouldn't have bothered Williams in the least. But now, for some reason, Varik sounded like a vulture ready to dine on the leavings. "Look, you hired me as a go-between, to try and persuade people here to sell to Nirvana."

"And you've done an excellent job. You've been amply compensated for your efforts."

"I'm not taking your money to cover up anything."

"Are you implying that I or anyone in the corporation is in any way responsible for Mr. Robineau's heart attack? If you are, Sergeant, I suggest you make your accusations formal, in which case I will phone our attorneys."

"Nobody said anything about Robineau. I'm talking about the water. And the land. Pollution."

Varik laughed, and it wasn't a pleasant sound. "Do you expect me to take you seriously? You, of all people, have little love for this town or the people in it, or even the environment. You've said so yourself."

This, Williams knew, was true enough. But something about Varik rubbed him the wrong way. "I may not be crazy about Chesborough, but I *am* a police officer and I'm warning you, Varik, I won't knowingly break the law for you or for anybody else."

"You already have, Sergeant Williams. Your superiors would not look favorably on your second job. Still, to set your mind at ease, let me assure you Nirvana is not responsible for environmental problems. This corporation is constructively dealing with a deteriorating global situation. I doubt you could initiate interest in an investigation on the basis that we're polluters; our record on environmental issues speaks for itself. But I do recommend you remember two things. First, investigations of any nature that focus on this corporation will surely focus on you as well. The other thing you should consider is that I am a busy man. I suffer fools not at all. When my time is wasted, I become annoyed. And when I have been annoyed, I am, I fear, very unpleasant to be around."

"Sounds like a threat."

"I'm merely expressing a weakness of character. A dangerous weakness I believe you should be aware of by now."

# Eighteen

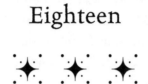

*Come. Farther.* He hears the words clearly and yet they are not like spoken words, more wind against sails.

The place is dimly-lit. Moist. Close. His body feels sticky.

Holding his hand, THE MOTHER leads him. They float downhill. Continually downhill. Her skin. Not soft, not rough. Neither warm nor cold. Eternal.

The scents. Of darkness. Of earth. Of flowers. Cloying.

Fear. Deep and twisting. Bottomless. Primal.

Run!

*You are not afraid!*

Gold walls flecked with glittering silver.

A flutter from the Otherworld.

Chatter. Laughter.

Eating. They tear into their food. Ravenous but unable to be filled. He understands.

*Serve the Greater Good,* she tells him, and he looks deep into her eyes. Opals. Eternal.

Varik jolted awake. The dream clung to him along with the clammy sweat adhering to his body. This wasn't the first time he'd had the nightmare. But he'd never been this far before, this deep.

He checked the clock. Glowing numbers read 6:00 a.m. He sat up and rubbed his eyes, then reached out a trembling hand to the glass of water. He felt uncomfortable, grimy, and wanted a shower. The phone rang.

He picked up the receiver. No one on the other end, yet the summons seemed clear.

Varik got up, went to his desk and unlocked the top drawer. He removed a packaged sterilized needle, a syringe, a short length of rubber and three of the glass vials. After he tied his arm, he fitted the needle and syringe together and pierced the vein on the inside of his right elbow; the vein in his left arm had collapsed. He plugged a vial into the syringe and, when it filled, another, until all three had darkened with his blood. Then he dressed quickly and picked up his sunglasses on the way out the door.

He walked one block, crossed a playground, and went down another two empty streets past the building marked CLINIC. Through the glass of the dome he could see that the night was not quite ready to capitulate to the sun. His mind crackled, alive with thoughts unconnected to emotion.

Perhaps he should inform Brenda. She would be on her own soon. He must make sure Sullivan went to visit Mrs. Robineau again.

Eventually Varik reached the restaurant. He crossed the drawbridge and entered the building, aware of feeling like a kernel of excitement about to pop. A second meeting. So soon! He felt honored, yet understood that this was as it should be. He was crucial to their success. He knew that. More importantly, THEY understood it.

Auxiliary lighting from the floorboards lit the hallway, dim but easy enough to see by. As he strode across the main room, heels slapping marble, all remnants of the dream with its terrifying images evaporated.

Varik unlocked the door to the smaller room and stepped inside. The fireplace blazed with fragrant red cedar logs, the only light. The three chairs facing him were occupied by pale figures, their features hidden in shadow. They sat, backs straight, heads poised, calm, immobile.

He stood before them feeling what he always felt. Awe. Respect. Titillation. And something else, a feeling hidden inside that refused to surface.

As a gesture of vulnerability, he removed his sunglasses and looked at them, one at a time. After a moment he took the vials of blood from his pocket and lay one before each like an offering. Time seemed frozen as he waited. The male in the center gestured, an acceptance.

This was Varik's second cue. Now he was permitted to communicate verbally. "I spoke with Mrs. Mowatt this evening before your arrival. I believe she's on the verge of selling."

The three did not react nor did they even give an indication of having heard what he said. None of the vials were touched.

"I expect her attorney will fax a letter today or tomorrow recommending the purchase. I've also prepared an Agreement of Purchase and Sale for the Robineau property. I'll have Sullivan take it over to Mrs. Robineau this morning. With our deepest condolences." He waited.

Varik was aware of the temperature. Cooler than usual. Vaguely he wondered if the air conditioning was malfunctioning. He'd have to speak to the custodian. The air plus the scent of flowers reminded him of something, something unpleasant. Whatever it was, he didn't want to think about it. Especially now. But he felt drawn towards identification, hovering on the edge of awareness—

Suddenly the one in the middle chose to honor him with

a communication. The voice, low, deep yet hollow, as though coming through an underground pipe. Its echoes filled the air with a ring that was neither pleasant nor annoying. More, Varik felt lulled by the sound. As always, he couldn't see lips moving.

*It suits us to migrate north, then return south. We acclimatize easily.*

Varik nodded. He let himself feel proud. When he'd first come across them he'd had the brilliant idea for a chain of Eternal Cities around the world. It took a great deal of convincing and, he had to admit, there were times he'd been afraid of them. Deathly afraid. But once he understood what they were, what they needed, what they could do for him, and they began to understand him . . . They shared a problem. Survival. And they recognized him as one of their own.

Finally he'd swayed them to his vision. Now, nearly a decade later, his dream of the cleanest environment money could buy had been eighty percent realized. But this was only one of his dreams. The best, still to come.

*The woman pleases you, as a mate.* The female. Her voice so similar to the male's but with a slight lilt. He looked at her and felt an attraction bordering on obsession. She turned her head slightly and firelight danced off her profile. He caught a tantalizing glint from her right eye. Although he could not clearly see her features in the poor lighting, in his mind he stored a detailed portrait that encapsulated her beauty. And yet, oddly, he also knew that the moment this conference concluded and he left the room, he would forget the details and be left with only an impression.

Varik said nothing. No need to speak. He accepted the fact that they could read his mind and he felt the power of that skill and the desire to possess it himself. He also knew he could read their minds, at least he was beginning to.

Without words, the female assured him that Claire would mate with him for life. Forever. Eternity.

He longed to be one with them, to sit on the triumvirate. To share the power, to control the future, to act beyond the scope of what ordinary human beings are capable of.

"When?" he asked, or thought he had.

*Soon,* she whispered.

He felt an urgency to share more, to open, to be blessed by them. Also, he did not want this time in their presence to end. "Sergeant Williams."

They remained silent and still, porcelain figurines.

"He has suspicions. About the City. About me."

A sharp sound came from the younger male and Varik turned towards him. This one leaned forward, wings quivering. His nose twitched, as if he was smelling the contents of the vial. Although his movements, too, were efficient and minimal, he possessed energy more erratic than the others.

*His service to the greater good has ended,* the voice said. Varik wondered where he'd heard those words and that sound before.

They gave him no instructions on dealing with Williams. Still, that was his job. He must decide. He would know their wishes.

A curt gesture told him he'd been dismissed.

As Varik recrossed the drawbridge and headed along the flagstone path, he became aware of his surroundings, as if awakening from a dream. This time the dream had been pleasant, filled with goals being actualized, longings he knew would be sated.

Through the dome he saw the rim of the sun break the horizon. He slipped his sunglasses on with a smile.

Claire would come to love him. Like everything else, that felt inevitable.

# Nineteen

Tuesday morning Gord, Claire and Bailie gathered at the Robineaus'. Colette's son and daughter had come in Saturday evening. Arrangements had already been made to ship Gilles' body to Québec City for burial. Colette would leave with her children this afternoon. "Forever," she said, then nervously dropped the rest of the bombshell: yesterday, she had sold her property to Nirvana.

Things are moving too fast, Gord thought. The weekend was a blur. He felt numb with grief. Hardly any sleep.

What a tragedy, for Colette. For all of them. And for him, not just the loss of a friend, but also the loss of an ally. And more. Gilles had been a father to him. Gord felt a guilt he recognized as unrealistic, the same guilt he felt about his own father's death: he should have been there.

Colette, her old face laced with pain, wearing a black dress with a white lace collar, sat at the table. In front of her lay her copy of the Agreement of Sale, signed and witnessed, and a check. Behind her stood Marielle and Guy, her children, both about Gord's age.

"If there's anything we can do, Colette, just let us know," Bailie said. Arms folded, he leaned back against the fridge door looking sad and worried.

Claire, also at the table, reached out a hand and

squeezed the old lady's. "Yes. Anything."

"*Je suis désolé,*" Colette cried. "I wish to fight no more. I feel I am letting you all down, you who are my friends. Gilles would not wish me to leave here, but I cannot stay."

Her daughter's arms went around her.

"We understand," Bailie said. "If I were in your boots, I'd do the same."

Gord scrubbed his face with his hands, unable to speak.

Colette said, "This place, I hate it now! The land was good but has become evil. I feel this for some time. The land, she does not support life." Something steely inside the normally shy old woman emerged. She lifted fierce eyes towards an obviously startled Claire. "*Quittez!* You must return to your home while you still may."

"We're leaving next week," Claire said.

Colette's hand crushed the Agreement to Purchase. "Sell them your land!" She looked from Claire to Bailie, and finally to Gord. Her eyes, red and glazed from crying, held a fury that startled him. She reached out a hand and he took it. "Gilles, he loved you like his son Guy. Sell. I beg of you." She broke into sobs.

Bailie left for his place, and Gord and Claire walked to hers. Two hours ago, on the way over, the morning air had been pleasantly cool but now, in the heat of noon, the sun scorched them with a ferocious intensity. The lake stank today, an omen, Gord thought.

"Claire, at the dock the other night, how did you know something happened to Gilles?"

She hesitated. "I can't tell you how. I just *know* things. Sometimes words come to me, other times images. Sometimes dreams. I've always been this way. I told you I knew something had happened to Bill. Well, I knew that about Lillian too. Since I've been back here the feelings are

162

stronger and that night I had a sense Gilles was in trouble. It's as though his spirit contacted mine and told me. I know this sounds strange."

"If I hadn't heard Lillian talk this way, it would."

She sighed. "I've learned to trust the voices and images, but I'm still uneasy with them. That's all I can say."

By the bank he noticed another squirrel, collapsed in on itself in death. "Are you going to sell?"

"What am I going to do with the land? Nobody else wants to buy it."

"But, after all that's happened . . ."

"*Especially* after what's happened!" Claire stopped and stared at him, anger flaming a face already pink from the heavy humidity and old griefs stirred up by this new one.

"Do I have to spell it out? They killed him for his land."

She looked at him like he was crazy and, at that moment, he couldn't blame her. "Gord, he died from a heart attack. The doctor said so, Sergeant Williams said so—"

" 'Sergeant Williams said so.' " Gord mimicked her bitterly, sounding like an adolescent, feeling like a desperate child.

"Listen to me, Gord! You're talking about murder, and that's a serious accusation. There's no evidence. None."

"What about what Colette saw?"

"What did she see? The birds Gilles was photographing? Flying shadows? There were no marks on Gilles besides the ones caused by branches and thorns. And we were all at the party, including Varik, Brenda, all of them. Or do you think they hired a hit man and dressed him up in a chicken costume to scare Gilles to death?"

She started walking again, her sandals angrily crushing gravel underfoot. "Gord, I can't buy this. You're paranoid."

They walked in silence for a while. Gord *felt* paranoid. He had to agree there was no real evidence that Gilles had been murdered. All he had to go on were suspicions, hunches. And he questioned his own motives. He and Bailie were the only holdouts now, not counting the Gwinskis, and he had no idea what they would or wouldn't do. Part of his reluctance to leave had been a commitment to the community. But, the community was deserting him, so why stay?

And what about Claire? He felt her slipping through his fingers while he stood by and let it happen. Maybe he was that obsessed prospector panning for gold so long that when he finally hits it he dumps the dust back into the river with the silt because he can't tell the difference any more. Was he so afraid of getting hurt he'd blow any chance of happiness?

He looked at Claire. Christ, he liked her. More than liked her. He saw potential there. He wondered if she cared about him as anything more than a friend. God, he had to make a move. Now. Before it was too late.

"I'm afraid," he confessed.

She stopped walking. "Of what?" Her voice softened.

"Being the only one left. Being alone. Being dead."

After a moment she said, "Well, I doubt Bailie will sell. And there are still people in Chesborough."

How could he tell her? There was so much more and he wasn't sure what to say. "Claire, look, I know you think I'm off the deep end. But look at me. Seriously. Look at me."

Her eyes stared into his face. He saw the suspicion in her gaze, but he didn't flinch. "All I'm going on is a feeling about Gilles' death. And the other deaths that have occurred. And the missing people. When Williams investigated the other night, I was with him. He won't admit it but

164

he's suspicious of foul play. I don't know if he'll take any action—he hasn't so far—but I saw him gather soil, water and blood samples."

"Sounds like standard police procedure to me."

"I saw him reading Gilles' journal. He took that and the film. I think Gilles stumbled on something. Maybe he photographed something or someone, and it was more than he bargained for, I don't know, but there's something strange going on here. I'm sure of it."

He stopped and took her by the shoulders. He wanted to tell her he needed her. But looking in her sky blue eyes unnerved him and he wasn't sure he wouldn't make a mess of things again. Instead he said, "The other thing was Gilles' face. My father died of a heart attack. I've known other people who have died that way, and yes, they all looked different, but the look on Gilles' face wasn't one of pain, or even fear. It was horror. He saw something that horrified him."

Claire's face reflected both pity and frustration. He dropped his hands and immediately she touched his shoulder. "Gord, I know what he meant to you. And what Lillian meant. Death is always hard. I told you before, I'm no stranger to it myself. It's easy to twist and turn things to try to make sense out of what's impossible to comprehend. We're here one minute and gone the next. Who can understand that? It takes time to assimilate all the feelings."

They were almost at her door. Soon it would be too late. Now was the time to say or do something. Let her know he cared about her. But the jumble of thoughts and emotions about Gilles, about his father's death, about holding out, about the possibility of murder involving the Eternal City, all of it demanded attention at once.

And intermingled were feelings for Claire. Feelings he had yet to express.

He had just screwed up his courage when, up ahead, through the forest of bush that separated the Robineau property from Claire's, he saw the limousine parked on her lawn. One feeling surfaced and wiped out all the rest—fury.

A small voice in the back of his mind assured him that he had let both of them down.

# Twenty

Earl watched through the trailer's grimy window as Sergeant Williams stepped out of the patrol car. His father stepped out of the other trailer, walked across the yard, kept walking, ignoring the policeman, who followed until they were both inside the work trailer with Earl and his mother.

Williams, standing in the doorway, looked up. A stuffed hawk, wings spread, talons extended, sharp beak gaping hung above his head. Earl had put in the beady glass eyes himself. Hooded eyes that preyed on what was younger, smaller, weaker. The hawk reminded Earl of Williams. He saw the cop's hand twitch.

"Earl, I need to ask you a couple of questions," Williams said.

Earl looked at his father. "Answer him, boy." The words barely hid the fury, but the eyes could not. Earl had been bad again. Real bad. He'd brought the cop here. Onto his father's land. And inside the work trailer. The big muscle in his left ass cheek spasmed; he could already feel the sting of the straps.

"You know Gilles Robineau. Around Lake Road."

"Yes, sir."

"You know he died the other night?"

"Yes, sir."

"Where were you Friday night?"

"Workin' at the gas station."

Williams's eyes narrowed. The fleshy lids sure did remind Earl of the hawk.

"The station closes at nine. Mr. Robineau died past midnight. Where'd you go when you left work?"

"Here."

"Is that right?" the policeman's voice threatened. Earl had heard that voice before, a couple of times. Both times that voice had been followed by a fist or two to his stomach.

"Yes, sir, it is."

Williams glanced at Earl's father to confirm or deny it, but his father had picked up a skinning knife and was already slitting the underbelly of a porcupine. Williams looked away, disgusted. "What time did you get home?"

"I came straight from work."

"That right Mr. Gwinski?"

Earl's father grunted.

"How's that?"

Earl's mother, staring out the window, fists balled, said, "The boy was home."

"Earl, you see anything that night?"

"No, sir."

"Look, we both know your history of skulking around the woods half naked, peeping through windows. I think you were out that night and I want to know what you saw."

"Didn't see nothing." But Earl had seen plenty. He'd seen THE FATHER with the Frenchman. Like he'd seen HIM with the old witch. And the Donaldson brat. And all the others. And he left Earl down on this painful earth again, where he could never be good. Never get it right. Where his bad thing always got him in trouble with the law.

With his mother and father. Where his bad thing brought him pain.

Earl's father began slicing the skin off the dead porcupine, using the little curved knife to cut it away from the muscle as one unit. Williams shook his head.

"Earl, you remember seeing something, let me know, you hear?"

"I'll do that, sir."

"You do that."

He watched the policeman drive away in his cruiser.

"Get ready," his father said, rolling up his sleeves, voice controlled, eyes blazing the way Earl's ass and the back of his thighs would soon be.

His mother unhooked the two flesh-colored straps from the wall.

As he leaned over the oil drum, Earl thought about what else he'd seen Friday night. It was different than with the old witch and the baby and the others. THE FATHER had left the Frenchman there. HE'd left the body. That was a good sign. THE FATHER was tiring of the others. They would die but not ascend. Soon THE FATHER and THE MOTHER would come for Earl and take him away from this pain.

The hard leather straps quickly found a rhythm and Earl's bottom jumped in time. He hadn't cried from a tanning in years, but today his eyes misted over. Through the haze of agony he watched like a movie in his mind THE FATHER and THE MOTHER leave the Frenchman's place and head to the back of the dome. And disappear. It was the first time he clearly saw where THEY went. Not to the sky, like he thought, but into the earth. That was another sign. They were close. The end was coming.

And he knew THEY'd come again soon and that he had

a lot of work to do first. THEY had shown him the way to redemption. He could help THEM. The dead would litter the earth and the chosen, like Earl, would be left. To be carried away in the arms of THE FATHER and THE MOTHER. At last. Forever. This purification was his final rite of passage. He could feel it in every crack of the searing straps. His earthly parents were whipping the last remnants of sin out of him. Pain sizzled through him, shooting the badness out through his pores. He closed his eyes and saw the white light expanding. Cleaning his insides. He was becoming clear. Empty. Like the animals, skin and nothing else. He felt ready for THEIR coming. Ready to help them in their work.

# Twenty-One

"This is not humanly possible," Jerry said.

David agreed. He picked up the box lid and compared the faded photograph with the half-finished jigsaw puzzle in front of them. The Puzz 3-D was of Habitat, a housing complex built for Expo '67, the World Fair held in Montréal.

"Bunch of boxes with windows," Jerry said.

"It's like somebody just threw 'em on top of each other." David tried to fit a piece in but the bubble was too big for the hole. "Damn!" He tossed it back into the pile.

"Got a pair of scissors?" Jerry suggested. "We'll *make* it fit."

"It's too boring. Want another Coke?"

"Yeah."

When David came back, Jerry was holding the photograph of Lillian on the mantle. David handed over the can and sat on the couch, stretching his legs out onto the coffee table. He took a noisy slurp from his drink. "What was she like?"

"Who? Lillian? Okay, I guess. She knew all this stuff about the woods, like things you can eat and what makes you better when you're sick and stuff like that. And she used to tell these great Indian stories, like how come skunks have white stripes on them. She liked to paint."

"We found some weird pictures she painted," David said. "Come on." He plunked his can on the table and climbed the ladder, Jerry right behind him. Upstairs he produced the ugly paintings.

Jerry whistled. "Nightmare! She didn't used to paint like this."

"That's not all." David went to a trap door in one wall, a storage space, and opened it. "I found this in here. Mom hasn't seen it yet."

He held the small canvas out. Jerry said, "That's Witch Rock. On the island. Where the cave is."

It was the same location as the photograph downstairs, but what a difference! In the painting, the dome took up most of the space. Behind it, the sun, the color of blood, had half set. A woman with white hair like Lillian's stood in front of the rock, and another woman that looked like David's mom stood beside her. The weirdest thing was a cloud mass that seemed to be coming out of the dome and not the sky. When you stood back it looked like the clouds had teeth.

"Creepy!" Jerry said, and then must have remembered this might offend David. "Sorry about that."

"It's okay. I feel the same way." He returned the canvas to the storage area and closed the door.

As soon as they were downstairs, David blurted, "Look, I'm gonna sneak into the City. Soon. You in, or what?"

"Sure I'm in."

"My mom'll be mad as hell if she finds out. Think Gord'll be mad?"

"I *know* he will. I'll be grounded for a week."

David sat down and picked up his Coke. "Nothing can happen to us in there, right? I mean, if we're caught, the security guards'll be pissed, but they wouldn't do anything to us. We're kids. Besides, I gotta go home in a week."

"Me too," Jerry said. "Okay. But let's get up early and go. We can be back for breakfast and our parents won't even know we went."

"Good idea!"

"We'll go in through the cave, okay? It's gotta lead to the city."

"Yeah."

"When should we do it?"

"How about Thursday?"

"Why Thursday?" Jerry said.

"I don't know. You wanna do it Wednesday. Wait! I know, let's do it Friday, 'cause I'm leaving Saturday and you're going back home Sunday so if our parents catch us they can't punish us too long."

"Yeah! Besides," Jerry said, "we gotta get our gear together. Agreed?"

"Agreed."

They gave each other a complicated five.

A knock on the door made both of them jump. They looked at each other and laughed nervously.

Mr. Varik from the Eternal City stood on the other side of the screen. David wondered if he'd overheard them. "Good afternoon, David. Is your mother at home?" he asked.

"Uh, no," David said through the screen. Man, this guy looked worse in the daylight. What was behind those glasses?

"When do you expect her?"

"Don't know."

Varik didn't look happy but he forced a smile. He reached into his suit jacket's inner pocket and took out an

173

envelope. "Please give this letter to her."

David looked beyond Varik. "Uh, here she is." His mother and Gord were coming up the road.

"Claire," Varik said, turning and reaching out a hand as she approached. "I'm so glad I caught you. I've brought a fax from your attorney. Come over for lunch and we can discuss it."

His mom looked at Gord, then at him and finally down at her shorts. "I'll have to change—"

"Nonsense. You look lovely. Come as you are."

"Well, David needs food—"

"You're both invited, of course," Varik said, but David got the feeling the guy hoped he'd just disappear.

"Let's go, Mom." He turned to Jerry and grinned, letting him know he'd check the place out.

# Twenty-Two

"The meal was wonderful, as always!" Claire lay her napkin on the table. "Just fabulous!"

"More wine?"

"Please." She held her glass out and Varik poured in more Cabernet Sauvignon from France.

The wine, the ambience, the company—everything was getting to her. Being waited on hand and foot. The finest food and drink. Incredible artwork all around them. The Castle definitely was a world class restaurant, and Varik a charming, urbane man.

"Okay, honey?" she asked her son.

"Sure." He sounded bored. Claire felt an impulse to reach over and throttle her child. He had not ordered the Rock Cornish Hen. He had not wanted the Duck a l'Orange. No, he wanted a hot dog.

"Perhaps you'd care for a dessert," Varik asked the boy, and raised his hand. As if summoned by a magic wand, a waiter appeared. "A dessert menu for my young friend."

David scanned a list of fifteen sweets and finally settled on a chocolate parfait when Claire explained it was a fancy sundae with liqueur.

"Claire," Varik said, "I wanted to tell you a bit about the Eternal City. I realize Mr. Roberts has a negative opinion—"

175

"Well, he does, but—"

"It's all right. I realize you're perfectly capable of coming to your own conclusions. Still, we're all influenced by those around us and I feel obliged to make certain you have the facts."

Facts. Why were these two men, Varik and Gord, as different as night and day, always trying to seduce her with facts. She wondered why neither seemed interested in other types of seduction.

A smile crept onto her face which Varik noticed. He raised an eyebrow—she could see it over the sunglasses. "I'm feeling good," she said, trying to get a grip.

"You know, Claire, years ago, when I was a young man, I had a dream that one day I would be wealthy and powerful. By the time I turned twenty-five I'd made my first million dollars. And at thirty-five I owned substantial shares in three of the largest corporations in the world. I acquired money, which is power. The world was at my disposal. But I wanted more. Can you understand that?"

What more could he want? she wondered, but nodded.

"More than a dozen years ago, when I first realized where the earth was headed environmentally, I decided to do something about the problem."

"So you built the Eternal City." She took a sip of wine. He was looking better and better.

"Cities. This is the third. There are more on the way. I have the answer, Claire. I've been able to do what no government has the political will to do, what no corporation, up until now, could accomplish. Singlehandedly, I've created a safe environment that is also economically viable."

The man's childlike enthusiasm was contagious. Claire found him delightful.

"Mom! Can I go for a walk?"

Claire looked at David and then back at Varik, who smiled benignly and gestured towards the door. "Okay, honey, but don't go far. It's getting late. It's . . ." She checked her watch, astonished that four hours had passed. "It's late."

After David left, Varik moved his chair around the table to sit next to her. Up close his face had the seamless look of youth, yet the skin lacked elasticity. His floral-scented after-shave got stiff competition from the abundance of fresh cut flowers throughout the room. He slid an arm over the top of her chair and leaned in. *My God!* she thought, *he's coming on to me!*

The idea of a man this close, this intent on her, had Claire almost gasping for air. It had been so long. Physical feelings hit her out of the blue. Heat rushed up her stomach and chest.

"The Cities," he continued, edging closer, "are more than you can imagine. No one unclean is permitted to move in."

"Unclean?" The word cooled her.

"I meant . . . in the sense of illness. Potential residents are screened physically and emotionally, and residents are monitored on a regular basis."

"Monitored? In what way?"

"Blood and other samples are taken and tests done routinely as the resident comes into the City. That way, we stop the spread of infectious diseases. If anyone shows signs of illness, we deal with it right away—for example, the blood pressure of one resident last week tested exceptionally high and he was admitted to the Clinic. It was for his own protection, and for the greater good."

Claire looked around but David was nowhere to be seen. Suddenly Varik took her hand and the contact startled her.

177

"Why do you wear sunglasses?" she blurted.

"Don't be frightened," he said. Still holding her hand, he took off the dark glasses.

Claire stared into light blue eyes, bright, the whites a little bloodshot, the irises flecked with yellow and black dots. Nothing exceptional. And yet something within her stirred, like a memory of a dream. Or something important but long forgotten.

"You're a brave woman," he said.

She had no idea what he meant.

He moved closer, insistent, and Claire felt herself succumbing but whether to his pressure or her own starvation she wasn't sure. He cupped her chin in his hand. His lips, when they touched hers, felt cool and firm. Intense. Her heart pounded. Behind her sexual tension she sensed a fear flickering that went beyond the temerity of a first contact after two years of celibacy.

She pushed him back gently and struggled to sound casual. "Why did you build this City? Way up here?"

He put the glasses back on but still held her hand. His tone became distant. "Because," he said lightly, "I intend to live forever. And what better place in which to attain that goal than the Eternal Cities around the world?"

She laughed. "I don't think genetics is quite there, unless you're talking cloning."

"Not cloning," he said, a little too seriously.

She decided a change of subject couldn't hurt. "Where are you from? Originally?"

"New York."

"I thought I recognized the accent. Do you still have family there?"

He leaned back slightly and she felt she had touched a nerve. "I was raised in an orphanage until I was seventeen, when I was adopted by an eccentric matron from Long Island. Her money was old and somewhat dirty, wealth amassed during Prohibition. As a child I knew both poverty and wealth. She was a strict woman, many said cold. Still, thanks to her, I received a fine education."

"Is she still alive?"

"She died when I was twenty."

"I guess the inheritance helped you get started in business."

"On the contrary. She left me her house. She had no living relatives, but the bulk of the estate went to charity."

"You must have been terribly hurt."

"Not at all. It was her prerogative to bequeath the money as she saw fit. Naturally I sued the estate. As a legally adopted child, that was *my* prerogative. I won roughly a third when the case finally settled out of court. But by then I was a millionaire in my own right."

He presented the facts in such an emotionless way that Claire suspected it was a perfectly memorized script he recited from time to time when needed. "Were you ever married?"

"No."

"Relationships?"

"There have been liaisons. My work has absorbed all my time. But now . . ."

He started to lean forward again when a voice on her left said, "Can we go now?"

"Certainly, David. Mr. Varik and I were just discussing the sale."

Varik had already moved back and Claire straightened her dress. "We'll just be a minute, honey."

"But I want to go now!"

"David, I said in a minute!" God, here she was feeling

guilty that her son had caught her in an intimate exchange with a man. "I'm sorry, David. Please sit down. I'll be finished very soon."

To distract herself, she said to Varik, "Since Mr. Bennett thinks the sale sounds good, I suppose there's no reason not to go through with it. Do you want me to sign the Offer now?"

"Legally you must sign an Option to Purchase first," and he pulled the legal sheets from his inside coat pocket. The fact that this lunch suddenly seemed a calculated move to get her to sign put her off. "I'll have the final papers ready for your signature and bring them to you this weekend."

"We're leaving Saturday morning. Why don't I come over Friday and sign?" She scrawled her name across the bottom of the original and three copies.

"Don't trouble yourself, Claire. It would be our pleasure to—"

"Besides," she said, standing abruptly, annoyed at the word "our" and its corporate implication, "I've been in the City three times now and I haven't seen the inside of an apartment. I want the intimate tour." Immediately she regretted the word "intimate."

"But not today," she added quickly. "So, it's a deal?"

"Very much a deal." He pocketed the papers and, instead of just shaking her hand, he kissed it.

"Well," she said, embarrassed, annoyed, feeling rejected in some odd way, "we'd better go." David leapt to his feet and was already halfway to the door.

Varik drove the cart through the city and out to the dock, chatting amiably, giving her more of "the tour." The boat was just coming into port and while they waited he kept his hand firmly locked near her elbow. Claire was beginning to feel uncomfortably possessed, the target of a man accustomed to getting everything he wanted and one who didn't seem to mind raising her personal expectations in the process of using her to conclude a business transaction.

"It'll be fun coming up for two weeks next year," she said. "You'll love the tennis, won't you, David?"

He shrugged and she felt furious, and abandoned. Why is he acting like such a baby? I have a right to a life, don't I? Is it too much to ask, a man paying attention to me? But she knew in her heart that wasn't it. David's hostility reflected some of her own feelings. Varik both attracted and repelled her. And through it all she could feel her own need and loneliness bubbling like a volcano about to erupt. Damn you, Gord, she thought, then wondered where *that* thought came from.

David ran up the ramp and onto the cruiser. Before she could follow, Varik pulled her back and into his arms. He was far stronger than he looked. He held her tightly, her hips pressed against his.

"Please," she said, off guard. "My son."

"You're more than a mother, Claire. Do you understand what I'm saying?"

She nodded. Instinctively she moved to peck him on the cheek, just to get it over with, but he turned so that their lips met. Firm flesh, pressing against hers, insistent. His tongue slid into her mouth and she became weak in the knees, afraid she would fall. Or rip off her clothes right there!

"Mom, come on! You're holding up the boat."

Before he released her, Varik whispered something about altering the two weeks to indefinitely, but she wasn't really listening to his words. Her body shook from terror and need, and when he let her go she stumbled.

She boarded as if in a trance, suddenly aware of the

warmth of the day, the rhythmic splash of water against the bow, birds calling to one another . . .

David avoided her on the boat. And would not talk with her in the limo. Once they were inside Lillian's cottage, Claire, ready to scream, said in a controlled voice, "Okay, what's up?"

"As if you don't know."

"Out with it!" She ruffled his hair but he pulled away angrily. "You don't like Mr. Varik, do you?"

"Do you?"

"I asked you first."

David got up from the couch and stomped into the kitchen. She followed and found him looking out the back door.

"David, *what* is going on?"

Suddenly he turned on her.

"He's a dweeb, Mom. A slimeball. Scum. He, like, died last year or something. How come you kissed him?"

"I'm sorry you saw that, David."

"Is that all? You're sorry I saw it? Aren't you sorry you did it?"

"Frankly, I'm not. David, you're old enough to understand. I'm lonely sometimes. That doesn't mean I don't love you and enjoy being with you. But I need to be with people my own age. With men my own age."

"Well, what about Gord? He's your age and he's a lot nicer than that guy, Varik."

Claire rubbed the back of her neck and sighed. "Gord isn't interested in me in that way. We're friends, that's all."

"Maybe you didn't give him a chance."

"I did." Oh, God, she thought, true confessions with your son. He's my child, not my confidant. "Look, honey, it's like this. We're going back home on Saturday; we'll come up here for two weeks a year, and that's that. But in the meantime, if kissing Varik makes your old mother feel young and attractive, well, lighten up. Nobody's being hurt. Not you, not me. And not your father. Nothing's changed. *Capisce?*"

He stared at her with distrusting eyes, a look that unnerved her. "Well, it's hot and I'm going to get a cold drink and sit in the shade. Want to join me, sweetie?"

"No!" he said coldly, bitterly, spitefully, and pushed his way out the screen door, making sure to slam it behind him.

Claire collapsed onto a kitchen chair. She hadn't dealt with that very well. With his feelings. Or even with her own. She sighed, thinking, I'm only human, wondering if David could accept that before the age of thirty.

# Twenty-Three

*July 4th: One other note. Gord Roberts was recently at the Eternal City. He confirms—there are no animals, domestic or wild, on Skeleton Lake Island. The dome, of course, would keep out birds. But one wonders how they rid the land of chipmunks, squirrels, skunks. More to the point, why would they wish to? Roberts, who considers Nirvana the root of all evil, insists there is a connection between Eternal City and all this devastation. I see strong evidence to support his claim. After all, the soil and water began deteriorating as construction started . . .*

Williams deciphering Robineau's journal, written in French. This was his third read of the journal, and he felt more uneasy each time. He took a Ramon Allones out of the small pine box on his desk and leaned back in his chair. He removed the cellophane, and clipped the tip, but did not light the cigar.

Atkins had driven over to Emerson's for a newspaper. The station was quiet. No need to hurry. Plenty of time to think. Too much time.

The record of fish and wildlife changes around the lake disturbed him. The daily tally of dead muskie, pickerel and bass washed to shore, when added up, became staggering. Robineau's well-kept notes documented what he had witnessed, particularly over the last few months: dead fingerlings, which meant recent spawns were being depleted. Ulcerated sores. Cancerous lesions. Stunted growth in the larger fish.

If Robineau's observations were accurate, and Williams had no reason to doubt it, Skeleton Lake had been deteriorating fast over the last two years. The color of money is blinding, he thought, but he knew it was more his desperation to get the hell out of Chesborough while he could still walk. Looking the situation squarely in the eye, Williams realized he might have been responsible for some of what was going on. Or, if not actively contributing to the problem, at the very least he'd sat back on his butt and done nothing to help.

He opened a small box of wood matches, struck one, and puffed on the cigar until the rolled tobacco caught. Normally the taste and the aroma gave him a lot more pleasure than they were providing today.

The locals had started coming to him in the spring, when the signs went up along the lakefront. Lillian Palmer. Robineau. A couple of the townspeople. Roberts, of course. They'd seen the dead fish, the dead animals, they'd smelled the water. They asked him and the Town Council to do something. But the council put it onto the provincial and federal governments to deal with it, suggesting only that residents get their drinking water from the natural spring outside town—most people did that anyway—and buy the chlorine filters the feds suggested. Now that he thought about it, by July nearly all of those same council members had sold their land. Damned convenient!

He'd lumped the complainers together—left-wing whiners like Roberts, angry at Nirvana for its success. Not only had he failed to see a connection to Eternal City, but he sure as hell hadn't wanted to line up with people who were, in his mind, losers. He still didn't see how Nirvana had been polluting, but at least he now accepted the fact that something was wrong and it started when they arrived.

Williams pulled the water and soil samples he'd gathered near Robineau's cottage out of his top drawer; the blood samples had already been analyzed by the coroner's office. It was Robineau's blood and no sign of anybody else's.

Robineau had been sending water and soil to the government since spring. Nothing. He'd been able to confirm the pH balance, though; the same as it had been for years.

He leaned back, puffing on the stogie. Williams had to face it; he was guilty of boot-dragging. But that was then, this was now. He intended to take action and he didn't give a good God damn what Varik or anybody else thought.

He lay the two vials on top of the desk, between Gilles' death certificate and his Journal. The coroner had certified the cause of death as myocardial infarction—his first guess—with the added information that Robineau's body was half rotted with metastasized cancer. If the old guy hadn't had a heart attack he no doubt would have been dead soon anyway. No external abrasions or contusions that couldn't be explained. No internal injuries. Estimated time of death checked out. The report should have been conclusive. The case file should be placed in the filing cabinet.

Williams took the envelope of photographs from his shirt pocket. Only one frame on the black and white negative developed. Grainy, out of focus, an odd angle. He could just make out something in the upper right corner, kind of like a hummingbird's wing, flapping so fast it became a blur. But white. An inverted negative. Didn't make sense, and the picture was too distorted to tell what the hell it really was. If he didn't know better he'd have guessed that was a human hand at the end of the blur.

Roberts said Robineau was photographing birds, that's why the scope, light enhancer, camera, the whole setup. Okay. What happened was obvious: Robineau'd tried to get the shot, had a heart attack, stumbled down the slope towards his back door, and died en route.

Yeah, obvious. And if there hadn't been so many obvious deaths in the last couple of years, Williams might have bought the package.

From the file cabinet behind him he pulled a thick brown padded government envelope, preaddressed to the Ministry of the Environment in Ottawa. He was just about to stuff the water and soil samples into it when the door opened. He'd been so preoccupied he hadn't heard the car drive up.

"Hi, babe," he said, standing immediately.

Brenda closed the door and let herself through the gate into the office. She wore white high heels and a red sundress with a halter top that showed the shape and fullness of her breasts through the fabric. As she moved towards him, he watched the sway of her hips.

Her warm wide smile didn't stop until she reached him, and their lips collided. He wrapped his arms around her bottom and lifted her into the air, kissing those breasts right through the dress, taking a fabric-covered nipple between his teeth.

"Whoa, tiger! Dinner first, dessert later."

"Just an appetizer," he said, letting her slide down in his arms so he could kiss her tasty lips again. Her skirt rode up in back and he reached under it. She wasn't wearing panties. He felt himself grow hard. He loved the way Brenda made him lose control. He hated it.

"Come on," she said, nipping at his ear lobe.

"Okay. Just let me clean this up." He started to slide the samples in the envelope.

"What's this stuff?"

"Death certificate. Other stuff. Gilles Robineau."

Brenda picked up the photograph, looked at it, then reached for the Journal and started to flip through the pages. He took the book and the picture from her hands. "Evidence," he said. "Wouldn't want your pretty fingerprints on it."

"If he had a heart attack, why do you need evidence?"

"Just some oddities. A case isn't closed til it's closed."

"What's in the envelope?" she asked, reaching for it.

He blocked her arm and she moved closer to him, letting her breasts rub up against his chest. "Tell me," she said in a little girl voice. Her big girl eyes laughed at the game they played.

"Just water and dirt samples, missy," Williams said, a little uncomfortable with the game but going along anyway.

"More evidence?" She kissed his neck and ran her tongue through the crevices of his ear.

"Un huh," he said reluctantly.

Now she had his lower lip between her teeth, pulling gently, grinding her pelvis into his.

"What are you gonna do with them?"

"C'mon Brenda," he said, holding her at arm's length.

She moved back, looking a little pissed. Both of them were silent while he cleared his desk and locked the drawer. He sealed the envelope, picked up his jacket and took her by the arm. "Let's go."

"Okay, Jack, what's the big secret? What's all this about."

"Police business, that's all."

"Anything that's police business around here concerns

the City and that concerns me, and should concern you. It certainly concerns *us*."

He looked at her a long minute. Finally he sighed and said, "The samples are from Robineau's property. He kept a journal. Looks like the lake's more polluted than we thought—seriously polluted—killing fish and wildlife."

"Jack, if that's true, the first thing the government will do is check the City."

"Well, there's nothing to hide, is there?"

"Of course not. But you know how ridiculous bureaucrats can be."

"I don't think it would hurt to have the water and soil checked."

She looked upset.

"Babe, sit down."

She stayed standing.

"I'm only doing this because it's my job. Look, the fish in the area, our wildlife, seem to be dying off. You know people are getting rashes from the water and it's not safe to swim in the lake."

"The government's already dealing with it."

"Maybe yes, maybe no. Robineau sent several samples this year and nobody ever got back to him. It's my job to do something. If anything's found, I'm the one'll be held responsible, especially if I did nothing."

"By that time we'll be in the Mediterranean, you'll be in charge of security there, and nobody will give a fuck what you did or didn't do in this shithole of a town."

"It's not just what other people think, babe, it's what I think."

"And you're willing to jeopardize your future, *our* future, because there might be some pollution in one small lake in a country where every other lake's dying of acid rain?"

He ran a hand through his hair. "I'm not jeopardizing anything."

"You will be if Varik finds out you did something behind his back."

"And how will he find out? You going to tell him?"

"If the government gets in here, I won't have to."

"If the government comes in and finds anything dirty going on, it's better for both of us not to be involved. I can get a job anywhere. There are plenty of resorts that need security. We'll go any place you like."

"Oh, right! And they'll pay you what Varik does. And what am I supposed to do, work as a waitress? Grow up, Jack."

"Come on, honey, I'm on your side. *Our* side. I just want things on the up-and-up." He kissed her forehead and pulled her close. The smell of jasmine hit him. "There's probably nothing to worry about in terms of Nirvana anyway. I just gotta check, that's all."

Slowly, Brenda let herself fall against him. "I'm just thinking about you and me. I don't know if you should send it or not, but at least wait until you've thought about it some more. Promise me that. There's a lot at stake. Sleep on it. Please? A day can't hurt. Just wait until you've thought about it."

She held him by the wrists, looking up at him over the top of her sunglasses, her wide green eyes sincere, persuasive.

Williams shrugged. "Okay. Consider it being thought about."

He half-turned and opened the bottom drawer on the left of the desk. He tossed the envelope in and shoved the drawer closed with his foot. What the hell, he thought. He'd mail it when he got back to the office in the morning.

# Twenty-Four

"Our attorneys are about to register the Deed on the Robineau property," Varik said proudly. "And Mrs. Mowatt has agreed to sell. She will come here Friday, the day before she leaves for Miami, and sign the papers."

He waited but the three before him were silent and still. He felt like a needy child. He wanted something from them, an acknowledgement that he had done well. Praise, even. Why were they withholding? He had given them the usual blood offering. Everything was going smoothly. Suddenly it came to him. Of course. He had more to tell. They had been aware of this even before he was.

"I've received word that Sergeant Williams is on the island."

A slight movement from the female. The younger male on the left twitched, but that was not unusual; his youth made him impatient, energetic. He in the center stayed perfectly still. Had Varik not understood what they were, the WAY they were, he would have been frightened by this non-response. As it stood, he felt impatient, a feeling that had never troubled him before. At least regarding them.

"Something must be done about Williams. He is no longer . . ." he wasn't sure how to put it, ". . . working towards the greater good."

There was no indication that he had been heard, yet Varik knew he'd been understood. He also sensed the solution to the problem, a termination of a contract, and that it might involve him. He wasn't sure he wanted to know much more.

The youngest made sounds, impatient, restless, hungry. Sounds that mirrored Varik's troubled mind. He became afraid and did not know why. Just as his fear threatened to mount to an unmanageable level, a calming voice said, *Be patient.*

It was her. Always her. Reassuring. Seductive.

*Change requires time.*

Yes, she would know all about that. She understood. As always. More than the others, she knew his heart and soul, even when he didn't know exactly what he was thinking and feeling. He trusted her more than the others. But, that was not strictly true. He trusted all of them. They were bringing him along. Helping him in ways that no one ever had. And hadn't he already changed remarkably? Soon the metamorphosis would be complete. Irrevocable. Without her telling him, Varik knew that then he could mate with her whenever he chose. And he would also have Claire. It was their way.

The one in the middle, the oldest, the strongest, the one who had guided him with discipline, just like a father, said, *The Son of God.*

And Varik knew that, finally, he had been named.

Eleven-forty-five. He should have been content. Relieved.

Everything he had carefully planned and worked so hard to create was beginning to actualize. His very existence would be altered irrevocably and he would have what few others had—the power of a deity. And yet he felt uneasy.

It was the dream. Every night it haunted him. Dragging him deeper and deeper into a dark maze of terror that could no longer be eliminated by sunlight. Or by waking.

Last night he had traveled the distance. Dread filled his body and yet he moved forward like an insect compelled towards a flame that would destroy it. The light blinded him so that he could only feel through his skin, the dampness, the heat.

And when he reached the end, instead of being consumed by the fires of hell, Varik entered a room. Large. Open. Noisy. The scent of flowers imbedded in thick air. Laughter. Music. Sounds of eating. A party. In his honor, no doubt. But inexplicable terror nearly suffocated him.

Varik checked his watch. Midnight. And noticed his hand shaking. He would have to sleep soon. And when he did he knew what would happen. Tonight, whether he liked it or not, he would come face to face with his hosts.

# Twenty-Five

Gord sipped his coffee and made a face. Cold. The fire had died down too. Faint embers amid grey ash. Just the way he felt.

Nearly midnight. He looked at Claire, then at Bailie. They both seemed exhausted. Could there be anything left to say?

On the other side of the room, the kids lay sprawled on the floor watching the latest *Hellraiser*. The emotionally embalmed Pinhead filled the screen. "I met a Welshman once, looked like him." Bailie nodded at the TV. He stood, yawned and stretched. "I'd better get a move on."

Gord walked him to the door. When he sat down next to Claire, she wouldn't meet his eye. She felt guilty. Good! Serves her right.

"I'm sorry," she apologized for maybe the fifth time. "If I'd thought you and Bailie were really going to make a serious offer—"

"We should've let you know we were talking about it," Gord acknowledged reluctantly.

"I wish you'd told me."

"So do I. I didn't realize you were going to sign right away. I wish you'd told *me!*" he snapped. Immediately he regretted it. "If you could only get out of it," he said in a milder voice. But of course they'd covered all that ground. If Claire reneged, Nirvana would probably take her to court. Besides, the amount of cash he and Bailie figured they could scrape together, *plus* financing through loans . . . They were still well below Varik's offer. A hopeless situation. Not only would she be sued but, even if she won, she'd have to wait maybe five, maybe ten years to get the case through the courts plus have to take a cut in the selling price when it was all over, and pay the lawyers, and meanwhile David might not have money for school . . .

He felt more than discouraged. "Crushed" struck him as the perfect word.

Losing didn't bother him, Gord realized. It was *what* he was losing. Not just a home. Something else. Something no other home he'd ever lived in represented. Just when he thought he'd sewn his life back together again, along came Nirvana to unravel the repair job.

He and Bailie were the only ones left on Skeleton Lake Road, besides the Gwinskis, and they just didn't come into this, never had—nobody knew their plans, if they had any. Bailie wasn't young, he wouldn't live forever. Eighty percent of the town had taken the money and run, with the rest likely to follow. Sure he could hold out, but what was the point?

Everything had changed. The initial attraction of living here had been the blend of isolation and rugged companionship he'd gotten from his close but not-too-close neighbors. Now he realized he'd had a hidden agenda all along. Something Claire had said the other day, a casual comment, that everyone else along the road was elderly. He couldn't help but think about that. This community had supported him emotionally the way parents support an only son. The way his father had been there for him. His dad.

195

He hadn't thought about him in a long time.

"This probably isn't a good time to mention it," Claire said, "and maybe it doesn't mean much, but David and I will be back next summer. We can still all get together."

"Doesn't mean much." Gord felt his temper surge. Damn her! She sells us out, becomes one of the ECbanites, and now she wants to be friends. What was this woman made of? He looked at her: Golden, untamed hair. Beautiful face. Clear eyes. Great body. No doubt about it, a fine surface appearance. She'll fit right in at Eternal City, Gord thought bitterly.

Who the hell could trust her, though? No sane man would, that's for sure. Lillian's basic honesty shone through, but there was also an element he didn't like. Maybe he was just a bitter loser.

"Varik's been pretty good to you." He watched her shift uneasily.

"I suppose so."

"Don't suppose. You got a better deal than anybody else around here, including Colette."

She jerked her head up. "Is that remark supposed to make me feel worse than I already do?"

"I don't know. Depends why you were treated so exceptionally."

"Gord, I don't like what you're implying."

"What am I implying?"

"That Varik and I . . . well, that there's something between us."

"Isn't there?"

"Don't be ridiculous!" But she looked away.

"Am I being ridiculous, or are you being evasive?"

"I don't have to put up with this interrogation. My feelings are my own business."

"And just what are your feelings?"

"For him?"

"No, for me!"

Claire looked as startled as he felt. She studied him for a moment, then got up from the couch and walked to the window.

After a pause she glanced back over her shoulder. "I like you. You know that. You're a very nice man, when you're not chewing me out."

"A very nice man," Gord thought. The ultimate insult. Verbal castration. She *was* being evasive.

And why the hell shouldn't she be? He'd been hesitating, no wonder she leaned towards Varik. Maybe she was getting from him what, up until this moment, Gord hadn't been prepared to give.

"I'm not sure how I feel about Varik," Claire said thoughtfully, as wide open with him as he was being closed with her. "He's attracted to me, and I enjoy that. And, I like him." She stopped and frowned. "Maybe 'like' isn't the right word." She went to the fireplace and stared at the dead fire. "He intrigues me. And he pays attention to me. I haven't had that in a long time."

"He pays attention to you because he wants your land."

"You want my land too, Gord," she reminded him.

"Not in the same way! Not for the same reasons!" he exploded and, oh shit, before he could stop himself, added, "I happen to love you and, unlike Varik, I can tell the difference between greed and love."

Impulsively he stood and moved up behind her. I must be crazy, he thought, wrapping his arms around her waist.

He half-expected Claire to turn and slap him, but instead she leaned back into him, almost sighing, as if to say, I've been waiting so long for this. "This is going pretty fast," she managed softly. "I wish I knew what I was doing. I'm so confused. I don't even know you. I have so many questions."

He could understand that. He'd been confused until a moment ago. But something—he didn't know what—gave him a sudden clarity that had been lacking. "Losing this place day by day is awful. It's like a slow death. It's the way my marriage ended. And Lillian and Gilles. And my father."

She turned to look at him, but he couldn't get it out, not right now.

"And you're mixed up in the whole equation. Nirvana is stealing you too, Claire, and I've never had you."

He kissed her lips passionately. Hers met his eagerly and the moment he realized how hungry she must be he felt his own starvation welling.

Gord kept her close to him. God, the smell of this woman, the combination of softness and firmness of her flesh.

"Claire, I haven't told you how I felt because I think that scares me more than the Eternal City does."

"You might have given me a hint."

He laughed. "You already thought I was crazy. I was afraid of confirming that."

"Well, maybe not *crazy* . . ."

"I've told you most of why I came up here in the first place, but not why I stayed. There are things I haven't told you. About my dad. I can't go into it now, it's too much and time's pressing in on me, but I will tell you. Soon."

"I thought you were keeping me at arm's length because I wasn't your type."

"Not at all! I was being selfish. I didn't want to get hurt again. Splitting up with Grace just about killed me. And you were leaving. Besides . . .”

"Besides what?”

He hesitated. "You aren't finished mourning your husband.”

Her eyes narrowed with anger for a moment then quickly widened as tears swelled over the lids.

"I'm sorry,” he said. "I know what it's like to lose someone who's a major part of your life.”

"It's okay,” she said softly. "You're right. I've been holding onto Bill.”

"I can't compete with him. Hell, I can't compete with Varik. All I can do is tell you how I feel about you.”

She looked relieved.

"But I have to tell you something else, too. Just because I love you doesn't mean I can walk away from this mess. They're stealing more than my home. They're killing my friends and destroying land I love. Claire, I don't expect you to understand or even accept it and, frankly, your approval doesn't matter, even now. But, I have to see this through to the end.”

"Why?”

"I'm not sure I can explain. But I've learned some things are worth fighting for. It's not your fight—I understand that now—but it was Lillian's and Gilles' and it is Bailie's and mine. I've got one more card to play, but I need your help.”

She looked wary, and a bit exasperated.

"Will you take Jerry for the night?”

"Is that all? Well, of course, but—”

"I'm going to drive to Ottawa. I should get there first thing in the morning, when the government offices open. I've got water and soil samples. From Gilles' property, and Lillian's. From the island. An old friend works in the lab at the Ministry of the Environment who, hopefully, will do me a major and fast favor. I want to get this stuff checked out right away."

"But I thought you'd already sent samples—"

"I have, Gilles did, we all did. We just get coddling form letters, it's 'being looked into.' I think Varik has been in there paying government people off. Look Claire, I don't use the 'L' word lightly. I haven't used it for a long time. I want you to wait for me."

"David and I have to leave Saturday morning."

"I know. Tomorrow's Friday. I'll be back tomorrow night, in plenty of time. Just don't sign the Agreement of Purchase until I get back."

"Alright, I guess I can put that off. But I promised Varik I'd come over tomorrow."

"Stall him." He grabbed her arms and said earnestly, "Claire, wait for me. Please. If worse comes to worse I'll fly you and David back from Toronto on Sunday and drive your car down to Florida myself. But I've got to give this one more shot. People have died. I can't just leave it all until I feel I've done everything I possibly can. Will you trust me on this?"

She hesitated, but finally nodded. "Okay. I'm as crazy as you; I'll wait. But, Gord, if you're not back by Sunday morning, I'm taking Jerry to Bailie's, and David and I are leaving."

He nodded, knowing it was the most he could ask of her.

"What do you expect to find?" she asked, moving his hands to her waist.

"Answers."

# Twenty-Six

Dry cold brushed David's arm, then a sharp prick. Pinhead! I'm *dead!* He raised a despairing hand.

"Hey! Wake up."

David sat bolt upright. "Whaa—"

A hand in the darkness clamped over his mouth. "Shssss!" It was Jerry's voice. "Come on, man, we gotta go."

A flashlight winked. The yellow beam played over his face, blinding him. "What time's zzit?" he groaned.

"Five."

He shoved the sleeping bag aside, wondering whose crazy idea this had been, then remembered it was his. "My mom hear you?"

"Doubt it."

David stood up and stretched. He'd slept in his clothes, which felt clammy. After he put on his running shoes and used the toilet, he grabbed one of the backpacks they'd loaded up the night before and hidden. He glanced at his cell phone but decided to leave it on the coffee table—who would he call anyway? He and Jerry quietly slipped out the front door.

"Wow!" he whispered. Inky sky. Silver half-moon. Glittering stars. Dark lake enshrouded in mist.

No sounds but their feet on soft grass, water gently slapping rocks, little animals scurrying in the underbrush.

They stepped onto the floating dock, which dipped and creaked beneath their weight. David felt excited and scared. If his mom found out, she'd kill him. Slowly and painfully. Taking a canoe out in the middle of the night without telling anybody was probably the worst thing he could do. The next worst thing was sneaking into Eternal City.

They pulled life jackets over their heads. "I feel like the Pillsbury Dough Boy," David said.

"You look like him." Jerry, down on one knee, looked up from untying a line.

The canoe was real tippy. David, standing upright at one end, nearly lost his balance. "Tah-dahhhhh!" He stretched out his arms, teetering like a tight-rope walker.

Jerry warned from the stern, "Hey, man, don't you know not to stand up? Kneel down. You'll capsize us."

"Aye, Captain!" David imitated the voice of Scotty, from the original *Star Trek*, and immediately crouched.

"Engage," Jerry added, updating. He pushed against the dock with his paddle and they drifted off in Lillian's canoe.

The shoreline disappeared in mist. The lake was calm; no waves. It's probably asleep, David thought. Ahead, the transparent dome rose out of the fog like a giant, green-tinged planet.

They paddled steadily, Jerry steering from the stern, occasionally trailing the paddle in the water to get the canoe back on course. Far away an owl hooted through the warm, soupy air. David began to sweat from exertion and undid the life jacket to peel off his windbreaker.

"What a stink, huh?" Jerry said.

"Like a toilet." David wrinkled his nose. The lake smelled worse than it ever had.

"It's always bad in the morning."

David yawned, just starting to wake up.

Jerry switched on the flashlight for a second. It barely cut through the fog. Nothing. Just the dome. They were close enough to see inside. The streets were dimly lit, no people in sight.

They moved quietly, cutting through the mouth of the Eternal City harbor, then rounding the island to the other side inside the ever-narrowing barrier surrounding the City. "There it is," Jerry whispered.

His flashlight lit up the sluice gate. Quietly, they paddled up to it then pulled their way around to shore. The canoe scraped bottom.

Jerry jumped out and David followed. They dragged the canoe up onto the bank and hid it behind wide-trunked trees. The dome was within reaching distance.

"Think it's wired?" Jerry whispered.

"You kidding? Know how much that'd cost?"

"Know how much this dome cost?"

Jerry had a point.

Inside, the City glowed with an eerie green light. The streets looked like something out of a dream. So quiet outside, so still inside . . .

They stood in front of the metal sluice gate. "Geez, it's like a sewer," Jerry said, a little too loudly.

"Shssh!" David warned. It seemed impossible but odor from the lake was actually being overwhelmed by what was coming from the cave.

The six foot metal sluice gate created a dyke, holding back the water. David jumped up and grabbed hold of the top of the gate. He pulled himself up so he could see over. Pretty dark in there. Within the barrier, the water level was much lower. David saw to his relief that the cave entrance was big enough for them to walk in, or at least walk bent. They'd get wet but it wasn't as bad as having to swim through the entrance underwater, which he'd been worrying about but hadn't said anything to Jerry. He didn't want to get real sick from swimming in this water, that was for sure. Still, fear rose from the pit of his stomach. Maybe it was the smell; he didn't want to go in there at all. But they'd come all this way and he couldn't weasel out on Jerry.

Jerry, half a head taller, crouched down and locked his hands together. David put a foot in and leapt while Jerry lifted. David grabbed the top of the gate. He scrambled over onto the other side. Seconds later one backpack flew over, then the other.

"Toss me the rope," Jerry called.

David got it out of the pack and tossed the line over the gate. He pulled as Jerry climbed noisily. Soon Jerry dropped down next to him with a big splash, knee deep in water.

"Man, we can almost walk through. We don't have to swim. This is cool."

"Yeah," David said.

They both burst out laughing and at the same time clamped hands over their mouths.

The craggy, rough opening emitted the powerful stench, and David wanted to puke. He flipped on the flashlight, noticed the batteries were low, and could have kicked himself for not bringing along spares. Still, they had *some* light.

This is what dying must be like, David thought. Both of them bent almost in half. Jerry led the way and David followed downward into the dark unknown. The damp tunnel snaked left and right, always descending. With each step he felt his stomach lurch. "Something's rotten," he whispered.

"What gave you a clue?" Jerry shot back.

"What was that?"

They stopped. A snapping sound, like a kite whipping in the wind. Then nothing.

"Must be a bird," Jerry said, but David could hear in his tone that he wasn't convinced.

It was cooler in here than outside, otherwise he couldn't have handled the stink; don't ever get a job working in the sewers, he told himself. He pulled the neck of his t-shirt up over his nose and mouth.

All of a sudden the tunnel opened up and they were standing on a level cave floor.

Jerry flashed the feeble light around. Walls everywhere and tunnels going in opposite directions. "Left or right?" he asked.

"Uh, left."

They moved along this new larger passageway, at least they could stand up straight. The air was cooler but even more fetid, if that was possible. Stalactites hung from the ceiling like sharp teeth. David ran his hand along the cold, rough wall. Suddenly his fingers slid through slime. "Ick!" he cried, snatching his hand away.

Jerry swung around quickly, dim light careening in all directions. "What's the matter?"

"I been slimed, that's what! Put the light here."

Jerry aimed the fading beam at his hand. Clear mucus dripped from David's fingers. "Yuck!" he said.

"Gimme that." David illuminated the wall, coated with stuff like snot. He let the beam sweep through the tunnel. The stuff was everywhere. Above them, both sides, even the floor, which had begun to feel slippery. He didn't have any choice but to wipe his hand on his jeans.

"Maybe this doesn't go to the City," he said, hoping Jerry would suggest they turn back.

"It has to. Where else can it go?"

A sudden noise! From the direction they'd come from. "Turn off the light!" David whispered.

They listened in the darkness. Scraping. Breathing. A lot of movement through the knee-high water. And a high, harsh sound that echoed through the tunnels.

David was trying to figure out what the sound reminded him of when Jerry grabbed his arm and yanked him hard in the direction they were already headed, deeper into the heart of the cold smelly darkness.

# Twenty-Seven

He stands naked among THEM.

Naked in THEIR brilliance. Excruciating, the white light of discovery.

The room is lavish. Opulent. Oppressive.

THEY watch him. Young. Old. Each exquisite. Sophisticated. Raw power.

Their eyes glitter, a million stars in the sky. THEY are hungry to know him in the most intimate ways.

The scent of flowers. Overwhelming. Cloying.

*Join with us.*

THEIR voices speak as one, a symphony, and yet he can distinguish between them. He hears HER, of course. Rapturous. The sweet tone of a mother. The seduction of a whore. Intense to his ears. Painful.

A banquet is taking place. Abundance. Food. Always food.

*Take. Drink. This is my blood.*

Freezing. Boiling. Liquid. Solid.

*Take. Eat. My flesh.*

Meat is presented. Red, dripping with the elixir of life.

*For the common good,* SHE assures him.

It is late. He is tired. But desire brought him here. SHE will not permit him to leave unsated.

Lust burns his gut. It drives him in one direction, towards HER. SHE forces him another way, towards HIM.

He is about to understand what he has become.

Varik screamed himself awake. Slick with sweat. Heart wailing within his chest. He could not find air.

He wiped his eyes. Tears? He must have been crying. He could not recall ever crying. His fingers covered his face, digging into the flesh, as sobs racked his body.

The phone rang. "Yes," he said, his voice a ghost of itself. The news was not good.

# Twenty-Eight

Williams opened his eyes. Still dark outside. He lifted his arm to look at the green glow of his watch face. Five-fifteen a.m.

Brenda lay beside him, sprawled on her back. Her red hair streamed across the pillow. Her breasts lifted and fell in the deep regular rhythm of sleep. The sheet covered most of her body, but couldn't hide firm nipples.

Jack couldn't believe how beautiful Brenda seemed to him at that moment. Limbs and features relaxed. Mouth slightly open. She'd be horrified to be seen like this, imperfectly coiffed, makeup not immaculate. And, in fact, he'd never noticed her quite this way before. Off guard. She had a naturalness that just wasn't there when she was awake. He found it more than appealing.

He slid out of bed and tip-toed to the dresser where he kept some casual clothes. Carefully he pulled open the bottom drawer. More by feel than by sight, he picked out a pair of grey jogging pants and matching sweat shirt.

All this silently, with an eye on Brenda. *Years of practice with Mary Ellen,* Williams thought ruefully.

His OPP issue navy pants and pale short-sleeve shirt were draped across the back of a chair. On the seat lay his utility belt with his gun, pager and flashlight. He left every-

209

thing there but his skeleton keys. No need to stir up suspicions if Brenda woke up.

Walking through the City was like floating through a dream. Halogen street lights threw an orange tint onto the grass and houses. The gunmetal sky had turned the photosensitive glass of the dome clear. Stars and a half-moon hung suspended outside the glass, although light from the east was already encroaching. Williams checked his watch again. The sun would rise within the hour.

Nobody out. No sounds. Not even insects. That was one of the comments in Robineau's journal. No animals at all in the City. And now that Williams thought about it, he realized he'd never seen any. Brenda told him Nirvana discouraged pets for two reasons: allergies, and the unnaturalness of keeping animals that belonged in the wild. Maybe he'd been love-struck at the time, but it had made sense. Now it seemed odd—not even a cat, or a canary? Walking through this island turned manicured, pristine park, Williams couldn't help feeling it was Eternal City that was unnatural.

So, what was his problem? Isn't this what he wanted? He'd been eager to get as far from rural living as he could. Eternal City looked like the perfect alternative, an urban setting, classy at that, right in his backyard. But the doubts grinding away at him all focused around this controlled environment.

He walked aimlessly, not quite sure what he was searching for. Everything looked normal: ideal homes, greener than green lawns (mowed to exact one inch standards), parkettes with swings and teeter-totters for the kids and benches and spouting fountains for the adults. Heaven.

He thought of Brenda, and how she looked while asleep. Maybe that was what he was looking for in her, a flaw he could love instead of an ideal he lusted after.

Eventually he came to a three story mock-Victorian house with bay windows. *The Clinic* it said outside. Brenda told him they called it that because a market survey indicated residents associated the word Hospital with sickness and death. But this place, she told him, had a fully equipped operating room. Hell, when he thought about it, the word Clinic scared him more.

He'd never been inside and decided this was as good a time as any to check it out. The building looked constructed from local birch, heavily varnished. Windows, flower boxes, geraniums in the neat yard, even a white picket fence. The door was unlocked so he went in. An attractive brunette about eighteen sat on a wicker sofa with floral upholstery on the seat. She wore crisp white shorts and a blue tank top and was reading *Elle*. She smiled, with a question in her eyes. "Hi. Can I help you?"

"Yeah. Got something for a headache?"

"Are you a resident?" she asked, the smile slipping slightly. He knew he didn't reek of wealth, just authority.

"I'm a guest. Of Brenda Lawrence."

"Oh!" The woman jumped to her feet. She was trim with a cute figure. The shorts were high cut. Pert and perky came to mind. "I'm Mandy Clark, night doctor here at the Clinic. Nice to meet you, Mr. . . ."

"Williams. Sergeant Williams." He didn't peg her as old enough to be a doctor.

They shook hands and Williams thought, if they're so eager to disguise this joint, maybe they should have made it look like a brothel.

"Now, you've got a headache. Would you like to come in to the examination room?"

He followed her swaying rear end down a hallway papered with flowered wallpaper and China plates hanging on it, past two rooms with closed doors to the back. They entered a white room, pristine, medical in appearance.

"Sit here, please."

He took the stool next to the desk. She pulled a stethoscope from the drawer and listened to his heart. Next she checked his ears and asked him to say "aah" while she peered down his throat. Her body so close, the tight shorts, warm sweet breath against his cheek . . . What in hell was he doing?

She removed the blood pressure band and jotted the numbers on the gauge onto a sheet stapled to a folder.

"Look, it's just a headache."

"Do you get them often?" she asked, still writing, as if searching for info that would prove he had a brain tumor.

"Once every four weeks. When the moon's full. Right on schedule."

She looked at him blankly, then smiled. "A joke."

"A joke," he confirmed.

There was a hard thump on the floor, the ceiling of the basement. They both glanced down, then back up at each other.

"Now, I just need your address," she said, returning to the form.

"I live in Chesborough. You can use Brenda's address and phone number."

"Fine."

"So, how about those aspirin?"

"Does aspirin work on your headaches? Or would you like something stronger?"

"Stronger is better."

"The pharmacy's closed but I think I've got some Advil upstairs. Be right back."

He watched her walk down the hall, turn and go up the stairs.

When she was safely gone he checked the other door in the room he was in. A back door, it led outside. He went down the hallway, looking into the two rooms he'd passed. Ordinary examination rooms. Quickly and as noiselessly as possible he hurried up the stairs to the second floor, forming an excuse in his mind. He would tell her he just remembered he's allergic to Advil.

The area on the second floor broke into two directions. The door to the left of the stairwell led to a recovery area. Six hospital beds. I.V. units at the ready. Cardio resuscitation equipment. Oxygen. The double doors at the far end probably went to the operating room. He heard someone walking across the floor above his head. Likely where they kept the medication. He hurried down the flight of stairs. He was nearly at the examination room when he noticed a small door under the stairs. He thought about it only a second before trying the door, then picking the lock.

Williams felt along the wall but couldn't find the light switch. Flicking on his keyring penlight, he closed the door behind him quietly. With any luck, she'd think he left.

At the bottom of the creaky wooden steps he found a regular, cramped basement. What'd he expect? Some underground laboratory manned by a mad scientist? Williams snorted. Well, he wouldn't have been surprised.

The unfinished basement was clean. Fuse boxes. Water heater. No furnace, of course, since the City used solar energy.

One door approximately beneath the examination rooms was locked, but that didn't stop him. Once the lock snapped, he opened the door carefully and peered through the crack. Williams wasn't prepared for what he saw.

A dimly-lit hospital ward. Spotless. Antiseptic. And crowded. A dozen hospital beds lined each side of the wall. In them lay people, all elderly.

He saw no attendant, so Williams closed the door quietly and walked down the middle of the room, not believing his eyes. Both sexes. Caucasians, mainly, but not exclusively. One thin black man. An Oriental couple side by side. An Hispanic lady with no teeth. An integrated chamber of horrors.

None of the patients seemed to notice him. Many appeared to be asleep, but not all. He heard coughs and groans. One old lady gasping for breath sounded like she was ready to croak. Whatever sophisticated medical equipment this clinic offered did not seem to be in evidence here.

The contrast between these pathetic people and the rest of the residents of Eternal City didn't escape Williams. He wondered what the hell was going on. In a City hyper-concerned about the spread of disease, this room acted as a breeding ground. Practically a mortuary.

He didn't know why but he expected to see Lillian Palmer here. But a quick scan of the emaciated faces told him she was not in this group. Suddenly, his instincts kicked in: he felt hostile eyes tracking him, and stopped at the foot of one of the beds. The patient—he couldn't tell if it was a man or woman—stared hard at him. Not *at* him exactly. *Through* him. Bright, burning eyes recessed deep into their gouged-out sockets, surrounded by parchment skin. Bone-sized arms rested outside the bedspread like branches lying on the forest floor, waiting to decompose. A clear, plastic tube was attached to each wrist. Two red rivers of blood dripped slowly. Bulging plastic bags hung below the level of the bed.

"Wait a minute!" Williams said aloud. He moved to the

side of the bed to examine the bags. Blood was flowing *into* them, not *out* of them.

Williams felt the old man's eyes again, and looked back at him. Milky irises, confusion. The ancient body trembled and he opened his mouth into an "O," like a silent scream.

"Jesus!" Unnerved, Williams put a hand on one of the man's arms. The skin felt icy.

Footsteps above. A pause. Shit! He didn't want a confrontation just yet. He'd better find out what was behind that second door.

Unlike the other doors, this one was unlocked. It opened onto a corridor of grey rock, a tunnel really, about seven feet high and wide enough for two people. Florescent lights lit the corridor every fifty feet or so. Chilly, sour-smelling air wafted towards him.

He walked the equivalent of half a city block until he reached a fork. Both dark branches looked pretty much like where he'd just come from and he suspected both led to another building. One branch sloped downward. And no mistaking it; the stench emanated from there. It made him hesitate.

Probably leads to a sewer, he thought. The City's illegally dumping waste; must be what's polluting the lake. Simple. Happens all the time with big residential complexes. But, damn it, he had to be sure.

He didn't feel like wading through shit but, on the other hand, it would be near impossible to get a court order to check out this place. He wasn't the only one in Nirvana's pocket. The bigwig politicians at the party the other night convinced him of that. Maybe if the soil and water samples turned up something. But, even then it might take weeks to get those bastards at the court to issue the right papers, plenty of time for Varik to find out what he was up to and haul away the evidence. And then there were those people, or what was left of them, having their blood drained out for no apparent reason and none of it replaced.

He was in too far. He'd lose his job, no doubt about it. No career with Nirvana he'd envisioned for himself seemed possible, he knew that now. But it wasn't the end of the world. He could resign the OPP before they fired him. Plenty of work in security, especially with his experience. Besides, he still had Brenda. He still had a life.

Hell, he thought. Not the best position to be in but not the worst either.

He pulled out his handkerchief and covered his nose and mouth. Then he headed down the narrow, black passage.

# Twenty-Nine

The tunnel curved sharply left, then flared out and up. "Pit!" Jerry whispered, stopping abruptly.

David accidentally bumped him from behind, and Jerry stumbled forward. David caught his arm as he wobbled at the edge.

They were so far underground this chamber should have been pitch black but instead it glowed with an eerie green light. Crystals embedded in the rock, Jerry guessed, his eyes adjusting. He'd seen it before, with his dad, when they checked out a cave at the petroglyphs.

Gradually, the ceiling, walls, and floor took shape. He wrinkled his nose. At least they found the source of the smell, that was for sure!

He noticed, or thought he did, movement. The walls seemed almost alive with shadows rippling over them.

"We can't stay here," David whispered urgently. Jerry scanned the wide route of the ledge. It circled halfway around the cavern wall. Every few feet huge boulders or out-crops of rock bulged like giant zits. The pit below emitted hot smelly vapors.

*Skreee! Skreee!*

"Jesus!" David said, his breathing ragged. "What's that?"

*Skreee! SKREEE!* Echoed behind them from the dark tunnel! Growing louder by the second.

Jerry tugged his sleeve. They ran along the ledge, the floor beneath them slippery. When they reached the first boulder, Jerry first, then David, dove behind it. The rock had a natural groove, big enough so they could press their bodies into it and hide. "Maybe they'll pass," David whispered in his ear.

"And then . . . ?"

"Don't know. Let's see who they are first."

"Man, I'm gonna puke!"

The illumination was good enough to see by but dim enough so that Jerry questioned what he saw emerging from the tunnel. Pale things on two legs. Buck naked. Then he noticed the wings.

He heard David's sharp intake of breath as fingers dug into his shoulder, forcing him to scrunch down further into the crouch. Don't worry, he thought, sending David a telepathic message, I'm *way* ahead of you.

Shuffling. Flapping. Loud as the cafeteria at lunch time. Jerry had to look. Carefully he peeked out from behind the boulder.

What the . . . ? People with wings? Their faces were all angles, with pointy chins and noses, sharp cheekbones. Pale hairless bodies. Like that anorexic girl at school who always looked hungry.

Most of them were adults, but there were some the size of teenagers, and younger.

By turns they walked to the edge of the pit, lifted their arms and soared a few yards over the stinking swill below, then landed along the ledge, like pigeons perching on a roof edge. Man, he thought, they walk *and* fly! And they're gonna see us any minute. Wings lifted. Fluttering, flapping, landing, walking, taking off again . . . He felt David trembling, or maybe *he* was shaking.

He counted fifteen, more still coming. A whole army!

One flew over the pit and perched near the boulder. A male, Jerry estimated it was about six-foot-two. The wing span astonished him.

As if sensing something, the creature cocked its head. Jerry didn't breathe. He closed his eyes and mouth, partly to keep from screaming, partly to keep from knowing his fate, praying the dark cavity in the rock would hide them. Wings flapped. He felt air waft towards him. The thing moved on again.

Creatures filled the cavern, screeching like vultures. The sound knifed his ear drums. They barely avoided colliding with each other in the confined space. Swooping. Soaring. Gliding close to the walls and to each other but managing to veer away at the last second. Sonar, Jerry thought, like bats. And they're territorial.

Despite himself, he found them fascinating, even beautiful. Their movements looked planned. Each had its own pattern and yet there was also a group pattern, like that science video he saw at school, simulating the intricate dance of atoms.

Now that his eyes had adjusted, he could make out more of the cave. The ceiling was so high he couldn't see the top. Thick needles of rock hung down and he wondered if they ever fell into the pool of filth below. They must. The smell that had gagged them since they got here was definitely from the pit but he wasn't close enough and he wasn't about to look over the edge anyway to see what caused it, just that brief glimpse when he teetered.

The wall farthest from where they hid looked weird. Suddenly he realized it wasn't just flickering shadows. That wall was definitely moving!

When he recognized what was hanging there, he almost yelled. Babies! Little babies with wings! Attaching to the rock like bats, hanging upside down. They didn't have the harshly chiseled features of the adults but instead looked gawky and sweet, the way the young of every species looks. And they looked human! Ohmigod, he thought, realizing that this place was a nursery. And that was bad news for him and David.

The baby bird-things squirmed like infants in cribs. The shrieks of the adults excited them and they made tiny cries of their own in response and flapped undeveloped wings as if imitating flight.

Another adult swept close to the boulder. Jerry and David both shrank. Jerry glanced back at the corridor where they entered. Only one creature, between them and the exit. It stood like a sentry on guard against enemies, enemies like Jerry and David. Its head jerked fiercely, right and left, up and down. Its eyes turned to the outer corners of the sockets so it could see to the side while facing front. Just like a bird.

Jerry felt they couldn't do anything but wait and hope they weren't seen. He hoped David had the same idea.

Eventually the frenetic movements of the flock died down. More and more of them attached themselves to the walls and ceiling. Hanging upside down, each stationing it-self near two or three young ones. He watched one wrap it-self in those enormous wings, cocooning for sleep.

The noise and rustling died. Almost an hour later, by Jerry's estimation, the flock was attached to the wall and immobile. All except the one at the tunnel that led to the exit. It paced and hopped and fluttered. David whispered, "Let's tackle it into the pit and get out."

Suddenly, the sentry swirled in their direction and snarled. Jerry jerked back. They'd been spotted! Oh, God, where could they run?

He grabbed David's arm and pulled him to his feet. The creature faced them. They were just about to turn when Jerry froze, mesmerized by what lay in the hollow of the bird-thing's throat. Lillian's amethyst necklace!

# Thirty

This was bad. Real bad. Williams didn't know how much more of it he was going to take. The deeper in he went, the worse the stench. He'd never smelled anything like it. He'd run across his share of dead animals, some pretty ripe. And he'd encountered more than one human corpse in an advanced stage of decomposition. But this was something else!

Whatever was in this tunnel reminded Williams of a trip to a slaughter-house he'd made when he was at OPP school. The course instructor wanted to give them an in-your-face experience. "If you can handle this, you can handle everything," he'd said. That place stunk of mass death too but, by comparison, the smell had been perfume. Here, rotting flesh and death piled on top of themselves. In the darkest recesses of William's mind, maggots squirmed through hollow eye sockets. Large, slow-crawling larva burrowed like slimy filth into grey, long-dead flesh. Adipocere at its best.

Cut it out! he ordered himself. Reality's bad enough.

The pathetic little penlight on his keyring—he could've kicked himself for leaving the utility belt at Brenda's—cast a ray of weak yellow nearly swallowed by the thick blackness. Mostly he felt his way along the cold slippery walls.

Williams walked for what must have been half a block when he noticed illumination fifty yards up ahead. An air current carrying a foul odor rushed towards him—this must lead outside. As a precaution, he cut the penlight. His steps became slow and cautious. He didn't know what to expect but he was pretty damn certain he wasn't going to like it.

The ceiling and walls suddenly opened up. He stopped short, and found himself at the slippery edge of a narrow shelf overlooking a huge chamber. His eyes adjusted, and he gripped the keyring to keep from dropping it.

The place reeked, but that wasn't the problem. Things. Bat-like, but huge and pale. Clinging to the glittering walls. Upside down, all sizes, like sickly pale pods.

Whatever the hell they were, they weren't aware of him. They should be. Any flying thing should have fled or attacked by now. Except for the occasional twitch and high-pitched squeak, these things were immobile, glued to the walls.

Their lack of response got to him. And the heat in here— a humid, fetid tomb. It was like listening to the dead decay. But these things were alive, sleeping, undisturbed even by the fumes that emanated from the pit forty feet below.

Cautiously he stepped forward to peer over the brink. Looked like a pond gone bad. Green scum floated on the surface like a thin scab over a festering wound. Breaks in the scum let him see a dark, murky sludge. Couldn't tell how deep it went or what the hell was in there. Hazardous waste, at the very least.

Half rotted carcasses of animals had risen out of the pool like miniature, wrecked islands. A raccoon's head. Half a fox. A dog, rigid in death. White bones bobbed to the surface of the dark mass. White bones that were . . .

Williams squatted down. Damn hard to see. Couldn't be

sure. He hoped it was a branch of a tree. He hoped it wasn't what he knew it was. A humerus, the hand at the end of it open, white bony fingers reaching up towards him. Pleading. Begging him to grasp it. For what? To be pulled up? To yank him down?

*SKREEEE!* An unearthly cry echoed around the cave, jerking him to his senses. Startled, he scanned the gloom. About fifty yards away . . .

What the hell . . . ?

A man? He couldn't make out much at this distance but something told him he'd seen the face before. Pale skin, white hair, slim but muscular. And, what the . . . ? Naked. A penis dangled between hairless legs. Arms spread wide. Arms? Hell, those weren't arms, they were wings! Wings fanning out for flight.

Williams' first instinct was to get the hell out of there. But whatever stood across the expanse of this cavern wasn't looking at him. It hopped and fluttered, excited, angry, trying to wake the others, no doubt, attention focused on a large boulder. Cringing behind that rock Williams saw Jerry Roberts and the Mowatt boy.

The thing threw back its head and screeched again. The ear-splitting sound from hell bounced around the walls. Out of the corner of his eye he saw frenetic movement along the wall.

The creature jerked its head grotesquely in different directions, bird-like. The boys stood up. The thing started towards them. Why in hell weren't they running?

No time to think. Williams grabbed a rock and fired it against the wall of the cavern. The stone pinged against stone, missing the creatures. The sound echoed and, distracted, the bird-thing turned.

"Over here!" Williams yelled, waving the boys around

the ledge. Smart kids, they didn't hesitate. The Roberts boy dodged around the boulders and jutting rock, the Mowatt kid on his heels. The creature still ignored them, for the moment. It lifted up off the cave floor and glided towards the wall where the rock had struck.

Williams backed up from the edge of the pit. He put a protective arm out towards the kids, waving them to hurry. Both gasped for breath, running full out, slipping on the slick surface as they rounded the ledge. Williams hurled another rock at the wall. This one grazed the left wing of the flying creature headed towards them. *SKREEE! SKREEE!* The thing swerved over the pit, struggling for altitude.

More stirring from the ones clinging to the walls. Fluttering. Flapping. Holy shit! They're waking up!

*SKREEE! SKREEE!*

One, close by, opened its wings and turned a sharp-angled, hollow-featured face in his direction. Malevolent eyes, like the empty glow of a florescent tube, fixed on his. Lips spread, exposing fang-like teeth.

It pushed away from the wall, wings spreading as it glided, then banked in the air. Gathering speed it headed straight towards him.

The second the boys reached him, Williams yelled, "Outta here!" He shoved the kids into the tunnel ahead of him.

They ran blindly. Williams felt the tunnel fork. The boys had already started down the left branch.

"Come back!" he yelled, but echoes garbled his words and they must have been too far ahead. All he could do was follow them, and fast. He hoped they weren't headed towards a dead end. The left tunnel transformed into another lighted corridor. At the end he saw a door with a crash bar. Jerry at the lead hit the bar running with both hands. The door swung inward and they were all through in seconds. Williams slammed it closed behind him and leaned against it panting.

They were in a room with a long table, some chairs, a fireplace. Dark paintings hung on the walls. And flowers. A whole shit-load. "Goddamn funeral parlor," he gasped.

As of one mind, the boys looked at the other door. "This goes to the restaurant," David said.

"We were here before. At the party," Jerry explained.

After what these kids had seen, after what *he'd* seen, nobody could be expected to be calm, and they were doing okay. "Let me check if anyone's out there," Williams said, opening the door a crack. The curtain that he realized had hidden the door during the party was pulled back; he could see the entire room. "Shit!" he muttered.

Varik stood ten yards away, issuing orders to the dozen men. The men were armed. M-16s. A.K. 60s. Williams didn't recognize any of these guys, but he recognized their attitude. Hard. Trained. Combat experienced. No ordinary security force. Ex-Army. Maybe goddamn mercenaries.

He didn't kid himself that they would be impressed by the fact that he was the law. In fact, it might piss them off. Varik had probably rounded them up to search for him. Williams eased the door shut. "We'll stay in here a minute."

"But they're gonna come after us," Jerry said, his voice trembling. Williams put a reassuring hand on his shoulder.

"We're trapped!" David said, close to tears. "Those things are gonna get here any second. We gotta get out of here!"

Williams glanced around. A vent, about head level in the paneled wall. Luck hung in with him; the grate was only plugged in, and he pried it out with his keyring penlight. The shaft wasn't big. Kid size. "Inside," he told them.

He boosted Jerry up, then David. "What about you?" David asked, on his knees, peering out as Williams pounded the grate into place with his fist. "Don't worry about me, son. Get back now, as far as you can. Keep outta sight."

He went to the door to the corridor and opened it cautiously. No sign of the creatures. Yet. Varik and his armed contingent were the immediate problem. Better them. At least they were human, and Williams understood guns.

He crossed to the other door. Just before he reached it, it opened.

Two guards stormed in, followed by Varik. The first man dropped to one knee, rifle up, SWAT style. At the same time an older guy, maybe fifty, stepped neatly in front of Varik, shielding him. They got the pro moves, all right, Williams thought.

He raised his hands up. "You guys know what the hell Varik's got under this goddamn city?" he asked abruptly, grabbing the offensive.

Varik's eyebrows lifted. "Suppose you tell them, Sergeant Williams," he snapped. The CEO looked like hell, like he hadn't had a good night's sleep in a week. He was still in control, though. Or thought he was.

"A nest of goddamn giant meat-eating bats!"

The two bodyguards snickered. Varik turned to them. "Wait outside, gentlemen. I'll call if I need you."

Once they were gone and the door securely shut, Varik said, "Sergeant Williams, you have caused us some concern. Brenda informed me of your plans to investigate Mr. Robineau's death, and a little over an hour ago Doctor Clark alerted security that you'd disappeared from the Clinic. I'm sure I don't need to tell you what this means in terms of any future you may have planned for yourself with Nirvana."

Brenda! She'd betrayed him. His heart skipped a beat or two. He couldn't believe it. On the other hand, yes he could. A small sad part of him wasn't surprised at all.

"So you've met our charter members, my friends," Varik said.

"Friends?" Williams laughed incredulously. "Are you nuts? You call those things 'friends'? They're not even human."

Varik's mouth twitched, and his left hand trembled as if he had Parkinson's. But the CEO of Nirvana Corporation seemed unaware of these physical aberrations. Definitely losing it, Williams thought. I can play with this.

When he spoke, however, Varik's voice remained strong and even. "History reveals that humanity has always perceived them in a negative light. Ignorant people relegate them to mere superstition while intelligent, although foolhardy, humans have hunted them throughout the centuries. I've managed to accomplish what no one before me has been able to. Not only have I entered into relationship with them but, in the near future, they are permitting me the honor of joining their ranks."

"Jesus Christ! You think they're vampires!"

"I'm not an idiot, Sergeant, a member of the ignorant masses. Those stories are myths, created by the charter members themselves, for protection. You see, they've always been with us. They've evolved through the millennia as our own species has but, of course, their population has been kept small, controlled breeding, if you like, out of necessity. The more of them there are, the greater likelihood of extinction. Especially on a planet our species has systematically poisoned. We are not only killing ourselves, but all life forms, including them."

It was as if Williams saw Varik for the first time. Body as

immobile as a corpse. Flesh pale and rigid. No wonder the man hid behind dark glasses. His eyes had probably glazed over long ago. Who knows when he fell over the edge? Williams knew one thing for sure, though. Varik wasn't going to climb back to sanity. Not in this lifetime.

The corners of Varik's precise mouth turned upward slightly. "Aren't they beautiful, Sergeant?"

"Beautiful?"

"A species with enormous strength as well as the ability to fly. A species that can pass for human and is virtually indestructible. You see, they live forever."

Forever, Williams thought. Oh shit. He didn't want to even think about Varik's mind. "So, these vampires, or whatever the hell they are. They drink blood? Human blood?"

"They prefer it, yes. But unlike the commonly accepted belief, they do not need to kill humans. A small quantity nourishes them. A vial. Less than ten cc's a day. Astonishing, isn't it?"

"And where are they getting the blood from?"

"Donors."

"Like you?"

The hand twitched. "Among others."

"What about the old people in the Clinic?"

"All residents of the Eternal City are donors, unknowingly, of course. There are so many diseases of the blood today. And other factors: pollution, pesticide-laced food, contaminated drinking water. All of it leads to poor health. Our blood is the most disease-free on earth. Preservation of the species is what this is all about. The charter members, *homo sapiens* . . . An excellent cause, don't you agree?"

Williams knew Varik was only being open because he had no intention of letting him out alive. Stalling seemed like a good idea. Maybe he could convince this nut that he believed him, was even on his side. A long shot, but basically his only shot. "If I hadn't seen them with my own eyes, I'd think you're crazy. Those vampires are real. Probably everything else you've told me is true too. Why do you want to be like them?"

"Isn't it obvious? I'm a man who has reached goals ordinary people have difficulty imagining. And yet when I die, all this dies with me." His hand swept the room. "We have an arrangement, the charter members and I. Because of me these Cities exist. They can live here safely, freely, come and go as they please. I provide them with not just all the blood they require but the purest blood on the planet. And, in return, I become like them. Eternal. The best of both worlds, shall we say?"

"Sounds good." Williams' mind raced. Let the lunatic think he was being won over. If he could get out of here and get some help, he'd have this psycho behind bars, politicians or no politicians. "Anybody else going to, uh, join these vampires?"

"Others have begun the process, yes. Brenda is one."

He struggled to keep his feelings off his face. "That's good to hear. If anybody should stay beautiful forever, it's her."

Varik said nothing.

"So, suppose I'm interested in joining this little party, now that I know what it's all about? How do I get in on it?"

"The point is, Sergeant, you cannot just *get in* on it. You must be chosen."

"Yeah. Makes sense. So, when can I go before the committee, or whoever makes the decisions? Or is that you?"

"It is not I, not at present, although very soon I shall be among those who decide."

Suddenly there was a noise from the corridor. Williams felt his heart lurch. Time. He'd needed just a little more time.

What crashed through the door was even more hideous up close than at a distance. All semblance of humanity had vanished from the angular face. The shrunken flesh of a corpse. Colorless hair streaming behind. Eye sockets ghost white. Ghosts that called to him. To join them. In death.

Williams screamed.

The bird of prey zeroed in.

Williams stumbled back against the wall. "Hey!" he said weakly.

It moved swiftly and silently to tower over him. Lips drew back revealing enormous fangs. Long. Sharp. Deadly. Fetid breath smacked him full in the face, and he reeled.

Before he could react, powerful talons buried themselves under his chin. He felt himself lifted two feet off the floor. He flailed, then grabbed the cool flesh to pry the hands away. Useless. He choked and gasped, his air passage punctured. Air that should have been going down his windpipe was siphoned off.

The thing clamped razor sharp teeth into the side of his neck. He'd never felt pain like this. Searing. Automatically his fists and legs punched and kicked, making contact, but the vice-like jaws had locked.

Varik's impassive face swirled in and out of focus.

Williams's body hit the floor. He became a carcass dragged by a ravenous animal back to its lair. He had a hazy awareness of the corridor. The brightness of the white light.

The white light of empty eyes.

*Jack.*

Brenda's voice. Sensual. Inviting.

231

*We'll be together at last. Join me.*

Pain vanished.

She nibbled at his neck, his arm, his back, his genitals. Williams felt joy. Heat drew him. All that remained was to slip into her humid darkness and lose himself. And when she called again, that's exactly what Jack Williams did.

# Thirty-One

For the umpteenth time that morning, Claire walked down the path and across the road to the lake. She shielded her eyes from the sun's glare and scanned the water. Where *were* those kids?

She checked her watch again. Ten thirty. Wait'll I get my hands on them, she thought. They both know better. And I *told* David not to take the canoe out alone. They'll probably be back any minute, hungry, acting as if I'm nuts to be so worried. They'll be back any minute.

*If* nothing's happened.

A wave of fear sliced through her and, to stifle it, Claire walked out onto the floating dock. The far-off drone of an engine carried across the lake. Maybe the canoe overturned, she thought. Maybe they ran into a submerged rock and sprung a leak. Maybe they drowned . . .

Hold on! She shook her head. This isn't doing any good. Standing around worrying was slowly driving her crazy; time for action.

On the slim chance the kids might be at Gord's, she drove there first. His house was deserted. Gord's boat, the *Devil-May-Care*, was tied to the dock. She checked the boat, then left a note there and on the front door. She returned to Lillian's and left a note there as well, then headed to Bailie's place.

On the way, she stopped at Eternal City's dock to question the captain and crew and the chauffeur; no one had seen David or Jerry.

Around the bend in the road, two miles past the Robineaus', just before the silver trailers glinting through the trees beyond, Bailie's stack-wall house came into view. His car was not in the driveway.

Like most of the cottages, the door was unlocked. Claire let herself in and left him a note. She drove for half an hour along the road, halfway around the lake. On her way back she stopped at the silver trailers.

There were two of them, Airstreams, old, half-rusted. She knocked on one, then the other, but the knocking didn't bring anyone out. Where the hell was everybody? Had the whole community mysteriously vanished?

Frantic, she drove to the OPP Station in Chesborough. A reed-thin young man with coarse blonde hair and a patchy beard stood behind the counter. She asked for Sergeant Williams.

"Not in today, ma'am."

"Well, maybe you can help me. It's my children. My child. And his friend. They're missing."

The man with the name tag reading *Sergeant T. Atkins* immediately pulled a pen out of his shirt pocket and a form from a box to his right. "How old are they?"

"David's thirteen. Jerry's a year older."

"How long they been missing?"

"Since nine this morning."

Atkins lay the pen down. "That's only three hours, ma'am. I realize that probably seems like a month to you but, ah—"

"I noticed they were gone at nine. They must've left a lot

earlier. *And* they took the canoe."

"Maybe they went to visit a friend without telling you. You know kids."

"I don't think so," Claire said firmly.

He nodded, and asked if either of them had boating experience.

"They both do. That's why I'm concerned. They should be back by now."

Atkins took down information about her and the kids, stopping to answer the phone twice. Finally he said reassuringly, "If something happened to the canoe, it would have been spotted by now. To me, it sounds like they may have dragged it up on shore somewhere, and went exploring. They might be lost in the woods, but that's pretty unlikely, there are roads every ten kilometers or so."

Claire nodded, not convinced.

"You and David argue lately?"

She thought for a moment and recalled the scene after the lunch with Varik, and other disagreements. "We differ occasionally, but David doesn't hold grudges."

"Boys his age often act rebellious, especially in pairs," Atkins chuckled. "I know my friends and I did. Pulled all sorts of wild stunts I never would have done alone."

Claire smiled despite herself.

"Mrs. Mowatt, I'm concerned but not unduly alarmed. Legally we need to wait twenty-four hours for a missing person. And we can't start a full-scale search right this minute anyway. I'm short a man today but I'll do what I can, make a few calls, alert people in the area. Do you have a cell phone?"

"My son does, but it's at the cottage."

"Alright, give me that number too. What I suggest is you go back home and wait. Keep the cell with you. Call me when they come in. I'll phone you if there's any news. As soon as one of the other officers gets in, I'll take the boat out and have a look around the lake myself."

"I'd appreciate that," Claire said.

Claire went to Lillian's first, picked up the cell, and left a second note. There was no sign that the kids had returned. At Gord's she made a cup of black coffee for herself and sat outside with the cell phone, in view of the lake but near enough to the cottage to hear his phone. The cell rang at two.

"Mrs. Mowatt? Sergeant Atkins. They home yet?"

"No," she said, feeling a sob crawl up her throat.

"Haven't heard anything here, either. I've called a few people in the area; they've called others. Word spreads fast. People will keep their eyes open."

"Thank you."

"I'm going to take the OPP search craft out and see what I can find. It's got a phone on board and I'll get the switchboard to patch me through to you if they turn up. I think you should stay right where you are. In case they come back."

*In case they come back?* Why didn't he say *when?* Please, God, she prayed, I couldn't bear it if anything happened to David. Suddenly she saw a gruesome picture of herself in black again, standing before a closed coffin, this time a smaller one. Then snippets of a life without him. The images were too real to fight off. "No!" she screamed, breaking down, struggling, unwilling to let this premonition be true.

Around four o'clock, Claire called Varik but was unable to reach him. She did get hold of Brenda, who promised to alert the staff and residents to be on the lookout. If only Gord had left a number where he could be reached!

By five Claire couldn't take the waiting. She drove west, past the turnoff to Chesborough, checking out the lake edge where they had first arrived. The road crawled away from the lake, towards the highway. She stopped at each house to ask if they'd seen David and Jerry. Then she drove east, back to the trailers. This time someone was at home.

One of the doors that had been locked stood open. She walked up the three steps, knocked and peeked in. The boy Earl, from the gas station, sat on a rusted oil drum in the middle of the room. The gloomy place reeked of harsh chemicals. Claire had a horrible olfactory déjà vu. The odor left her feeling vulnerable and frightened.

As her eyes adjusted, she realized that every surface was littered with bottles and rags and parts of dead animals, mainly heads. Heads lined the walls—elk, moose, deer— and smaller creatures stood stuffed and mounted for table display. Here and there were odd pieces she couldn't iden- tify—two things on the table that looked remarkably like human hands. She refused to step inside.

Earl turned towards her, straddling the oil drum. He continued to wipe down two thick flesh-colored straps. Even in the poor lighting she could see that his eyes were glazed and she wondered if he was drunk, or on drugs.

"Excuse me," she said, "I'm Claire Mowatt. I live along the road."

"They said you were comin'."

Atkins must have called.

"Have you seen two boys? Both thirteen. One is Jerry Roberts, the other my son David. He has—"

"Sure did."

Claire's heart skipped a beat. "This morning?"

"Nope."

"Well, when did you see them?"

237

"Before sunrise."

She felt sick. "Where were they? In the woods?"

"Nope."

She could barely control herself. "On the lake? Please, just tell me where."

"Our FATHER in heaven took 'em. You know that."

Her hand flew to her mouth. She had to grab the doorframe to keep from falling. "What exactly are you saying? Are you saying they're dead?"

"Nope."

"Then where are they?"

"Eternity."

"Eternity? You mean heaven?"

"Nope. I mean, eternity. You know like I know, cause THEY told you same as THEY told me. Where I'm goin'. Where you're goin'."

He knew nothing. He was crazy. But his eyes, the way he looked at her, undressing her, the way he licked his lips as if she were a piece of meat and he was oh-so-hungry . . . She felt disgusted.

"Where are your parents?"

He pointed and nodded at the other trailer.

Claire backed down the steps and he followed her to the door. He was barefoot, wearing only pants. When he reached the doorway and the natural light, she noticed his body was painted red and his clothes splattered with the same color. Leather dye, probably. She hurried across the littered yard and knocked on the second door. Behind her she heard a sharp crack and turned.

Earl held the straps together at both ends taut, close to his ear. He moved his hands together to separate the layers of leather into a large "O," then yanked them apart so the skins would snap together. Again and again. "When THEY

238

choose you, you gotta be pure before THEY take you. You know that."

The cracking more than his words unnerved her. She tried the door handle. Something vibrated through the rusted metal like a warning. She did not want to go in there. Not now, not ever. But the boys might be inside.

She steeled herself and turned the knob. The door opened out.

The odor of putridity shoved her back. She forced herself to look inside.

Blood. Everywhere. Body parts. The head of a man, eyes wide, mouth gaping, black tongue lolling . . .

She fell back off the step.

Behind her the cracking intensified. It's not red dye he's covered in, she realized.

The immense carnage left Claire lightheaded. Her body began to shake. Afraid and revolted, she had to fight her body to keep from running to the Jeep. Earl was insane. Any second he could turn on her—he was only a few feet away. But she had to be sure her son, and Jerry, were not here. She went inside.

Blood and gristle everywhere. The bodies had been severed into parts and seeing the limbs separated from the torsos—the entire room began to look unreal. Most horrifying were the missing parts, the things she hadn't wanted to recognize in the other trailer. Hands. Four of them.

Shakily she stepped over the human debris to check the small bedroom. No blood. The violence had occurred in the main room. Stupidly, she'd left the cell phone in the Jeep. She searched the trailer for a telephone, but couldn't find one. There was, however, a woman's breast in the kitchen's tiny sink. On top of the television she found a man's genitals, and nearly vomited.

Nothing that looked like her son. Or Jerry. But she couldn't feel relieved. Outside the door a madman waited.

Claire could barely control her shaking. She forced herself to open the door. Earl stood in the yard, between the two trailers, still snapping the flesh-colored leather. Most of the blood painting him was spread across his exposed stomach and the front of his pants. His eyes glittered. She didn't know what he was seeing, but it wasn't her.

She forced a smile onto her face, stepped down the steps and said, "Yes, Earl, you're chosen. You're to wait right here. THEY'll be here soon."

His face lit as if a spotlight had been flicked on.

"Yes, ma'am. Oh yes, ma'am," he said. "And thank you."

"Wait right here, now. THEY want you to wait here."

She fought with herself to keep from running past him to the Jeep. Anything could throw him off. Besides, the top was down—she wouldn't have a chance.

She got in and started the engine. Earl stood watching her, his face glowing. He started walking towards her, still snapping the leather.

She backed down the road quickly, crushing a taillight against a tree, turned and hit the gas, leaving dust in her wake. With enough distance to feel secure, she picked up the cell and shakily punched in 911, which put her through to the OPP office.

When she returned to Gord's, Bailie was waiting.

She told him what she'd seen while she drank the big shot of whiskey he'd poured for her.

Claire got on the phone, struggling to focus, and called the OPP again, this time asking to be patched through to Sergeant Atkins. She repeated what she had told the other officer, and then told him she was sure the boys were not in that trailer. "Mrs. Mowatt, I think this is unrelated to your missing boys. I've scoured the lake and I'm afraid there's no trace of that canoe. In a sense, that's a hopeful sign. Even with a leak, it should still float. And they could've hung on a bit and swum to shore—it's not that far. My bet's they dragged it out of the water and hid it behind some bushes, that's why nobody's spotted it yet. Our concern at the moment isn't a drowning. I do think they might be lost in the woods. We've had two dozen boats out on the water and as many cars on the road. We'll do what we can before dark. Hopefully they'll be back before then. But I have to tell you, after eight-thirty, quarter to nine, it'll be too dark to do anything until sunrise."

"And at sunrise?"

"Well, it's a bit soon, but just to cover all bases, we can get equipment in from Bali and drag the lake. First things first. I've sent an officer to pick up Earl. We'll keep you posted. That situation's gonna take most of our manpower, I'm afraid."

Claire felt herself losing it. When she got off the phone she walked down to the water again. How could such a natural setting breed the violence this area has seen? Everywhere, people dying in unnatural ways.

The dome sparkled in the afternoon light like an emerald. But it was not an emerald, it was glass. Glass that played tricks on the eyes, one minute reflecting the environment, the next transparent. Glass that covered a City that held the chosen few.

"I'm going to see Varik," she told Bailie, jumping into the Jeep and heading towards the Eternal City's dock.

# Thirty-Two

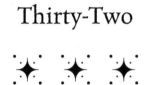

David felt like a human popsicle. He and Jerry had been shivering for hours. Now their teeth chattered uncontrollably.

It hadn't taken long to realize that the shaft they were hiding in was part of the central air conditioning unit. Cold air flowed through the dark, corrugated passage like a fast-moving stream of ice water. Jerry, further in, was getting the worst of it. His body shielded David's from the cold. But David's body had shielded Jerry from seeing what had happened in the room.

During those horrible nightmare moments they pulled deeper into the airshaft. Still, David had seen and heard everything through the grating.

Varik.

Williams.

And . . . it.

Even after Sergeant Williams was dragged away, struggling, groaning, Varik stayed in the room a long time. Just standing there. Motionless. Staring into space behind those dark glasses. Smiling. Just smiling. A couple of times he mumbled. Once he laughed. Through it all, David trembled uncontrollably.

Finally, after a long time, the man who was in charge of

the Eternal City silently put the table and chairs back where they had been, as if the place was not covered in blood. Then he left the room.

The room had been empty for hours. Had been most of the day. Ever since . . .

For a long time he and Jerry were afraid to talk. And when they started talking they whispered softly, Jerry in his ear, David turning his head as far as he could. They were too scared to leave their hiding place. But they couldn't stay here forever. The cold was lethal. The muscles in David's back and legs ached from being scrunched up for so long, and his skin felt numb.

Jerry tapped him on the shoulder. "We gotta do something."

"I know."

"What?"

David shook his head. He stared out through the slats at the room where something unbelievable had happened. Where he'd seen a guy get pulled limb from limb. Then dragged back down that tunnel where those things were waiting . . . waiting to . . .

His body spasmed, from the cold, from stark fear. He bit his lip, hard, to keep from making the sound that had been building up in him for hours. Maybe somebody would come and rescue them. Maybe this was all a dream. Maybe his dad was still alive.

# Thirty-Three

By the time Gord returned to Chesborough on Friday, it was nearly seven at night. He had made good time on both the drive up and back. And he'd accomplished more than he'd expected to in Ottawa.

Talk about luck! First thing this morning he caught Peter Ferguson, his old roommate at Laurentian University. Last they'd talked, eight years ago, Pete had been working for the Ministry of the Environment as a lab technician in their testing center.

Arriving in Ottawa just after nine a.m., Gord found the laboratory without much difficulty. He was in the foyer, just about to approach the reception desk, when he thought he recognized Peter standing in front of the elevators. Who else could it be? Skyscraper tall. Old-fashioned wire rims. White lab coat. "Ferg?" Gord called.

The man turned around. His curious glance swept the room like a search-light, settled on Gord, passed him, then shot right back. "Gord?"

"Roomie!"

"I'll be damned!"

They grinned and whooped like teenagers, then awkwardly fell into a bear hug. People passing by smiled.

It took a few minutes of chatting, exchanging brief recent histories, before Pete finally asked, "What the hell're you doing here?"

"Looking for you."

"Mission accomplished."

"It's more complicated than that. I need to get a rush on some soil and water tests."

"What kind of tests?"

"To determine what poisonous substances, if any, are in there."

"Hmmmmmm," Pete said, rubbing his chin. "Normally you'd have to go through regular channels; submit the samples, wait ten days."

"Tried that. How do I break through the red tape?"

"You mean, whose ass do you have to kiss?"

"Exactly."

"Well, the director's about the only guy who can authorize this kind of thing. See, the tests you want are pretty comprehensive. It's not just one area of the lab the samples would go to. We can do a micro bio reading on this floor but, depending on what we find, we may have to send it upstairs."

"What's the director like?"

"Tough son of a bitch," Pete said, soberly. "Doesn't break the rules for just anybody."

"Who *is* this guy, anyways?"

Peter folded his arms, drew himself up to his full, imposing height, and said, "You're look'n at him."

"You're the director?"

Pete's grin widened. "And my ass is just aching to be kissed."

Downtown Ottawa was just a short, five minute walk from the lab. Gord spent the day killing time. He strolled

245

up and down Sparks Street, the outdoor mall and took in an afternoon Van Damme double feature at an almost empty, smoke-filled dive of a theatre. The results would take twenty-four painfully long hours, which meant he'd have to drive like hell to get back to Chesborough the next evening. He called home. No answer. He wished he'd been on top of things, had Claire stay at his place. She needed to know he'd be a bit longer than expected. And, he wanted to talk to her.

Peter and his wife had him over for dinner that night and finally he met Peter again for lunch the following day at a French cafe near the Ministry.

"The soil's okay," Pete said. "More acid than alkaline but not out of line for the area."

"And the water?"

"Damnedest thing." He bit enthusiastically into his *croque monsieur*. "It's polluted, all right. Coliform bacillus."

"If you remember, I failed chemistry. What's that?"

"A bacteria that comes from a variety of sources. Dead fish. Decaying plants and animals. Rotting food. This coliform is the product of feces."

"Feces? Shit? Literally?"

"Well, shit, when it breaks down, produces the coliform bacteria."

"What kind of shit?"

"No way of knowing yet. Got to run some serial tests. Plug into the international data banks. Complicated. It'll take a few weeks."

Gord gave his friend an exasperated look.

"The thing about coliform is, you can identify the type of animal, even the species. But, like I say, it takes time."

"Could it be farm animals?" Gord pushed.

"Doubtful. We've had enough cases of farm animals polluting small town water supplies that I'd recognize most of the common strains. And we're talking about a huge increase of coliform in a short time, and therefore a big increase in waste. There'd have to be a corresponding jump in population. Had a lot of tourists up there lately?"

"We've got a new residential complex, people moved in this spring."

"Eternal City. I read about it. How many residents?"

"A thousand. Fifteen hundred max."

Pete shook his head. "Have to be ten thousand or better. And that complex has its own sewage treatment system, doesn't it?"

"They say."

"Nope, I'd recognize human coliform. By law," Pete explained, "the acceptable limit for coliform in drinking water is zip. In lake water it's one hundred organisms per one hundred milliliters of water for swimming. What's in this sample is way over six thousand per mil. That's dangerously high. Anything over one thousand causes skin rashes, ear, nose and throat infections, gastrointestinal problems. Any unusual outbreaks of illness in Chesborough? Flu symptoms?"

Gord told him what the residents had experienced and about the signs warning against swimming.

"With a count like this, the local health people should have notified us."

"People have been sending samples up here for months."

They looked at each other with the same thought: payoffs. Gord said, "If *people* aren't polluting, and it's not farm animals, what else can be causing it?"

Pete's mood sobered. "To tell the truth, Gord, I want to collect more samples and get further tests run. We need to test three times before the count is verified. But from first glance all I can tell you is that this is very weird." Pete looked pissed. "If I get my hands on the guy who let this by for a few bucks . . . Gord, I don't know if I'm making myself clear, but the reading I got, and again, I'll have to retest to make sure a mistake wasn't made. Well, I wouldn't even want to live near that lake."

"This is beginning to spook me," Gord said. Too many shadows from the edges of his consciousness began solidifying.

Pete scratched his head absently. "Only time I've run across such a dramatic increase in coliform was in Venezuela. A year ago, on a research project, I visited caves inhabited by thousands of vampire bats that had recently migrated to the area. They excrete guano."

"Guano? Isn't that bat shit?"

"Bat shit and bird shit. Unbelievably potent stuff. High voltage ammonia smell. Half a mile south of El Tigre, all the farms store rainwater in big cisterns. Now, rainwater kept in separate storage tanks shouldn't be polluted. The water in those cisterns was almost as high in coliform as what's in this sample. It was the bats flying overhead every night. Their droppings falling into the water."

"Vampire bats? In Chesborough?"

"Probably not. I'm talking about bats indigenous to tropical climates. Yours are the fruit- and insect-eating variety. Mice with wings. And the population's a drop in the bucket compared to what they've got down south. If it *is* bats—and remember, until further tests we don't know—they'd have to blanket the skies to produce this much toxicity. Nobody's reported swarms of bats, have they?"

Gord shook his head. "Although, Pete, all summer we've been hearing these strange calls at night. Never able to spot anything. Gilles Robineau, one of my neighbors—he died last week—got pretty excited. He was a naturalist and thought maybe there was a new species of bird in the area. Maybe they're shitting in the lake."

"Could be. But, again, there would have to be thousands of them. Or," Pete laughed, "they'd have to be bigger than you and me."

As the waiter cleared their plates and served coffee, Gord said, "What's the next step? From your end?"

"Well, my people will take more samples, we send them up for comparison testing. We should be able to identify the species."

"And if not?"

"That's unlikely. But, say we can't. We send samples to a couple of labs in the States and Europe. Among us, we've got samples of just about every known type of coliform bacteria on file. If that doesn't produce anything, we'll put out the word to small labs around the world. Maybe some technician's got something in the store that hasn't made it into the records yet."

"How long?"

"Earliest, say, three weeks. If we can identify it here. If not, your guess is as good as mine."

"Suppose you can identify it. Then what?"

"Either way, the count's so high I've got to write a report and send it upstairs. Then, who knows? Government moves slowly but eventually they'll get on the ass of the local health people. Try to organize your neighbors. The louder they yell, the faster they'll be heard. And, damn it, make sure nobody goes near that water!"

Gord hesitated but decided to go for it. "What if there's a cover-up? At the top?"

Pete studied him. "Still the old radical, aren't you?" he asked, bemused.

"I know I sound paranoid," Gord said, "but megabucks have changed bank accounts up there. I've seen at least one federal notable with a smile on his lips like he'd just had a good time in bed with the corporate sector."

"Doesn't shock me but, hell, I don't know how or why that'd happen, Gord. I can see a local guy greasing his pocket. But Skeleton Lake's not exactly a hot spot of activity, even with that new residential complex. Still, worst case, say somebody owns a new Jaguar. All I can do is slip you a copy of the report—and you better swear it didn't come from me because I'll accuse you of theft. But, hey, you know as well as I do, it wouldn't be the first time information's been leaked to the media."

Gord burned rubber all the way back from Ottawa. He could hardly wait to tell Claire the news. He felt terrific. He'd been amazingly lucky, really, but, hell, he deserved a break for a change. And he'd had several breaks lately, especially Claire.

He turned onto Skeleton Lake Road, immediately surprised to find Bailie's car in his driveway. As he switched off the ignition, a grave-looking Scotsman hurried out the door.

Despite the intense humidity, Gord suddenly felt cold. Bailie's eyes seemed tired. He put a hand on Gord's shoulder.

"Jerry and David are missing. Since this morning. With the canoe. The police, the whole area's out searching."

Deep down, Gord felt something shift. Every other concern receded. "What happened? Where's Claire?"

"She's gone over to see Varik. And that's not all. The Gwinski boy murdered his parents. Claire found them. Come inside. You could use a whiskey."

Gord checked his watch. Seven-thirty. An hour, maybe an hour and a half before darkness set in. He followed Bailie inside, but not for a drink. He went to his bedroom and got the 12-gauge shotgun from his closet. Bailie stood in the doorway silently, watching him rummage in his dresser for the box of shells. He loaded five shells into the shotgun and crammed his pockets with the rest of the ammunition.

As he boarded the *Devil-May-Care*, Gord checked the sky. The sun would set within the hour. He'd better hurry.

# Thirty-Four

David finally put into words what they both had been thinking—"Man, we gotta chance it."

Jerry's teeth knocked together. "Yeah. I know it too."

But David was reluctant to leave. The air shaft felt safe; the outside didn't. Still, they'd better escape while they had the chance.

He pushed out the grate. "Shit!" he said, as it slipped from his grasp and hit the carpet with a thud. "Fingers are numb," he whispered. They waited. Nobody came running into the room.

David eased out of the opening and jumped down to the floor as quietly as possible. Jerry followed fast. Both of them could hardly stand. Pain cut through David's cramped thigh muscles. "Let's move around, get the circulation going again. Ow, ow, ow!" David sucked in air through his teeth. He winced, limping as he tried to walk.

"Pain's a good sign," Jerry reassured him, his face showing what he felt. "Everything's thawing out."

The pain cutting through David's calves was bad, but getting away from the relentless icy wind in the shaft was worth anything. The deep cold in his bones began to subside but he still shivered. He alternated rubbing his arms and kneading his locked leg muscles.

The room looked pretty much the way it had when they'd run in here with Sergeant Williams. Furniture in place. Flowers in vases. The crazy paintings hanging where they were. The big difference—blood. Smeared on the wall right beneath the shaft. Embedded in the carpet. A trail to the door leading to the corridor. But, if you could just *pretend* the blood wasn't there, Jerry thought. Or, if you could pretend you didn't know how it got there . . .

"Locked," Jerry whispered. He'd just tried the door to the restaurant.

"How do we get out?" David whispered back, afraid he already knew the answer. He looked at his watch. "What time's the sun set?"

"Don't know. Nine, maybe."

"Those things were going to sleep when we came in." His voice sounded unnaturally high in his ears.

"You think they sleep during the day?"

"Maybe."

"Varik said they're vampires. Vampires sleep at—"

"That guy's hard drive crashed!" David said. "Anyways, it doesn't matter what they are. We either freeze or starve to death, or they find us. We gotta chance it."

"Okay. Let's get going."

Jerry opened the unlocked tunnel door a crack. The brightly-lit white light of the corridor blinded him after the hours of darkness in the air shaft. Along the floor were large smears of dried blood that he refused to look at it. "Man, I do not want to go in here."

But he went first, David on his heels. Within a minute or two the white corridor ended and they entered darkness. Soon they were moving along the tunnel by feel, fingertips scraping the jagged rock wall one second then slipping through slime the next.

The tunnel grew colder. David's eyes adjusted to the dark. They moved faster. Suddenly he became aware of sounds. Frightened, he grabbed Jerry's shirt and they stopped. "Listen!"

"Listen. Listen. Listen . . ."

"Just echoes," Jerry said.

"Echoes. Echoes. Echoes . . ."

They stood perfectly still, hardly breathing, the silence unnerving. Up ahead water dripped.

Eventually they reached the fork. One route led downward, back into the bowels of the island where the vampire things were. The way they'd come in. The other route turned left.

"Where do you think this goes?" Jerry whispered.

"Maybe nowhere."

"I say we try it."

"Agreed."

They turned left, David in the lead this time. Eventually they came to another lighted corridor with another door at the end.

David cautiously pushed down on the metal bar and eased open the door a crack. He peered in.

Rows of hospital beds. Old people lying in them. Two of the creatures were in there and David panicked and almost slammed the door shut. But he managed to control himself. Just long enough to see one of them pick up a large bag of blood and drink.

From somewhere he had the presence of mind to slowly and quietly close the door. He paused for a moment, long enough for his body to spasm.

"What?" Jerry whispered.

David put a finger to his lips and pulled Jerry down the corridor and stopped just before the darkness. He turned.

His face must have been a mask of terror because Jerry's eyes widened in horror. "You're scaring me, man. What was in there?"

David just shook his head, unable to put it all together. "Them." He didn't say anything more to Jerry, especially that he didn't believe they'd get out alive.

# Thirty-Five

The second he spotted Claire with Varik on the Eternal City's dock, Gord's blood began to boil. When Claire noticed him, she waved. He felt Varik's eyes, sharp as the sight of a gun, targeting him.

He maneuvered the boat alongside the pier and threw a waiting dockhand a line, then jumped out. Claire ran into his arms.

Gord buried his face in her hair and let himself feel her body tremble against his for a moment. "Thank God you're back," she whispered. "They were gone when I woke up," she tried to explain, lifting a tear-coated face.

"I know, I know," he said gently. "Bailie told me everything."

"I'll never forgive myself if—"

"We'll find them."

Varik stood motionless off to the side, a voyeur in the requisite sunglasses. Gord wondered if he was imagining it, but the man looked odder than usual. Overnight his face had lost its rigid intensity. When he lifted a hand, it quivered. Rather than projecting control, he looked barely able to hold on.

No, Gord decided, it wasn't his imagination. The head of Eternal City had shipwrecked. His crisp suit was rumpled. His hair disheveled. Lines and puffy skin made up the once-ageless face, as if whatever held the skin taut had suddenly given way and everything collapsed into pre-plastic surgery slackness.

"Seen or heard anything?" Gord asked him.

Varik shook his head.

"They could have snuck past security and gotten into the City."

"He's checked," Claire said. "So did Sergeant Atkins. They haven't come here. Oh, Gord, what if Earl hurt them?"

He didn't want to talk in front of Varik. "We better head home. Bailie told me Atkins has organized a group of volunteers to search the woods."

Varik hadn't moved much while they were there talking. Suddenly, his arm jerked up. "The papers, Claire. You haven't signed them."

"Later," Gord said, pulling her across the dock and onto the *Devil-May-Care*. Still rooted to the spot, arm extended, Varik seemed to be watching them turn around in the harbor. Finally, as they accelerated, Gord saw him turn and walk back towards the City airlock. Stiff-legged, arms swinging out-of-sync by his sides, his jerky gait reminding Gord of a puppet. "Is he on drugs or what?" he asked Claire.

"He's acting strangely," she said, "but not at all aware of it."

"Do you think he knows where the kids are?"

She gave him a penetrating look. "Yesterday I'd have called you paranoid to suggest that."

"And now?"

She glanced away. "I'm not sure anymore. All I know is I have a feeling they're here, on the island. Something Earl said to me."

"Let's take a quick run around the island before it gets too dark to see," he suggested, altering course.

Claire stood at the wheel beside him, worried eyes scanning the shoreline. The sun vanished quickly, leaving behind a sky of crimson tendrils. A half hour more and even this light would fade to nothing.

"I want to check the back of the island," he told her.

"The police boat checked the lake, but let's look again."

"What about the cave? The kids were talking about it last week and Jerry's tried to get me over here several times."

"I mentioned that to Atkins," she shouted. "Varik told him the cave's flooded. The kids wouldn't be able to get in."

"Did Atkins check it out?"

"I don't know."

The *Devil-May-Care* slowed. Gord cut the engine and let the boat drift in close to the concrete barrier. They could see over it to the sluice gate beyond. They could *just* see over the gate—the water level was low; the cave entrance was not submerged. "I'm going in there."

"I'll go with you."

"We've got to hurry." Gord tucked the bulky waterproof flashlight into the waistband of his shorts. He pulled the *Devil-May-Care* close to the barrier, until concrete scraped the sides.

"What's that awful smell?" Claire wrinkled her nose as Gord heaved her up to stand on the railing. She grasped the top of the barrier and tumbled over into the water. Gord followed immediately.

He gave her a boost and she went over the gate—he heard her splash down onto the watery bank. He followed right behind.

He crouched low and entered the black mouth of the cave, using the powerful flashlight beam; they could see very little. "This is definitely where the stink originates!"

"I can't believe David would go in here."

"Knowing Jerry, it wouldn't surprise me." The powerful white beam led them into the intensifying smell. It filled Gord's sinuses and caught him at the back of the throat, making him want to gag. He felt along the cool slimy walls of the tunnel. This is a sewer, he realized, likely the source of the lake's pollution.

Eventually the tunnel opened up into a huge cavern the size of two Olympic swimming pools, and at least they could stand up straight. Green crystals embedded in the walls cast a low illumination. He switched off the flashlight and they could still see.

"Gord!" Claire whispered, touching his hand. "What are those?"

"What?" Then he saw them. The myriad of pale shadows squirming along the walls like huge insect larva. Clinging. "Jesus," he breathed. Large ones. Small ones. All sizes. Hanging. Twitching. Stretching.

"Are they bats?" she asked.

"Don't know, but certain people in Ottawa will be extremely interested."

He switched on the flashlight again, and played it around the cave. The beam caught one creature in the face. Its sharp, angular features gave it a feral look. The eyes blinked open briefly. Pure white. Were they blind? It twisted away from the beam.

He turned the flashlight to the ceiling. More of them. Hundreds. Shuffling. Jerking. Definitely waking.

The chamber reminded him of the body of a huge spider, with tunnels branching out like legs. The belly was a deep pit, obviously the origin of the powerful stench. He moved cautiously forward to the edge of the ledge and looked down.

Below, a pool full of . . . full of . . .

Caught in the beam of his light were bones. More bones than he'd ever seen in one place. All types, in various stages of decomposition. When he saw the skull and jaw bone of a dog, with patches of red fur attached . . . No! It couldn't be. Mouche! A little groan escaped his lips.

Claire grabbed his hand and moved the light to the left. Clearly visible were the remains of a body. A man. Only some of the features had been eaten away. It took him a moment to identify the hair, the build.

"Sergeant Williams," Claire whispered.

"Mom!" The sound echoed across the cavern. Instinctively Gord jerked the flashlight in the direction of the voice. Two terrified faces came into view.

"David!" Claire screamed. She was already running around the ledge.

About to follow, Gord heard a hiss to his left. He swung the beam along the walls. "No! Claire! Don't!" he yelled. Too late.

The creature had spread its wings. Feathers stretched from the knees. The span was incredible, at least six feet. Quickly Gord crisscrossed the walls with light. Others had their white eyes wide open. He flashed back to the first one. Suddenly it dove towards Claire.

"Hey!" he yelled, holding the light on its hideous face, hoping to blind or at least distract the thing. The humanoid mouth opened. Two rows of jagged teeth, strings of saliva connecting them, snapped angrily in his direction. The creature hovered in mid-air like a bee.

He could see its body clearly now. Part human, part . . .

other. Male. Anatomically correct. But there were features that belonged to an alien species. But where on earth had he seen that face before? A snapshot clicked into memory. That white hair, perfectly coiffed, body encased in an expensive summer suit, coat draped over shoulders to obscure certain non-human features. Of course, the party! He shook his head in disbelief and, for a moment, felt stunned by this clever freak of nature that could span two worlds.

With two lightning flaps of its wings, it glided towards him, hands that resembled his own reaching out. Fingernails, no talons, aimed at his throat, ready to tear him to pieces.

Gord stooped and felt for a rock but came up with only a handful of pebbles. He hurled them at the thing swooping in on him and, at the same time, aimed the flashlight into those dead white eyes. It swerved to the right, screeching in pain and outrage.

"I've got them!" Claire yelled. "We're coming." Her voice echoed around the chamber.

The creature turned back to him. Gord found a rock the size of a baseball and pitched it. The bat-thing veered again, shrieking.

*SKREEE! SKREEE!* The cry stabbed into Gord's eardrums. "Hurry!" he called to Claire.

Suddenly the creature turned and headed their way. They stopped dead. "We can get out this way!" David shouted. "Into the City!"

"Go!" Gord called back across the chasm. "I'll find you!"

As he watched the kids and Claire disappear down a dark tunnel, he heaved another rock at the creature. It soared around the cavern as if considering who to pursue.

Gord retreated backwards to the corridor he'd entered by. He aimed a volley of rocks. "Eat these, freak!" That got its attention.

The thing zeroed in on him, eyes blazing white fire. Gord turned and ran.

Outside, he clambered over the gate and clumsily over the barrier. He had to swim to the *Devil-May-Care*, relieved when finally he climbed the rope steps to the deck. The engine kicked over. Stalled. Kicked over again. Caught. "Thank you *God!*"

Fierce purple streaked the sky. Water the same color churned white froth at the stern as the vessel backed away. Gord kept his eyes glued to the cave entrance. He hoped the thing hadn't taken after Claire and the kids instead of him. Where the hell *was* it?

He left the wheel to get the shotgun and cracked the barrel to check that it was loaded, then propped the gun against the railing within reach.

Above, a sound. A loose sail in the wind. He sensed movement.

*skree! skree! skrEEE! SKREEE! SKREEEEEEEEE!*

It glanced off his left shoulder, sending him reeling. He grunted, the wind knocked from his lungs, but regained his footing.

The shotgun had been knocked over and slid across the deck. He started for it. Suddenly he was slammed sideways. His forehead crashed into the rail. He toppled and landed on the deck again, on his back. His shoulder stung and he risked a glance at it. Blood. Three or four razor blade cuts. Deep as hell.

High in the sky he saw a pale, hawk-like shadow circling. He had to get to that shotgun!

Gord climbed to his feet and turned. Earl Gwinski stood before the cabin door, pointing the shotgun barrel at Gord's chest. "It's gonna be me this time, not *you!*" he screamed.

Before Gord could say or do anything, a loud *SKREEE* forced his glance skyward. The thing plummeted. Spiraling down, straight down. A rainbow of colors.

The mesmerizing movement of otherworldly wings.

A familiar voice. *Gord!* Kind. Firm. Strong.

He couldn't tell where the voice came from, only that he recognized it immediately. His dad.

*You were wrong, son. You shouldn't have left me alone.*

Gord felt his head nodding in agreement.

*But I forgive you. I love you.*

Pain seared his heart. The dark knowledge opened up sadness and guilt. He had left his father all alone to die but his father had *known*.

*Gord. Son! I miss you.*

"Dad? Where are you?"

The form shimmered in the black sky. It became a recognizable face. The familiar square jaw. Sandy hair and eyebrows. Eyes crinkled at the corners. Warm eyes that looked down at him with affection. With hopelessness. Eyes that had stared blankly into his own when he found his dad dead. Heart attack, the doctor said. But Gord knew it was suicide. His dad had just stopped taking the nitroglycerine pills. Grief overwhelmed him. Then. Now.

An ear shattering blast shot him back to reality. He felt startled, yanked out of a dream. His father's face still hovered above him, but now new images appeared, superimposing themselves over those beloved features: The cave. The pit. Mouche's skeleton. Williams—what remained of him. Jerry and David. Claire!

"You said I was next!" Earl, sobbing, face turned to the

sky, fell onto his knees. "You can't take him. It's gotta be me this time."

Gord looked up. His father's face dispersed like a cloud. Behind it loomed another face, a grotesque parody of human features. Yet Gord still felt his dad's presence. Calling. Reaching for him. Begging Gord to join him in death.

The thing dropped to striking distance. But it had come for Earl, not him. The creature's head rammed into the boy's crotch. At first Gord thought only fabric that had been ripped away. Until he saw the blood. Gushing. He looked up. Earl's genitals caught in that hideous maw!

An insane smile spread across Earl's face. His crazed eyes leaked tears. He opened his arms wide and the creature swooped low, claws digging deep under the collar bone. It spun as if to show Gord its grotesque face—razor fangs chomped bloody flesh.

Earl's features had become beatific. Tears coated his cheeks, giving them a translucent quality. He screamed the words "Yes, FATHER, take me! Thy will be done!" over and over.

As the creature lifted Earl into the sky, the shotgun slipped from his grasp. Gord dove for it.

He grabbed onto the trigger and fired the four remaining shells, then broke the barrel and reloaded. His finger hugged the trigger again. The blasts deafened him. The butt slammed against his injured shoulder.

The creature flew backwards through the air. It hovered, wobbled, then spun out of control, all the while clutching Earl's writhing body. It ascended a little, then hurtled down fast, splashing into the lake, taking Earl with it.

Gord grabbed the rail to steady himself. His shoulder blazed as if it had been attacked by a swarm of wasps. The pain helped him focus. Finally, he stumbled across the deck and looked down into the water.

Murky lake. Light too dim to see much. His legs threatened to buckle. Where the hell was it?

The thing surfaced, Earl nowhere in sight, and Gord got it in the shotgun's sight. One wing flapped desperately; the shotgun pellet must have hit the bone or cartilage or whatever was in there, and the thing couldn't lift off. Gord watched it sink, surface, and sink again. A death struggle. A sudden realization swept over him that the thing was drowning. Instead of being elated, Gord felt a powerful sadness well up.

He checked the sky, automatically loading the 12-gauge to full capacity. No image of his father hovered above. But the despair of loss and guilt clung to him.

What had just happened made no sense. All he knew for certain was that he had to get into the City, and fast. If he could ram the barrier and the gate, he could flood the cave. Drown the newborns for sure. Maybe all the others. *If* the boat could do it without breaking apart.

But what if that trapped Claire and the kids? He hoped David was right about there being a route from the cave into the City. But if they could get out through the City, why were they in the cave? And if Claire, Jerry and David could get out that way, so could these creatures.

Gord stared at the now translucent dome looming before him. The back of a row of townhouses stood fifty yards inside. The cave had to connect to the City. No doubt about it. And he also had no doubts Varik knew the route.

He thrust the engine into forward. The *Devil-May-Care* circled, then gained speed. The sweep created a wake that he cut across. He held the wheel steady and braced himself. The boat headed straight for the concrete barrier and hit it with a loud crash. It took another two rams before the bow crashed through to the sluice gate. Then, WOMP! His body slammed into the wheel. The boat shuddered and stopped, the engine grinding rough and furious, about to give it up.

The vessel lay wedged in the cave opening. The sluice gate was down, the concrete a kind of vice holding the *Devil-May-Care* in place. Gord thrust the engine into reverse. Metal shrieked. Water gurgled and poured past the hull into the cave, rising quickly. The entrance swallowed wave after wave until it was completely submerged.

He backed up the damaged boat with great difficulty, and turned her. The throttle read *Full Speed* but the old girl barely moved at quarter speed. The hull had taken a few hits, and water flooded the deck. She would go down soon. He had to get out of here, fast. But the worse part was, his dad's voice continued to flood his brain, urging him to stop. Forever.

# Thirty-Six

David and Jerry fled through the tunnel and Claire followed them blindly, running, stumbling in the dark, falling onto the slimy, smelly floor and getting up to run faster.

The wild cries of the creatures dimmed as she ran, but not by much.

By the time they reached a lighted corridor, her legs felt leaden and it was as though she moved in slow motion through a dream.

David hit the crashbar and slammed through. Jerry, then Claire. Out of breath, the boys leaned their backs against the door as if blocking it. Claire doubled over, hands on her knees, gulping oxygen. "Where are we?" she gasped.

David moved across the room and tried the other door. "Still locked. It goes to the restaurant."

"Help me with this," she said, struggling to drag the massive walnut table across the room.

"It won't make any difference," Jerry said. "It doesn't stop them at all." Still, they helped her push it against the corridor door.

"Mom, what're we gonna do?" David asked.

She looked around the room. There was no place to hide. Surely someone would be in the restaurant. Maybe they could just bang on the door until . . . But then it hit her. There was no way those things could live under the Eternal City without people knowing about them. Without Varik knowing, she thought bitterly.

"It wore Aunt Lillian's necklace," David said.

"What?"

"One of the vampires had Lillian's amethyst around his neck," Jerry explained.

"Oh no!" Claire said softly. The implications hit direct and horrible, but there was no time to dwell on them now. She had to protect the children. But how?

David said, "They killed Sergeant Williams, ripped and tore him apart."

"Oh, honey," she said, pulling her son close.

"They dragged him out. Back there," Jerry added. Claire pulled him in too.

"How did you two get away?"

"We hid. In the air conditioning." Jerry pointed to the duct in the wall.

"Sergeant Williams made us go up there." David told her. "But he couldn't fit."

"I want you kids to go back up there."

"Mom, no!"

"It's freezing, Mrs. Mowatt," Jerry said. "And you can't fit."

"I need you hidden and safe. I have to know you're safe before I do anything. I'll get Varik to let me out of here."

"Williams tried that!" David's voice was despairing.

"I have a relationship with Varik. I don't think he'll hurt me. At least I can buy some time, maybe get away. And don't forget, Gord will be back with help soon."

"If he's okay," Jerry said.

"He has to be, Jerry. You have to believe that."

"Mom, this isn't gonna work . . ." David said.

She cut him off. "This is the way it has to be. I love you both. Trust me."

Claire helped them up into the air shaft and plugged the grate back into the opening. Then she took a deep breath and pounded on the door with both fists.

Without warning, the door burst open. Three men with guns pushed in. She could see five more outside.

Before they accused her of anything, Claire said, "Thank God you're here. I got locked in. I'm looking for my children."

"Gentlemen," a familiar voice came through the door, followed by the man.

"Varik!" said Claire. "Thank God you came." She rushed to him and took his hands in hers.

His face was impassive, yet still pale as a corpse. She realized he'd regained some equilibrium, despite the still-rumpled suit. She didn't know if any of it was good or bad news.

"Claire," he said gently. Icy fingers grasped hers. With a flick of the hand he dismissed the soldiers. When they closed the door he turned to her. In the back of her mind she held the thought that the door wasn't locked now.

"What are you doing here?" he asked. He seemed glad to see her, but slightly wary.

"Gord took me home and I brought a boat out because I wanted to check the island's shoreline. I found a cave and went in . . ." Claire let the sentence trail.

His face betrayed nothing. Again, she couldn't tell whether that meant he would side with her, or not. "My children. I can't find my children."

"Yes," he said. "We've *all* been looking for them." A puzzled expression crossed his face. "But I'd been informed you found the children. Is that true, Claire?"

"No. I came through the cave but they weren't there."

"*They* let you through?" he mused, more to himself than to her. The "they" obviously referred to those animals hanging from the cavern walls. So he did know about them. A chill raced up her spine and she struggled to not let the reaction show on her face.

"Why don't we go into the restaurant," she said. "Maybe we can have some wine."

He ignored her for a moment but then, for no apparent reason, grinned as though pleased. "Claire, there's something I want to share with you. About my life here. My plans. For us."

Startled, she wondered if the man was going to propose.

"I've told you how I built this city. My financial genius enabled me to create an empire. But there's more to the Eternal Cities than you know. Than you can imagine."

Or want to, she thought.

"Oh, Claire, I have plans!" He removed his glasses and once again pale blue eyes gazed into her own. The pupils were dilated. He wasn't talking to her, that was clear. She felt that same pull, as though a connection existed that, if she could plug into it, would make sense of all this.

"You'll join me," he said. "We'll live together. All of us."

An hour ago, Varik had been teetering at the brink of insanity. Now, Claire realized, he had lost his balance.

"It's for the greater good," he was saying. "The two of us. Forever. With the others, naturally."

"Who, exactly, are the others?"

"The charter members, of course," he said matter-of-factly. "You saw for yourself. I've already begun the change, as you can no doubt tell from my eyes."

He thinks he's becoming one of them, she thought.

"A painless process," he explained, his fingers playing with the sunglasses. "They require a single vial each, twice weekly. The City provides many donors but it is the exchange of blood that initiates the bond. I am their child, their creation. As you will be." His eyes misted. "We'll belong to each other. You. Me. Them. And we will never die."

His mood had dissolved into soppy sentiment. Claire decided to go with it. Keep him talking. Wait for an opening.

"The charter members," she ventured. "They're amazing, aren't they?"

His eyes glazed over, as if he'd retreated to a private memory, both fascinating and horrifying. His features took on the soft dreamy quality of a child. "They're like nothing I've seen before. Superhuman strength. The grace of birds. The wisdom of the brightest our species has produced. They live forever and, they look so much like you and me they can pass for human."

"How did you meet them?"

"It was nothing short of a miracle. I stumbled on them by accident, in the rain forests of Brazil five years ago, researching an investment. You see, that's one of their homes—in the caves, among the trees up in the highest mountains. But with the forests being clear cut, they were pushed further and further back until there was nothing left. Naturally they distrust humans. Look what we've done to them. And our kind, we fear them like peasants terrified of vampires. But they're children of nature, the same as you and me."

"Let's go into the restaurant and you can tell me how you made contact with them." The glassy gleam in his eyes frightened her. It reminded her of the way Earl looked.

"I respected their powers. You see, with their intelli-

271

gence, they master languages easily, but not oral expression. They prefer to communicate mentally. Telepathically, if you will. They understood my intentions immediately and trusted me, just as I trusted them. When I learned of their difficulty, their need for security, for a healthy food source, I came up with the idea for the Cities. It benefits both species. And they are grateful. They're willing to create others. Myself, for example. And you."

Varik leaned forward, right into her face. "They love, too, Claire. Oh yes, they have much love to give. Why, only today, this morning with Sergeant Williams . . ."

His pale face drained of the remaining color and his eyes floated towards the top of his head. "If only you could have been here," he whispered, his tone rising. Tears spilled over his lower eyelids.

Clearly he was horrified, and repressing that in favor of thinking what had happened to Williams was a good thing. Claire realized he must have watched them murder Williams. He's mad, or under their spell, she thought, aware of her body shaking. But either way, it didn't matter. She had to get out and find help and she had to do it now.

In an instant, even before the noise at the corridor door, she felt them coming. Fluttering sounds. A squawk. Another squawk.

Before she could move toward the restaurant door, the corridor door imploded. Two winged figures glided into the room like demon angels straight from hell.

Claire screamed and instinctively jumped behind Varik. He still held one of her wrists and grasped it so tightly she couldn't break away. His body shook. One of the creatures floated to a halt in front of Varik. The thing was male—the genitals made that clear. Over six feet tall. White, rage-distorted face. And lying in the hollow of its throat like a perverse trophy was Lillian's necklace. It was all Claire could do to control her screaming.

"My friends," Varik said.

The creature made a sound, harsh, angry. One arm raised and the wingspan stretched to the ceiling.

Varik released Claire to open his arms in greeting.

Claire dove for the restaurant door and yanked it open.

"Mom!" David shrieked, "look out!"

# Thirty-Seven

Through the slots of the grate David watched them take Varik. They dug their talons deep into him. Ripping. Slashing. In seconds they brought him down. Dragged him out into the corridor, the way they did Sergeant Williams. And the whole time Varik just grinned.

Behind David, Jerry shivered. He couldn't see anything, but David saw it all. And he couldn't stop looking. Yesterday, Williams had been screaming and trying to fight them off. But Mr. Varik didn't struggle. It's like he *wanted* them to kill him.

His mom got out the door. He hoped she'd be okay. That those guys with the guns wouldn't hurt her. He hoped she could get help.

He heard a noise. They were coming back. Not the same ones, others. A dozen streamed through the room. Vacant white eyes glistening. Needle-sharp teeth.

They poured into the room and through the other door and into the restaurant. He heard screams. And gunfire. But mostly screams.

His mom must have gotten out by now. She had to. Because if she didn't . . . if she didn't . . .

He wasn't going to go there. No! He had other things to

think about. Like the creature, the one wearing Aunt Lillian's amethyst, that returned and had just turned cold white eyes in his direction.

# Thirty-Eight

BROTHER. FATHER. GOD.
SISTER. MOTHER. ETERNAL LOVER.

Varik stretched his arms out. "Let me join with you," he begged, and trembled.

This time was for him. Just him. THEY told him this wordlessly, in the way of THEIR kind, now his kind.

Arms surrounded him. Hands clung to him, pressing past skin, beyond muscle, reaching into his bones. "Yes, yes!" he cried at the pain of this caress, knowing that between them there would soon be no separation.

A small voice called "Claire," and, momentarily, THEY paused. "Please," he cried openly now, afraid of being abandoned, that THEY would initiate another as THEY had initiated Williams instead of him. The memory of past abandonment engulfed Varik.

THEIR eyes, white, unspoiled life itself, returned to renew him. Tears of joy, of release. His body shook.

THE MOTHER and FATHER led him down past the light that scorched his eyes, the light he knew must burn THEIRS—he knew everything about THEM—and into the blessed darkness. Moving easily, they flew together, the cool night air gently slapping his cheeks to keep him alert. The scent of flowers filled his body.

Love. Yes, at last he understood love.

And the room he had dreamed about. With a million lights. Or were they stars? The floor a black ocean, everlasting. And floating in that obsidian sea were tiny images, so many, all of mankind like grains of sand.

Tonight THEY were few in number and absently he wondered where were the others. Where was the young male? He was surprised and delighted to see two children. He searched the crowd of faces among the stars, expecting to find Claire's son and the Roberts boy among them.

Of course THEY were ravenous, especially these young. It was only natural. Everything about them was so natural.

Suddenly he felt exhausted. THE MOTHER understood. SHE knew him so well. HER eyes caught his. HER face, sternly loving.

*Do not struggle.*

Yes, struggle would change his body chemistry. SHE pressed him to the cool, wet floor that reminded him of HER moist embrace. Although he shivered, he tore off his clothes and lay naked before them. Naked. Like them. Offering himself.

*To the Greater Good.* THE FATHER commanded and HE must be obeyed.

One by one they came to honor him, enveloping him in soft white bodies. Sweet cherub faces. Kisses sharp and many. Forever. And above him, watching, pleased, THE MOTHER and THE FATHER, their faces so human, blessed him. Forever.

# Thirty-Nine

The *Devil-May-Care* barely cut a wide turn around the island. The boat was three-quarters submerged, the motor sputtering as the life drained out of it.

The Eternal City's harbor blazed with light. Sporadic shouts echoed across the water. Gord heard a siren wail from somewhere inside the City.

Departing craft, frantically leaving the City, blocked his battered boat. Gord wove in and out of the traffic, maneuvering to port, mooring behind the OPP launch. He leapt onto the dock as she went down.

A mob of people surrounded Brenda and Sullivan, both of whom looked frightened.

Bailie, Sergeant Atkins of the OPP, and five or six officers were pushing their way to the Eternal City officials. Atkins spotted Gord.

"Hold on, Roberts!" he yelled, eyeing the sinking remains of Gord's boat, then the shotgun he cradled. "Things are a little out of hand here," he said, reversing course. When he reached Gord he held out a hand. "Maybe you better toss me that weapon."

"I need it," Gord said, tight-lipped. He skirted Atkins and elbowed his way towards Brenda, Atkins on his heels.

"Something's loose in this city!" a woman shouted, her

voice shrill and ragged, "and Nirvana's covering it up!"

"My son, Claire's son, and Claire are in there," Gord said loudly, coming face-to-face with Brenda. He pointed the shotgun at the airlock.

"Impossible," she said.

"Quit lying!" Gord snapped. "This place is falling around your ears and you're still pretending nothing's going on."

"Nothing *is* going on." Her eyes sparkled, unnaturally bright.

Gord appealed to Atkins. "Ask her why everybody's leaving. Ask *them*, for chrissakes!" He nodded to the crowd.

Sullivan's hands went up in a placating gesture. "There seems to be some animal inside the perimeter. Harmless, I'm sure. People are upset. Naturally. City security is looking into it. And, of course, I understand your feelings about your son, Mr. Roberts, but I assure you, he's not in here. Frankly, you're just adding fuel to the fire."

"I don't have time to argue," Gord shouted. He turned to Atkins. "Look, I was just in the caves under the City. Williams is dead."

"Dead?" Atkins said, shocked. "How?"

"Killed. By whatever's loose in the City."

Brenda's hand fluttered up to her mouth. Her face lost its color.

"Claire's got the kids. They're being chased by . . . by . . . creatures with wings." As he said the words he saw their faces change.

"I fought with one," he tried again. "That's how I hurt my shoulder. Creatures, like birds or bats. Huge. And they look almost human."

No use. At best he sounded like a character in a "B" movie. They obviously thought he had lost it.

There was no time to waste in persuasion. He lifted the shotgun and pointed it at Brenda.

"Put down the gun," Atkins said.

"Gord, take it easy!" Bailie said.

"I'm going in for Claire and the kids and no one's going to interfere. Back up. All of you. Not you, Brenda. Stay where you are."

Fear swamped her face. "You can't—"

"Where does the cave exit to?"

"I assure you I don't—"

Gord slowly lifted the barrel and pointed it at her face. "No more corporate bullshit!"

"Gord . . ." Bailie pleaded.

"Roberts," Atkins warned, "just put the gun down now, before you're sorry."

"No one's believed me about a lot of things around here," he said, addressing Brenda. "Maybe you'll believe this. If I don't hear where that cave exits within sixty seconds, this dock will be painted with your brains."

The second-in-command of Eternal City stood paralyzed, a child caught in a lie.

"Look in my eyes and tell me if I'm bluffing."

Brenda looked like she was going to call his bluff.

"Ah, what the hell . . ." He cocked the hammer.

"No, please! Don't kill her!" It wasn't Brenda but Sullivan who said it.

"Don't tell him anything!" Brenda ordered.

"There are two exits," Sullivan stammered. "The Clinic and the restaurant."

Gord lowered the shotgun a little, and glanced at Atkins. "I'm going in. Sullivan's coming with me."

"We'll all come with you," Atkins said.

"I don't know what these things are, but they're big. And

280

they kill. You better radio for help."

Once through the airlock, they commandeered three carts and proceeded deep into the heart of the Eternal City. The wail of the siren grew louder. People were running as if for their lives. A man and woman in matching striped pajamas stumbled by.

Gord heard a rumbling and looked up.

A pencil-thin crack of deep purple sky appeared down the center of the roof as if it were the first cut of a surgeon's scalpel. One of the dome's panels was slowly retracting. He figured the siren probably had something to do with that.

Just as they reached the drawbridge, a figure raced from the restaurant doorway.

Claire! Alone.

Gord braked and jumped out. Within seconds, a stampede of yelling men with guns streamed out behind and followed her across the drawbridge. At first he thought they were chasing her, but then realized they were running away too.

Claire's face was twisted hysteria. She didn't notice him and he grabbed her as she ran by. "Claire!" For a moment she fought him, her eyes wild. She stared for long moments, uncomprehending.

"It's me!"

She stopped struggling as recognition washed over her. "The kids!" she gasped. "They're trapped. Those things are streaming through the tunnel. I don't know how many. They have Varik."

"Varik?" Brenda said.

"Where are the kids?"

"In an air shaft. A room inside the restaurant."

A loud shriek made them turn. A long figure materialized in the restaurant doorway. At first glance, human. At second glance . . .

"Holy shit!" Atkins muttered.

Translucent wings lifted and fell. The creature held something in its mouth. Ripped, human flesh. Bloody meat.

Gord raised the shotgun and fired.

*SKREEEEEEEE! SKREEEEEEEE!* The thing dropped what it held and danced sideways like a crab to the edge of the drawbridge. It teetered. Wings fluttered furiously for a moment then relaxed at its side. Gord fired again. The creature had an uncanny ability to dodge bullets, as if it knew where they would go! How could that be?

A volley of bullets split the air as Atkins and his men fired. The creature stumbled left, then right. But when the pungent smoke cleared, incredibly, it was still standing.

"You'd need an elephant gun to pierce its hide," Atkins said.

The huge wings began to unfurl. The legs took several odd steps forward. The creature lifted off the ground. It flew high above the restaurant, bullets firing, out of sync by one second.

Silently they watched it circle one of the turrets. Suddenly it dropped downward.

"Brenda, no!" Sullivan yelled.

Before anybody could stop her, Brenda had run onto the bridge. She stopped in the middle, arms flung wide in receptivity. A look of devotion painted her face. Rapture mixed with madness.

Sullivan started after her but Atkins held him back.

Arms and eyes still raised to the heavens, Brenda fell to her knees as if offering a pleading embrace to the thing that descended. The creature's speed increased as it neared.

Guns fired, but it was out of range, and when it got

within the scope of what the guns could hit again, it seemed to anticipate the bullets.

Brenda was snatched up into the air. Her scarlet hair streamed in the wake of current created by flight. The look of bliss embedded in her features had shifted to confusion and terror, but she made no effort to resist. The creature bent its face as if to kiss her; they were too far away to see what was really happening.

Horrified, Gord and the others watched as, moments later, her body, limp, fell from the sky. It hit the moat with a splash.

Silence filled the air, until Gord suddenly said, "They can't swim! The one I shot drowned. If we could get it into the moat—"

"Where'd you shoot it?" Atkins asked.

"Where? I don't know. The wing, I think."

Atkins lifted his rifle and aimed carefully. He fired four shots: wide of the mark, dead on, wide, dead on. One hit a vulnerable spot. The right wing collapsed. The thing dropped fifteen yards in a second. It glided to the draw-bridge on one wing and landed shakily.

It raged, hissing and clawing. All traces of humanity had vanished from its features. Wings down, the injured one protected, it stumbled to the center of the bridge, thirty yards from them.

Gord, Claire and the others backed away, but not far enough that Gord couldn't see clearly what was hanging around its throat. An emotion he did not have time to identify swept him. He raised his shotgun and fired, and ran.

"Hold your fire!" Atkins ordered again.

As Gord raced across the bridge he reloaded, then fired again. Blood still flowed from the injured wing but Gord knew he hadn't inflicted further damage. The thing was too smart, too anticipatory. And that wasn't Gord's goal. As he neared the thing, he flipped the shotgun and used the butt to whack upward at its temple. The features turned astonished. Then murderous. Gord knew better than to look in its eyes.

He slammed the butt into the side of its head again and again until he'd knocked it off balance. It catapulted off the bridge and plunged into the moat.

Atkins was already by his side. Gord heard the others running across the wooden planks. They watched the creature flounder on the surface. Gord felt the pull of those eyes as images of his father infiltrated his brain. "Don't look in its eyes," he said, fighting to keep his mind under his own control. The thing struggled, swallowing water. A flicker of resignation crossed its face just before it sank like a rock.

Gord, breathing hard, tried to come to grips with the adrenalin surging through his body and the powerful images threatening to overwhelm him. "Where's the air shaft?" he gasped.

"In a room just off the restaurant," Claire said. "But we'll never get through. There must be three dozen in there."

"I flooded the cave. That's driven them up." He turned to Sullivan. "Can we get to that room from the Clinic?"

Sullivan nodded, unable to speak, his face grey ash.

Atkins ordered his men, "Raise that drawbridge and keep 'em in the restaurant. If they try to take off, shoot for the wings."

Except for two OPP officers stationed at the bridge, everyone else piled in the carts for the agonizingly slow ride. Gord briefed them on what had happened to him at the cave entrance. "I think they have some kind of mind-meld abilities."

"Varik said they're telepathic," Claire said.

"You mean they mesmerize us?" Bailie asked.

"Worse. They promise things. Eternal things." The faint memory of those promises sent a painful longing through his body. It was as though they had offered what he had always been striving for and yet hadn't been aware of. Something from the dark side of his soul he hardly knew existed. He wondered if he'd seen something human beings aren't meant to see. The depths of his unconscious? The divine? The memory of what they showed him was gone, but what lingered, what tormented him still was the desire.

As they approached the Clinic, another white-shadow emerged from the building and took flight. Soon it was high in the sky, too high, Gord felt, for fire power to do any good. A rifle blasted beside him, leaving his ears ringing.

The creature plummeted.

"Atkins," Bailie observed for all of them, "you're a damn good shot!"

Sullivan led the way inside. The main floor was empty. Atkins sent a man upstairs. The basement door had been flung wide open and cautiously they descended.

Gord couldn't believe the carnage. The ward was painted crimson, textured with bits of human tissue. Gutted bodies lay sprawled against bloodsoaked hospital sheets. Organs had been torn out and half eaten. Matted hair clung to the ravaged shells of what had once been human heads.

But he felt most horrified by the eyes. Every last one had been gouged out, as if the creatures favored these parts. Blood and gore oozed from gaping sockets.

Claire turned absolutely white.

Bailie stood frozen.

While Atkins did a quiet examination of the scene, Sullivan retched in one corner.

The door to the corridor stood ajar, and Atkins approached it cautiously. "Holy Jesus! What a stench," he said. "There's likely more in there."

They left the lighted section of the corridor reluctantly. Atkins switched on a powerful flashlight. Walls smeared in red made a grisly trail coaxing them further into danger.

"Watch for ricochets if we have to shoot," Atkins warned.

"And don't make eye contact," Gord said. "Somehow, they can get to you through the eyes."

He added up the facts: At least half a dozen creatures had left through the restaurant and were now in the City. Plus the one leaving the Clinic. And one must have been seen by residents earlier. They might escape through the opening in the dome, but it would be a while yet before it was wide enough. In the meantime, he could only guess what destruction they would cause. He figured that many, especially the young, had been caught by the flood in the cavern. That left those still in the restaurant, the ones they would encounter in this tunnel, and any in the room where David and Jerry hid.

"Any other exits from that cave?" he asked Sullivan.

"Not that I know of."

If the kids hadn't been killed already, they were trapped. Of course, so were the creatures. And, Gord thought, once we get there, we won't be in a great position either. There's no way we can drown them in the restaurant. Even if bullets damage their wings, they will anticipate the trajectory. And even if we hit one or more, they'll still be able to walk, and crawl, and bite, and claw . . . Yes, he thought gloomily, we are in a lousy position. But what alternative did they have? They had to get Jerry and David out, and the sooner the better.

They followed the intoxicating stench of death, a smell that revived images of his father.

# Forty

Camouflage. That's what the flowers are for, David thought. To hide the rot. A raw hamburger gone bad.

There'd been a lot of movement. Through the room. Out in the restaurant. Human screams. Gun shots.

Then, quiet.

The bird-thing wearing his aunt's necklace stopped in front of the grate. David held his breath. Milky eyes peered through the openings but David got the feeling it couldn't see him but knew from other senses that he and Jerry were there.

The grate was yanked out. The sharp-angled face shoved in. Angry, alien features. From a nightmare.

It screeched at them. Jerry, behind him, jumped. Apparently the creature wasn't worried about making noise. As a unit, David and Jerry hobbled backwards, fast.

"The opening's too small for it to get in, right?" Jerry's voice, laced with tentative hope, sounded high and girlish.

David felt hysterical, like he just wanted to laugh and laugh, and then scream forever. "Yeah," he said, trying to convince both of them.

And it was true. The thing tried to reach in, but the wings attached to its arms made that impossible.

But what neither of them had considered was a smaller

creature. A child thing. Their size. One that fit as neatly into the shaft as they did. That was as savage as the adults. Like the one that came scuttling towards them now, fangs bared, jaws snapping, talons slashing the air in killing fury.

David screamed and Jerry joined in. But the young creature just kept coming.

# Forty-One

"There's the room," Claire whispered.

The group crept out of the shadows into this new, well-lit corridor. Atkins motioned the other officer to join him up front. Claire and Gord kept to their heels, while Bailie and Sullivan brought up the rear.

The splintered oak door hung off the top hinge; Claire's stomach constricted. She heard the sound of a wing flapping.

*SKREEEE! SKREEEE!* vibrated through the stone tunnel, clawing at her eardrums.

Atkins flattened against the wall and motioned for everybody else to do likewise. He aimed his rifle at the doorway.

Muffled scuffling sounds. A whimper. Young. Terrified. Human.

"My God!" Claire whispered wildly. No one had to tell her it was her son. She darted forward.

"Hold it!" Atkins ordered in a hoarse whisper, trying to grab her, but she broke his grip and barged past, Gord right behind her.

The door smacked back against the wall. Her momentum carried her three or four steps in. A large female creature, white body, half skin, half feathers, slick with clear mucus, faced Claire. Her wings twitched enough that the feathers created a breeze.

Gord lifted his shotgun. The creature snarled and Claire gazed into a mouth full of serrated fangs.

The female held Jerry and David before her like fleshy shields. Their heads had been pulled back, necks exposed to switchblade talons poised to slash their jugulars. Lillian's amethyst hung around David's throat.

Gord aimed the shotgun.

"Don't!" Claire cried.

The female's eyes glinted white sparks. Her jaw snapped rapidly.

"Mom!" David sounded weak and frightened. The thing, in a slow movement, drew a talon down his neck. Blood beaded from the cut and he groaned, but Claire could see that the wound was superficial.

Just as Gord cocked the trigger, Claire stepped in front of him. "You'll hit the kids."

Behind her, she heard the others enter the room. Sullivan, his studied veneer long ago ruptured by fear, sounded shocked. "They'll kill us all. I thought they just needed a little blood. I didn't know," he moaned.

"Be careful," Bailie said, quietly. "She's desperate, that one."

"I'm desperate, too," Gord said.

Claire saw movement. "Look! Her young." Two small creatures that reminded Claire of baby vultures peeked out from behind the female's wings, white eyes fierce yet round and receptive.

She felt an odd power in the presence of this creature. She realized that she'd somehow been connected to these beings, on a psychic level, since the moment of her arrival. Maybe before.

It occurred to her that Lillian may have believed the

same thing, and it did her in. But whatever they were, threatening them was no way to proceed. This creature had the advantage. She had David and Jerry.

"I want to try to talk to her," she told the others, "but I don't want any interruptions. No words, no weapons." Her challenging gaze moved from man to man.

"Nothing to lose," Atkins shrugged.

"There's plenty to lose," Gord said. "Claire, you don't know what you're saying. She'll promise you things—"

"I won't fall for it. I'll resist—"

"You won't be able to resist. They promise to take you away from pain. From life. I don't know how to describe it."

The thing in the corner gave a shrill cry.

Claire shook her head impatiently. "Somebody's got to try. She'll kill them in a split second unless we can work out something."

"Then I'll talk to her."

"No! She'll trust me. I'm a mother, too. And a widow." Claire turned away from him.

She inhaled and exhaled, took two deep and slow breaths, trying to still the doubts and fears careening through her mind. She took a cautious but deliberate step forward.

The thing hissed, spitting saliva across the six feet that separated them.

Claire stretched out her hands slowly, not to touch, more as a symbol.

This female was mammal, she had given birth. She had witnessed death. She had human features. Claire looked into her eyes.

Such colorless orbs chilled her. The vacant intelligence of an insect. Totally alien. Not like me, she thought. Cold-blooded. The way Varik had looked when they first met. And yet there was a connection, she could feel it to her bones.

She hoped her innate respect for all life forms would be enough to carry her through the terror, and yet, this one had put Lillian's necklace around David's neck. She probably killed her aunt. What hope did Claire have of surviving? She snuffed out that fearful thought, which led nowhere but to more fear.

This creature emitted waves of ferocity. Claire had no sense of whether or not she was getting through. She sent thoughts out like a spider spinning delicate silk threads, struggling to bridge the barriers of species. There was nothing from the other side to grip onto. Yet Varik had, so it was possible. They understood him and trusted him enough to leave the rain forest and migrate. But in the end they killed him, she reminded herself.

A black tongue, long, lizard thin, darted from the mouth. The little ones behind her fidgeted. They seemed curious and, despite their savagery, Claire saw the appeal of the young. A mother would love them. She appealed to that mother now. She stilled her mind, as Lillian had taught her to do when they had tracked deer in the woods.

*You have young. You are holding my young,* she thought.

The creature cocked her head to one side.

Encouraged, Claire took a small step forward. *Don't hurt them,* she thought, and said, more as a warning to the others in the room, "We won't harm yours."

The jagged mouth snapped open and shut, a blur of razor fangs. The room filled with a loud *Skreee!* but to Claire's ears the tone had softened.

Out of the corner of her eye, Claire noticed Atkins lift

his rifle. She signaled slowly with her hand. The barrel lowered.

*You want to survive. We want to survive,* she urged. "Give us our children, and you and yours can go free."

"Now, just a minute . . . !" Atkins began.

Staccato gunfire erupted in the restaurant. Wild screeches! Reinforcements, Claire guessed. The scent of fire; grey smoke began to seep into the room from the restaurant.

Some cellular connection to her flock must have made the creature understand that a mass slaughter of her kind was taking place. Her head jerked birdlike, frantically, from the door to the restaurant to the door to the corridor. As the smoke became more intense, she grew increasingly agitated. Claire feared there was no more time.

*Help us! We must survive. For the greater good.*

The words rippled through Claire's head. She felt the thin muscle between her scalp and cranium vibrate. She made an instant decision, and turned. "I'm taking them back through the Clinic and helping them escape the City."

"She's under its control," Gord said.

"No! I'm not. It's the only way to save David and Jerry."

Gord looked at her, his eyes brimming with fear and loose adrenalin. He looked at Jerry, then David. Talons, poised at their throats. He must know better than the others that it would take only a fraction of a second to sever the vein. How could she explain to him, to any of them? Despite everything that these beings had done, she understood them in some way he could not.

"All right," he said, "but I'm going with you. The dome? Will it still be open?" he asked Sullivan.

"Should be. But you'd better hurry. The system's automated. It's designed to protect the environment. Unless it receives instructions through the main computer, the panel closes within a half hour. Only Varik and Brenda knew the codes to keep it open."

Gunfire from the restaurant had stopped. Grey smoke billowed under the door, the acrid smell of wood on fire, the sweet odor of charring meat. "We've all got to get out of here," Bailie said.

*Come,* Claire thought, concentrating hard. *Trust me.* She motioned the large creature to follow.

It/she moved hesitantly, body almost gliding, head jerking nervously in every direction, clutching David and Jerry as she shoved them in front, her young clinging to her back beneath her wings.

Claire led the way through the tunnels to the Clinic, past the remnants of the slaughter, averting her eyes, the creature, and the others following her.

When they reached the living room on the main floor Gord looked through the window and pointed out the SWAT team positioned on the lawn. The streets were otherwise deserted. Atkins, Bailie, Sullivan and the other officer left first. They ran across the grass to the commanding officer.

Above, the dome opening seemed wider than when Claire had last noticed it. But if Sullivan was right, the roof must be retracting. From this distance she couldn't judge whether the space remaining would be enough to allow the creature and her babies to get through.

Gord stepped out of the Clinic first, then Claire, and finally the creature and the four offspring. It looked up, calculating the opening just as Claire had done, and made a decision.

After a moment Claire said, "She insists we get away from the guns. She wants just me to follow. Stay here."

From the way Gord looked at her, she knew he was worried about the toll the mental link-up was taking. "I'll be okay," she said.

He didn't like it but she could see he knew they no longer had a choice.

The long-legged creature strode across the lawn, and Claire struggled to keep up, trying to be near her son and Jerry. They had gone about a block when they turned a corner, out of view of the weapons.

The creature stopped in the middle of a playground and turned. *We have a deal,* Claire told her.

Precious moments passed. She could sense the dome closing. Suddenly the thing released David and he ran to Claire. She held him tight but Claire's relief was short-lived.

*My other child,* she pleaded.

*He is not your offspring.*

Claire wasn't prepared for this. *He . . . he is like my offspring. As all the young of your kind belong to you.*

The creature did not move.

Jerry sobbed loudly. Claire's heart pounded hard.

My God! If she kills him . . . She nipped that thought, unwilling for it to be read and used against her. "I need my other child," she said firmly. *As you need both of yours,* she thought. A glance told her the opening of the dome was narrower than even moments before. "Please. There's not much time."

Claire looked into the blank whiteness of those eyes. No sign of recognition. Nothing she could feel coming from it. Nothing but radiant white light.

An image came to her, so quickly she forgot that it had not always been there. Like a hologram—she, David, and Bill. Not the past, but the future. Her life as it would have been. As, she now realized, it could still be.

Bill turned to her and smiled. He reached out for her. "Join me, Claire," he said. "There's something greater in store for us. The three of us. Don't let this chance slip away. I miss you. I love you."

Her heart ached with joy and pain. Hot tears of longing streamed from her eyes. She understood. This had to be real. It was for her, a gift from a universe that had been moved by her pain. When she touched his hand they would be together again. At last. Forever.

"Mom! No!" David's voice sliced through the image. Bill's face shimmered. The edges, like a burning photograph, turned ragged, collapsing inward. Still, she felt the warmth of Bill's body pressing towards hers. She sighed, aware she had been holding her breath.

The reality before her superimposed itself onto the fantasy. One winged arm reaching out for her. Claire understood the promise clearly. She could have Bill. Any time. But not on this earth.

Jerry sobbed once and Claire looked at his face, crinkled with terror. This boy was part of her future.

"Give me my child!" she demanded, tears exploding from her eyes. The memory of Bill, the longing for him, sucked at her like a vortex that had opened in the sky.

A gun blast.

Everything happened too quickly.

Claire lunged, whether as an act of sacrifice, offering, or heroism, she did not know.

The creature looked to where the shot originated then glanced up. In a fraction of a second she took flight.

As she lifted off the grass, Claire snatched Jerry out of her embrace.

A demanding *SKREEE!* called the two young, who followed hesitantly, as if they were flying for the first time.

Claire shoved David and Jerry to the ground and shielded them with her body. Something horrible was about to happen; she felt her heart about to shatter.

Gord watched the three creatures soar straight up, heading for what from the ground looked like only a cut in the dome. The mother's wings stretched wider than the span of both young together. The slickness that covered their bodies became iridescence when the bright lights from the City hit the skin.

He had taken a chance. On Jerry's life. Thank God it worked. His body shook from tension and the shotgun barrel dropped to the ground.

The mother swooped back and down creating a diversion, stalling until her young ones could gain altitude and fly closer to the pencil-line space.

Suddenly the loud blast of another gun startled Gord.

"No!" Claire screamed.

Sullivan fired again.

"We had a deal!" Claire screamed.

Gord heard a longing in her voice that re-ignited his own. Before he got off a third shot, Gord tackled Sullivan to the ground.

Claire watched as the large creature spiraled. She plunged twenty feet before she could right herself. Then she flew low, setting herself up as a barrier between the bullets and her young. Claire felt sure she had lost the use of one wing because her flight pattern became erratic.

The babies neared the closing panel, directly overhead. Now they were out of firing range. They reached the opening. First one, then the other slipped through the crack.

Their mother struggled to soar but the damaged wing kept her from reaching the altitude necessary. And, Claire realized with horror, she could no longer fit through that opening. Finally she plummeted, first slowly, then faster as she weakened.

She hit the ground with a loud crack. Claire heard running from all directions but she got there first.

The impact from such a height had been tremendous. The chest cavity had cracked wide open. Internal organs were smashed and scattered all over. Bloody brains oozed from the shattered skull, itself broken in a dozen places. Limbs were twisted and broken, ribs sticking up through the chest, the pelvis smashed.

But those white eyes were open wide, staring up at the sky, the intelligence of the creature assuring it that its progeny had survived.

She called to Claire still. There, in the purity of the white glow Claire saw Bill, her life, her whole world as it should have been. She watched the promise of heaven fade until the light behind the eyes dimmed and finally was extinguished.

Gord knelt beside her, his arms around her, her children clinging to her side. They were all safe. But why did she feel that a part of her soul had just shriveled?

# Forty-Two

As Gord drove south along Highway 11 towards Toronto, Jerry said, "I don't wanna go back to school."

"Me neither," David said.

The boys were in the back seat of the Jeep, he and Claire up front.

" 'Course," Jerry added, "considering where we *might* be, the alternative isn't so bad."

Gord glanced in the rearview. They had come out of this remarkably unscathed. They're resilient. Of course, it's only been three days. Probably the repercussions will hit later. Bound to be nightmares, at least. For all of us.

He checked his watch. Five hours to make the airport. Lots of time to drop Jerry off with his mother. And then for Claire and David to catch the evening flight to Miami. The drive would take him two days, three if he didn't push it, and he didn't feel like pushing anything right now.

From there, well, who knew what would happen? Between him and Claire, him and David? And Jerry would be affected. Gord decided to fly back to Toronto in a week to check on his son.

He turned towards Claire and felt a surge of affection. Maybe it'll work out. He reached over and brushed her cheek with the back of his fingers.

Her smile upset him. Maybe it was just his imagination but it seemed slightly mechanical. Suddenly his body went cold. He couldn't put a finger on it. She had some grey hairs that hadn't been there a week ago. New lines on her face. They were all the worse for wear. But that wasn't it, not what bothered him.

Something felt . . . missing. She seemed preoccupied. He remembered a luster in her eyes that was no longer present. It saddened him that it was gone. And made him angry.

"It's all so hard to believe," Claire was saying. "Their exceptional intelligence."

"You could say the same about humans," Gord reminded her.

"Their ability to fly. Their physical prowess."

"You're right," he agreed, noticing she'd left out what he considered the creatures' most unusual and attractive attribute, their supernatural mind control powers.

"They're not like anything else on earth." The longing in her voice disturbed him.

"For centuries, they've been the best damned kept secret in the world."

"I wonder why they allied themselves with Varik, how he was able to convince them to let him build the Cities?"

"What Varik told you was probably true. The destruction of the rain forests threatens them with extinction. They had to trust him. They may have to trust us again."

"They just want to survive."

"At our expense," he reminded her.

"As we survive at the expense of other species. Maybe our survival depends on them in some way, who knows? What about the two that escaped? Think there's more?"

Gord wanted a cigarette, but he'd thrown them away. Maybe this time for good. "The government people figure another four got out of the City. Maybe more. They think those things will probably head back to South America, back to the rain forests. By instinct. That's safety, as they know it. They can breed there. One of the media guys told me this morning he heard off the record that the governments of six countries are going to support scientific research to study the corpses. Once they know more about what they're dealing with, they'll go in and study them in the field. Of course, they'll be talking to us again. And again."

"Do you think they'll find any? When they go looking?"

Their eyes locked in silent agreement not to verbalize the hope they both secretly entertained. Gord saw the obsession in Claire as strongly as he felt it in himself. It didn't matter to him that he *knew* they had killed. And that what they promised was impossible. What he had been offered, the feeling tone of it was so extraordinary. He had been offered heaven. He just prayed that he would land with his feet on the ground, that for both he and Claire reality would again be good enough to substitute for the ecstasy they had tasted. You can't live in the land of ecstasy, he thought, but it's nice to visit once in a while.

At that thought, Claire turned sharply in his direction. He wondered if she could read his mind.

They were all silent as they took the ramp for the 401. Suddenly Claire sighed. That longing, again. He was afraid of what she would say. But her mood had lifted. "You know, I could really use a holiday."

He laughed. "You're not the only one, Lady."

Her eyes softened. The sparkle had reappeared, and it lingered.

"I'd love to go away over Christmas. Two, maybe three weeks. A luxury resort. On the beach. Not the Caribbean, though. West. Maybe Hawaii. All the comforts and nothing to do but loll in the sun."

"Sounds idyllic. And expensive. Now that Sullivan's given back the signed offer, for better or for worse you're still a land owner in the Great White North."

Claire laughed. The music on the radio ended. It was replaced by an ad and the four listened tensely until the last lines: *Eternal City Four. Hawaii. Open this Christmas. A new concept in living. Life will never be the same.*

"Hawaii, huh?" Jerry said. "Boy, Claire, you know how to pick 'em." He and David laughed nervously in the back seat.

Then David said, "Hey, Mom, can we get the tape deck fixed?"

Only Gord noticed the solitary tear threatening to slide down Claire's cheek.

Suddenly she reached out and viciously punched the radio button to "off." She swiped at that tear, blew her nose, took a deep breath and said softly, "On the other hand, be it ever so humble . . ."

"My very sentiments," Gord said, "exactly!"

# About the Authors

Award-winning author Nancy Kilpatrick has published in the fantasy, dark fantasy, and mystery genres. Her 26 books include 14 novels (among others, the popular *Power of the Blood* vampire series); 5 collections of her more than 150 published short stories; and 7 anthologies she has edited, including *In the Shadow of the Gargoyle* and *Graven Images* (Ace Books). She has just completed *The Goth Bible* for St. Martin's Press, a non-fiction book on the gothic lifestyle (2003). She has won several awards for her work, including the Arthur Ellis Award for best mystery story. Born in the United States, Nancy has lived in Canada about one half of her life. Currently she dwells in a gothically-decorated apartment in Montreal with her black cat Bella. When not writing, her favorite activity is travelling the world and visiting castles, cemeteries and ruins with her photographer companion, Hugues Leblanc.

In his youth, Michael Kilpatrick published newspaper articles on tennis and travel. He was also one of Canada's world-class tennis professionals. In 1992 he published the short story "A Major Malfunction" in the young adult anthology The Blue Jean Collection (Thistledown Press). Currently he teaches high school in Toronto, Canada, where he lives with his wife and two children.